BLUE HALO SERIES BOOK FIVE

NYSSA KATHRYN

An NW Partners Book
Cover by L.J. Anderson at Mayhem Cover Creations
Developmentally and Copy Edited by Kelli Collins
Line Edited by Jessica Snyder
Proofread by Amanda Cuff and Jen Katemi

❀ Created with Vellum

Some loves are impossible to leave behind...

Cassie Webber had it all. A man who loved her, a mother and sister who were all the family she needed, and a job she adored. Until, in the blink of an eye, everything changed. Now her mother and Aidan are gone, and her sister's in danger. Cassie's willing to do anything to save her—including marrying her best friend and returning to a place she vowed to leave behind. She nearly succeeds in extracting Mia before everything changes yet again—and Cassie herself is the one whisked away.

Following a life-changing kidnapping ordeal, former Special Forces Operator Aidan Pratt has thrown himself into the new security business he's embarked on with his teammates. He uses his military training and a host of enhanced skills to keep people safe, all the while trying to escape the memory of Cassie, who moved on without him during his two-year absence. But the universe has other plans, and before he knows it, Aidan is hired to rescue the very woman he's trying to forget.

With Cassie back in his arms, the full extent of her peril becomes glaringly clear, and Aidan will burn down the world to keep her safe. After all, danger has never scared him...but losing Cassie a second time? Aidan can't fathom anything more terrifying.

ACKNOWLEDGMENTS

Thank you to my A team. The people who take apart and put my book back together, better and stronger than it once was. To my editors and proof-readers, Kelli, Jessica, Amanda and Jen, you are the people who make my books reach that next level. Thank you.

Thank you to my ARC team. You are my cheer squad, and I am eternally grateful to have you.

Thank you to my readers, you always ensure the next book gets written. You're amazing.

And my husband and daughter. You two give me the life and space I need to create these stories. When I'm stretched thin with a deadline, it's you guys who do it touch to make sure I get where I need to be. I love you. Thank you for all you do.

PROLOGUE

 *ne Week Ago*

AIDAN PRATT WALKED into the Blue Halo building and climbed the stairs. It was late, and they'd spent the day dealing with that damn doctor kidnapping and almost killing Carina. Not to mention the motorcycle club attack. He was ready for the day to end, but if there was a meeting about a new security job *now*, at this hour, it had to be important.

The one good thing that had come out of the last twenty-four hours was capturing Ilias Forman, the fucking *hired gun*, as he called himself. Aidan and his team had done what was necessary to get as much information as they could from the asshole before handing him over to the FBI. Apparently, he actually lived in Idaho...but there were similar guys in a dozen other states. Men who had been part of Project Arma, just like Aidan and his team. Men who had been given the same experimental drugs. Made stronger. Faster. And a dozen other things.

He pushed into the reception area. The text had come from

Callum. Over the last few months, Callum had taken over a lot of the administration and technical side of the business, but the entire team helped whenever and wherever they could.

When Aidan stepped into the conference room, Tyler was there too—he and Callum both looked solemn.

Shit. What was wrong *now*?

Suddenly, his chest seized. "Is it Cassie? Did something happen to her?"

At the thought of anything happening to his ex, everything inside him ached. No. Not ached. It tore him to fucking shreds.

Cassie might not be his anymore, she may have chosen another man, but that didn't mean his heart just forgot about her. The woman still owned him. And not a day had passed—or would ever pass—when he didn't think about her.

Tyler shook his head. "As far as we're aware, Cassie's fine."

What the hell did that mean? "As far as you're aware?"

Callum nodded toward the empty seat. "Sit. The call's about to come through."

"What call?"

"Will you just sit your ass down?" Tyler sighed, shaking his head.

Aidan dropped into the seat at the end of the table. Something was going on. And his team needed to tell him what it was, right the hell now, before he lost his damn mind. He was not a patient man. Never had been. But especially when it came to Cassie.

Callum tapped a few keys on the laptop. "We got an urgent job request. I spoke to the guy briefly, but he said it needed to be *you* who took the job."

"Why me?"

"That was my question, too."

When Callum didn't offer anything further, Aidan blew out a frustrated breath. That short patience of his was about to snap. "What else did he say?"

"That's the thing. He wouldn't tell me shit. All he'd give me was his name. And the name of the woman he wants protected."

Again, his friend stopped before providing any information that would be useful. The air tightened in Aidan's lungs as he asked, "And what were those names?"

Before Callum could answer, a Skype call came through on the large monitor on the wall, and all three of them looked up.

The man who appeared on the screen had every muscle in Aidan's body tensing, his hands fisting, and his eyes narrowing.

Damien fucking Webber.

Cassie's husband.

Also, Cassie's childhood best friend. A man Aidan had always liked. A man he'd never suspected would one day take his woman and make her his own.

The craziest part of it all was, Aidan had *approved* of the man's friendship with Cassie. Neither of them had ever given him reason to believe they felt anything more for each other.

"What the hell do you want?" he asked quietly, his voice so low it would be impossible for Damien to miss the anger.

The man's features were shadowed as he stood outside, in the dark. "Hello, Aidan. It's nice to see you again."

Nice? Aidan could think of a lot of words to describe this moment, but *nice* wasn't even in the vicinity.

Callum leaned forward. "What can we do for you tonight, Mr. Webber?"

Aidan tried not to flinch at the guy's last name. Now Cassie's last name.

"I can't talk long." His gaze skirted somewhere above the camera, then back again. "I also can't give many details. But I have a job I need Aidan to complete."

The last thing Aidan wanted was to work for this guy. "What do you mean, you can't give many details?"

"I don't have the time. They could be watching."

Aidan frowned. "Who?"

"I told you. There's not enough time." He shot a look around again, like he expected someone to join him...or find him. Then he looked back at Aidan. "I need you to kidnap Cassie this Friday at ten p.m."

Aidan's jaw dropped. Callum and Tyler straightened in their seats. Whatever he'd been expecting Damien to say, it wasn't that.

"I'll send you the location to grab her from. I need you to hold her for a week at a safe and hidden location. But you need to make it look like a real kidnapping. No one can know the truth."

It took Aidan a moment to respond. "You can't be serious."

"I assure you, Aidan, I am." For a third time, Damien looked beyond the camera, once more scanning his surroundings.

Aidan leaned forward. "I am not going to *kidnap* Cassie. First of all, that would fucking terrify her. Second, we're not in the business of staging fake abductions."

Damien stared straight into the phone's camera. "It's the only way to save her."

"Save her?"

There was a short beat of silence. "If you don't do this, they'll kill her."

Aidan's insides iced over. When he spoke again, his voice was low and deadly. "You need to give me some fucking details, and you need to give them to me now."

"I've already been on this call too long. I'm going to text you the address from this burner phone, then I'm going to destroy it. You won't hear from me again, and it's important you don't try to contact me."

Burner phone?

"How do we know this isn't some setup?" Callum asked.

Damien's gaze never left Aidan's. And finally, he saw something other than shaky composure in the man's expression. Desperation?

"I love Cassie. You know I do. That's why I need *you* to do this for me. You're the only one I trust to do whatever it takes to keep her safe."

His words hit like rounds to the chest. Hell, he'd been shot. This was worse. Hearing the man say he loved Cassie... Hearing that she was in danger...

"Even if I were to do this, there's no way I'd go alone."

"Then bring a friend. Hell, bring your whole team! Just as long as you shelter her somewhere safe. I need to go." Another flicker of his eyes. "This isn't a setup or a joke or anything else. This is life or death. Whether you believe me or not, I'm going to send the information and then just hope like hell you're in."

The call ended, and the man disappeared.

For a moment, Aidan sat there, not sure what the hell had just happened. The only thing he *did* know was that he could never let harm come to Cassie, regardless of whether they were together or apart. He needed her alive and safe more than he needed anything else on the damn planet.

CHAPTER 1

oday

Cassie Webber sipped her cold glass of sparkling apple juice. The liquid fizzled on her tongue as she cast her gaze around her living room.

Why were they all still here? It was almost ten o'clock, so yeah, not late for most, but for her it was definitely late. She was tired. She'd done her job. She'd hosted this week's "family gathering". It was time for them all to get out of her house.

She smiled absently at something Damien said to the group of people around them. He'd always been a great host. Able to plaster a smile on his face when needed. Say all the right things and nod at appropriate moments. Cassie had gotten better. But tonight? She'd stopped listening several laughs and five sips of juice ago.

How long had she been on her feet? Two hours? Three? Whatever it was, it was too long. She needed to lie down and rest before her legs gave out on her. She'd sat down periodically, but it wasn't enough. And it wasn't just being on her feet that was causing her to feel lightheaded. No. It was the stress.

Damien's arm was around her waist, just as it had been for the last half hour. He knew she couldn't stand for long periods of time. Not without repercussions. Everyone did. So why were they still here?

She rubbed a finger along her forehead as her gaze caught on Mia across the room. Her sister was in a group with three other people, laughing. One of those people was Sampson. He and Mia were growing closer. Her sister was already head over heels in love with the guy. Had been for years. Mia had admitted to sharing a few kisses with him recently, but they weren't officially dating yet.

When their gazes connected, Cassie tried for a smile. She hated seeing her sister standing so comfortably among all these people. Among Elijah and his brothers.

At the thought of Elijah, her gaze almost drifted over to him. Almost. It took everything in her not to look. Because then she'd have to use the last scrap of strength she had to not reveal her absolute disgust in the awful person she saw. Awful was actually too kind a word for him. The man was pure evil, and he deserved a special place in hell.

She took another sip of juice and tried to concentrate on the conversation, but when Olive Hollow excused herself from Mia's group and headed toward the bathroom, Cassie straightened. She'd been waiting for a chance to talk to the woman alone all night.

Cassie leaned into Damien and whispered in his ear, "I'm just going to the bathroom."

Worry flickered through his light brown eyes. "Are you okay?"

She gave him her most polished smile. One she'd perfected over the years. "Of course."

With a light press of a kiss on his cheek, she stepped away and moved through the crowd. Her heels clicked against the marble tiles, and the sparkling apple juice rolled in her belly. When she reached the guest bathroom, she washed her hands at the double sink, watching the closed toilet door from below her lashes.

The second it opened, Olive paused. Only for a second. Then she moved forward and washed her hands beside Cassie.

"You're still okay for this Wednesday?" Cassie asked under her breath.

There was a stutter in Olive's breathing that was barely discernible. Her gaze rose to the exit, shooting around the room before returning to the water. "Isn't there—"

"No. There are no cameras in the bathrooms." Or her bedroom. It was the first thing she'd checked after moving into this house. Something she *still* checked periodically. She needed to know the safe spaces where there were no watching eyes or listening ears.

The woman hesitated. The pause had unease crawling into Cassie's gut. This couldn't fall through. The woman had to show up.

"Detective Shaw will be there," Cassie whispered. "He'll sit at a table beside us with a recording device. No one will know what he's doing but us. You and your mother will be safe, I promise." She needed Olive's testimony and any evidence she had, but there was also no way she'd put the younger woman or her mother in danger.

Another moment of pause. Then, finally, Olive gave a small nod. "One o'clock at Vaserelli's Diner."

She almost sagged in relief. The Cassie of a few years ago *would* have sagged. But the new Cassie had gotten good at keeping her emotions in check. "See you then."

Cassie turned off the water and headed toward the kitchen, internally grimacing with each step. Man, it really *was* getting hard to stay upright. She should have rested more before everyone had arrived tonight. But no, instead she'd been on her feet, too worked up about Elijah and his brothers being in her house to sit still. Now she was paying the price.

Damien had also been acting strangely all day. She'd pestered him about it, but he'd told her nothing.

She stepped into the kitchen. It was all white and open, in a very Hamptons style. Big and beautiful. Most people would kill for a kitchen like this. She hated it. It was a reminder that looks could be deceiving, and the most beautiful place might not be what it seemed.

All she wanted was out. Out of this house. This life. All of it. And she would be. Soon.

Mrs. Alder turned from where she loaded the dishwasher. The woman was ostensibly a housekeeper, gifted to her and Damien by the organization after their wedding. But she wasn't really. No, she was less of a housekeeper and more like *Cassie's* keeper. She had no doubt Mrs. Alder reported everything she saw and heard back to Elijah.

"Could you please start collecting empty cups?" Cassie spoke with the formal, impersonal voice she always used with this phony woman. "I think people are just about ready to leave."

The older woman lifted a brow. A couple of years ago, that simple brow lift had terrified Cassie. Not anymore. Now it felt more like a challenge. A challenge Cassie would win.

"Don't you think Elijah should be the one to end the party?"

Her skin crawled at the mention of the man's name. She might have to remain around these people, but it didn't mean she had to go out of her way to speak to their *leader*.

"This is my and Damien's home, and we're ready to go to bed. So please go around and collect the glasses."

Mrs. Alder's eyes narrowed. The older woman started to leave the room, but before she stepped out, Cassie added, "And Mrs. Alder—do not question me in my home again."

There was a small huff of irritation from the woman, then she left.

Good. Ten minutes, and they'd better all be gone. Though realistically, she didn't even know if she had ten more minutes left in her.

Cassie had suffered from neurally mediated hypotension since she was a kid. Sometimes known as the fainting reflex. It basically meant that if she stood for too long, her blood pressure dropped, and she fainted because of a miscommunication between the heart and brain.

But it wasn't just standing too long that caused her to faint. Ha. If only her life was that easy. No. Her blood pressure also dropped if she was stressed, which was essentially her whole life for the last two years. Too much heat also affected her, so long hot showers had never been an option.

At the thought of heat, she tugged the high neckline of her dress, suddenly aware of how hot she was. Her gaze skittered to the back door. Then, not caring that Mrs. Alder would scold her later, she moved over to the trash and lifted out the half-full bag.

A normal person could just step outside their house and empty the trash without a second thought. Her life wasn't normal. Hadn't been normal for a while.

Before Mrs. Alder could return, Cassie slipped out the back door. The second the cool breeze hit her, she sucked in a long, deep gulp of air. God, she missed being outside and in nature. Once upon a time, she'd lived for morning walks. She'd take her dog, Felix, to the woods and they'd just get lost in nature.

Her heart hurt at the thought of Felix. He wasn't the only loved one she'd lost in a short time frame.

Swallowing, she moved to the side of the house. She dumped the trash but didn't go back inside right away. Instead, she stood there, looking up at the two-story house. By all appearances, it was a dream home. Right in the center of Salt Lake City, grand and beautiful. But to her, it was a prison.

Not for long, a voice whispered in her head. Wednesday was the beginning of the end.

Scrubbing her eyes, she headed toward the back door. She'd almost reached it when a prickling at her nape had her stopping. It felt almost like someone was watching her.

Frowning, she turned her head to scan the large yard. No one. No one that she could see, anyway.

She took a step toward the door, but the prickling became almost a burn.

God, what *was* that?

Suddenly, something came back to her. She'd gotten this same feeling not long ago. She'd been out to lunch with Damien, sitting at an outdoor table, and she'd felt it. But it hadn't made her wary, like how she felt under the eyes of Elijah's men. She'd almost wondered if—

No. She couldn't think about him right now. Because every time she did, every time the man crawled into the crevices of her mind, she wanted out. She wanted to walk away from everyone and everything and return to him.

But she couldn't. Not now. She was too close, and this was too important. She needed to finish this. Not just for Mia, but for everyone.

Her gaze flickered across the large yard one more time.

When she was feeling weak, she thought about him. And those memories tormented her thoughts.

He'd been her everything. Then he'd disappeared, and everything had fallen apart. It was the start of the end of the happy life she'd known. And every day after that, it had only gotten worse.

When a wave a dizziness rushed over her, her body tilted. She would have fallen if an arm hadn't suddenly slipped around her waist. A familiar arm.

Damien looked down at her, his eyes yet again worried. "What are you doing out here? It's freezing."

"Just taking out the trash and getting some fresh air."

If she'd said that to anyone else, she'd be met with disapproval. Maybe some suspicion. Damien knew she was at the end of her rope tonight. He knew that cold helped the hypotension.

"Come on, let's get you inside," he said quietly.

He led her to the door and was just opening it when his gaze lifted and skirted around the yard. Did he feel it too?

Five minutes later, people finally began to say their goodbyes and filter out. The hardest goodbye was always Mia. She hated seeing her sister go back to the compound. She hated her sister being anywhere *near* Elijah and his brothers.

Mia was only two years younger than her, but Cassie had always seen her as her responsibility. Especially after their mother had died when Cassie was only ten and Mia seven, and they'd gone into foster care. Hell, a lot of the time, Cassie had been the only person taking care of Mia.

Cassie pulled her into a hug. "Stay safe, little sister."

Mia stepped back and smiled. "Always."

She swallowed and watched her sister leave. She hadn't told Mia anything because knowledge made you vulnerable. If Elijah ever found out what Cassie knew, what she was trying to do, she'd be dead by morning.

The last person to say goodbye was the man himself. Bile crawled up her throat when he pressed a kiss to her cheek.

"This was a lovely evening, Cassie," he said after straightening. "Thank you for having us over."

Like she had a choice. Elijah had asked, and no one said no to the man. Members living outside the compound often hosted dinners at Elijah's request. He made them seem like simple family gatherings, but she knew the truth. It was his way of watching those not living with them. Because the cameras and spy maids weren't enough.

She forced another fake, polished smile to her lips. "Of course, Elijah. Thank you for coming."

His gaze lingered on hers a beat too long. It always did. "This week is a special one. It's your thirtieth birthday this Sunday."

She didn't need the reminder. Thirty. She was turning *thirty*, and she was nowhere near happy. She was hopeful, though. Hopeful that her thirties would be better than her late twenties. Hopeful that certain scumbags would be locked up for the rest of their days.

"It's very exciting."

"We'll see you then for your ball?"

Ah, yes. Her big ball. "You will. I'm really looking forward to it." *Not.*

"Good."

Damien's arm slipped around her waist. "Thank you for coming, Elijah."

The men shook hands, and Damien turned and headed toward the stairs as Elijah stepped out, leaving Cassie to see him off. She frowned. That was odd. Damien was normally far too conscientious to leave her alone with the man.

No matter. He was heading down her porch steps with a final wave before she closed the door. Then she almost sagged. Not just because she couldn't stand the man, but because he was a powerful enemy. He was the leader of the group. Their *Holy Leader*, as he often referred to himself. A man who considered himself as close as mortals could come to God.

He was the leader of their cult. And she was going to make sure he paid for his crimes.

CHAPTER 2

The moon cast a dim glow over the back of Cassie and Damien's house. The place was fucking huge, with a massive outdoor patio and a big-ass pool.

How the hell did they afford a house like this? He worked in finance and she didn't work at all. Not anymore. She *had* been an executive assistant at a big law firm when Cassie and Aidan had been together. She'd loved the job. Why she'd given it up, Aidan had no idea.

Another damn question he had for her. One of many.

Like why armed guards sat in cars on the street, watching the place. Why there was a high-tech camera planted on the front door and surrounding the property.

"The front door just opened. People might be starting to leave," Tyler said through the earpiece.

About damn time. And cutting it way too close. Damien had told them to enter the house at ten p.m., but there was no way they were performing an extraction if there was still a house full of people at go time.

Tyler watched the front, while Callum and Liam were

stationed on either side of the house. Aidan stood behind a large bur oak tree that sat at the back of the huge yard.

Damien's words came back to him.

If you don't do this, they'll kill her.

Fuck. The words felt like acid in his chest.

Cassie had been his entire world. Then he'd been taken, held hostage by the people who ran Project Arma, and just months after he'd disappeared, Cassie had married someone else. But there was no off-switch on his emotions. No way to shut them down. He loved her. He'd always loved her.

"You okay, Aidan?"

Aidan could have laughed at Callum's question. He was about to kidnap the woman he still obsessed over. Touch the woman he hadn't touched in years. Would anyone in his situation be "okay"?

"Ready." Lie. Big-ass lie that his teammates would see right through.

Callum said something, but the words faded when the back door of the house opened and Cassie stepped outside, trash bag in hand. His world stopped. Every part of him stilled and tensed. Even his breathing paused.

Cassie. *His* Cassie.

She wore a high-necked, long-sleeved black dress with black stockings. The dress fit her like a second skin, showing off every curve. Her hair was pulled up into a tight bun, which was strange. She'd always hated wearing her hair up. Said having it down was like a part of her soul being free.

But that wasn't what really had his gut clenching. It was her face. Her eyes. Eyes that haunted his dreams. They were a jade-green shade that lightened and darkened with her mood. Very few would be able to see her eyes so clearly through the dark and the distance. With his altered DNA, he could see everything, right down to the small marring of her brows.

She dumped the trash, and he expected her to walk straight back inside. She didn't. She stopped and looked up at the house.

He couldn't see her face anymore, but the action was strange, and he was almost certain he saw the muscles in her back tighten.

What's going on in your head, Cass?

When she turned back toward the door, she scrubbed her eyes. That's when he noticed she wasn't quite so steady in her heels. Not only that, but her breaths were too shallow. She almost seemed to be struggling to remain upright.

Fuck. She looked tired. Was it stress? Or had she been on her feet too long? He was all too aware of the NMH. Hell, how many times had he forced her to rest, made her leave a party early—or not go to an event at all—when she wasn't in a good way?

Too many.

"She's tired," he said quietly to his team. "I think she's on the verge of passing out."

Not good. For a second, he considered calling this entire thing off. But then those damn words repeated in his head again.

If you don't do this, they'll kill her.

Damien had given them no details. But he reluctantly trusted the guy. He'd been best friends with Cassie since they were kids, and even though Aidan hated that he'd married her, he *did* trust Damien with Cassie. If he said she needed to get out, he believed him.

"What do you want us to do?" Liam asked.

The team knew about Cassie's medical condition.

"We get it done quickly," he said quietly. "If she passes out, I know how to take care of her."

Rest would help. The woman always needed rest.

When Cassie stopped and scanned the yard, Aidan shrank back behind the tree. She wouldn't be able to see him, but she was looking out at the yard like she knew someone was there.

Can you feel my presence as strongly as I feel yours, Cassie?

He wouldn't be surprised. The connection between them... God, it had been like nothing else. Exactly why he'd been so damn shocked that she'd married another man.

When she wobbled on her feet, Aidan almost gave up his cover.

"Stay down," Callum said quietly through the earpiece.

Damien stepped outside and slid an arm around her.

He ground his teeth, clenching his hands into fists. Her husband. The man was her damn *husband*. His insides coiled at the reminder. She shouldn't be married to Damien. She should be married to *him*. That had been the plan. Marriage. Kids. They'd spoken about all of it so many times.

You gave up on me so quickly, Cass.

Six months. He'd only been missing six damn months when she'd married Damien. Had it all been a lie? Their entire relationship?

She would have seen him on the TV when news of Project Arma broke less than a year ago. Everyone had. But she hadn't come to him. She hadn't contacted him at all.

Damien's arm remained around Cassie the entire walk inside the house. The lock clicked as loudly as a gunshot in the quiet night air.

He didn't plan to enter the house through the back door, though. No. When Damien had sent this address—an address Aidan already had—he'd also given them instructions on which windows he'd leave unlocked.

"People are filtering out," Tyler said quietly.

He shot a look at his watch. Five minutes. Five minutes until he'd be infiltrating the house. Five minutes until he'd be taking Cassie.

His legs itched to go to her now. But he shut it off. He switched *everything* off. He had a job to do. Get in. Get her out. Make sure she stayed safe.

Aidan stared at his watch for the remaining few minutes. Then he heard Tyler's voice.

"They're out, and it's ten o'clock. Time to move."

CHAPTER 3

The front door closed, and Cassie rested her head against the wood for several precious seconds. Finally. Bedtime. She was going to pass out in her bed and not open her eyes for a full twelve hours.

She turned to see Mrs. Alder cleaning the living room. Usually, she'd offer to help, because even though she didn't like the woman, she'd been raised with manners. But tonight, she was just too dang tired.

"Good night, Mrs. Alder."

The woman lifted her head and gave her an assessing look. "Good night." Then she got back to work.

Cassie could have laughed. She should probably be used to the woman's calculated glances, but something told her she'd never get there.

A smile played at her lips as she started up the stairs. She'd had one job tonight—confirm Olive was still good for Wednesday—and she'd done it. Her years of misery were finally about to pay off.

She yawned as she reached the top of the stairs, heading to her bedroom. She took one step into the room—and stopped.

No Damien. Strange. When he disappeared as she closed the front door, she'd assumed he'd gone upstairs, just as exhausted as she was from hosting people he didn't trust.

She moved over to the connected bathroom and stuck her head inside. Nope.

"Damien?" she called out. A moment of silence passed. Nothing.

Very strange. Maybe he was in the kitchen helping Mrs. Alder, and she'd just missed him.

She moved over to the dresser mirror and sat, watching her reflection as she removed her earrings. Wednesday could be her last day here. Her last day in this house, pretending to care about an organization for which she had nothing but resentment.

Would Detective Shaw move that quickly? Would he arrest Elijah and his brothers and anyone else involved on the same day? That was a question she needed to ask him. Her gaze shot to the bathroom. Her burner phone sat hidden in there. It was how she communicated with the detective.

Then another question popped into her head. One that was equal parts exciting and nerve-racking. Once she was out—what then?

Would she return to him? Just show up at his house and say, "Sorry about the whole marrying another guy thing, but here I am..."

Aidan. The name was a whisper in her head.

She'd never forget that feeling of seeing him on the news. Elijah didn't allow members to have TVs or radios in their homes. She'd been out to dinner with Damien when she'd looked up at the TV mounted in the corner, and there he'd been, on the screen.

She'd been so shocked, she stopped breathing. Damien told her later that she'd gone so white, he'd thought she was going to pass out. Every part of her had wanted to go to Aidan. God, it had been like a physical pull on her limbs. But she couldn't, not only because they always had eyes on her, but because it would have ruined everything.

So she'd forced herself to stay here in Utah, all the while expecting him to come to *her*. To ask her why she'd married another man. To find out what the hell was going on.

But you never came.

She dropped the earring to the dresser and closed her eyes before touching the necklace under her dress. The necklace Aidan had given her on their anniversary, the week before he'd left on that final mission. On the pendant was a common hackberry tree. The tree was *their* place. The site of so many memories. It was where they'd shared their first kiss. Where he'd first said he loved her. And where he'd given her this necklace.

She still remembered the moment he'd slid it around her neck. The kisses he'd pressed to her skin as he whispered in her ear.

"The tree is one of the toughest in the US. It can survive strong winds. Pollution. Drought. Heat." She touched the spot where he'd kissed her neck. *"It can survive whatever the world throws at it. Just like us."*

Her eyes flashed open. He hadn't counted on Project Arma. And she hadn't counted on Mia running back to the cult.

A shudder rippled down her spine.

For a moment, she wondered what would happen when he saw her again. How would he look at her? With anger? Resentment that she'd married someone else? What if he was dating another woman? Or worse, also married? The idea had shards of ice puncturing the lining of her stomach. He had every right to date and marry, but it didn't make it any easier to accept.

Blowing out a long breath, she rose to her feet. Yep. She was definitely lightheaded.

Quickly, she reached for the hem of her dress, but before she could tug it off, something sounded from another room. It was the floorboard beneath the window in the guest bedroom. She knew it well, because she'd stepped on it many times.

Frowning, she dropped her hands and stepped into the hall. "Damien?"

Silence.

The fine hairs on her arms stood on end, and an uneasy feeling began to churn in her gut. Someone had definitely stepped on the floorboard, but if it was Damien, he would have answered her call.

Her head swam with the need to lie down, but she pushed through the dizziness and moved forward.

"Hello?"

Nothing. Not even a whisper of sound. Slowly, she opened the guest bedroom door.

A cool breeze hit her skin. Her gaze zipped across to the open window. Had Damien left it like that? Maybe an animal had jumped in. They got a lot of squirrels around here.

She stepped into the room.

An arm suddenly curved around her waist. She opened her mouth to scream, but a hand covered her mouth. The hold wasn't rough, but it was firm and strong. Impenetrable.

Heat pressed to her back.

For a second, she was so shocked that she went completely still. Then the man tugged her toward the window. Holy crap, was he going to throw her out of a second-floor window?

Fear snapped Cassie out of her shock, and she acted. She struggled against the body behind her, shoving her elbows back into him, stomping on his feet. But the guy didn't so much as grunt at her attempts.

Her fingers brushed against something cold. A knife strapped to his thigh. She yanked the weapon out before bending her elbows and aiming it for the asshole's shoulder. He quickly dodged the blow and reached for the knife.

The second his arm released her waist, she tried to twist her body, but the hand on her mouth kept her head in place. The knife disappeared and the arm returned around her.

No! She couldn't let him take her!

She pulled and twisted against the hold, and even as darkness edged her vision, she continued to fight. Even as the last scraps of her energy fled.

She wouldn't stop. Not until she passed out cold with the effort.

The darkness almost consumed her—then she heard a whisper in her ear.

"Stop fighting me, Cass."

Her limbs froze. That voice… A voice that had haunted her for so long. Drowned her in her dreams.

"You're safe."

More hauntingly familiar words. Then the world went black.

AIDAN PARKED the car outside the cabin. He'd swapped cars twice on the way here and watched the rearview mirror the entire drive. There had been no tail, so even if on the off chance whoever was watching Cassie through those cameras at her house had inexplicably recognized him through the ski mask, there was no way they'd find him here. Cassie was safe from whatever was going on. At least for now.

He turned his head, and for a moment, just watched the gentle rise and fall of her chest as she slept in the back seat. At each car change, he'd checked her heart rate and breathing. It had been even. He was used to her fainting spells, and he knew that when her body was ready, she would wake up. Didn't mean he liked it, though. Each and every time, it scared the hell out of him. Like it did right now.

He climbed out of the car. Before going to Cass, he moved to the cabin door and unlocked and opened it. Then he returned and reached for her in the back. The second she was against him, a war raged in his soul. A war between wanting to distance himself from the woman, and tugging her even closer.

The smell of wildflowers mixed with vanilla hit him like a freight train. For a moment, his breath stopped, and he was thrust back to a different time. A time when she was his. A time when upon waking, she nestled into him.

Fuck. He needed to shut it down. The woman was married to another goddamn man. *Had been* married to him for over two years. Sleeping in his bed. Waking up with him.

A dark jealousy tinged with rage began to simmer inside him. That's what he needed to hold on to. That was better than the desire. Rage was a familiar emotion. And it was a hell of a lot easier to navigate.

He made his way up to the cabin. It was cold, and when a gust of wind hit them, a small moan slipped from her lips, and she snuggled into his chest.

Instinctively, he tugged her closer.

Stepping inside, he strode through the living room and straight into the only bedroom at the back of the house, then lay her on the bed. The second he pulled the covers over her, she rolled into a ball and pulled up her legs. She'd always done that. And once upon a time, he'd pulled her against his body and held her.

Shit. He needed to stop. Stop remembering everything he'd forced himself to forget.

With gritted teeth, he moved over to the fireplace. *Focus on that, Aidan. Focus on warming the place up, and not on her.*

There were two fireplaces, one in the living room and one in the bedroom. The team had made sure the place was fully stocked with firewood, food, and water. There were enough supplies that they could hole up here for a month if needed.

He got to work on the fire, but the entire time, her soft breaths sounded through the quiet space, calling to him. Her heartbeat, which he hadn't been able to hear when they were together, now beat loudly thanks to his enhanced hearing.

He'd thought Project Arma would be the most painful experience of his life. It wasn't. It was returning to his family and being told by his mother that Cassie had married Damien six months into his disappearance.

The pain... Fuck, it had been like nothing else. He'd rather take ten bullets to the gut than be told that news again.

Once the fire was set up, he lit the kindling. The flames danced in front of him. Then he turned and looked at her again, because how could he not? It was Cassie. His Cassie. The woman he'd vowed to marry. The only woman he'd ever loved.

He drew closer, and like his hand had a mind of its own, he reached down and brushed a strand of hair from her face. God, her skin was still just as soft as ever.

A soft hum slipped from her. Then a whisper.

"Aidan..."

His breath caught in his throat at the sound of his name on her lips. No one said his name like her. Not a single damn person. *Why* had she said it? Because she'd recognized his voice before passing out tonight? Or because she recognized his touch just now?

He was tugging his hand away when she reached out and latched onto his wrist. Her eyes didn't open, and her breathing didn't change. But that touch... It sent an arrow from his hand right into his chest.

He didn't move. He didn't breathe.

The hand on his arm grew slack. Dropped away.

The warmth where she'd touched dissipated and turned cold. Then his phone rang from his pocket. Cursing under his breath, he stepped out of the room to answer it.

"Callum. Everything all right?"

The guys had followed him halfway, making sure they were safe and no one followed. Then they'd separated.

"Everything's fine on my end. You get to the location okay?"

Depended on what okay meant. He sure as hell didn't feel okay. His blood was rushing through his veins way too fast. "Yep. We're here."

There was a small pause. "We ran the plates."

Aidan's fingers tightened on the phone. They'd taken note of the license plate of every guest at her house, and the guys back in Cradle Mountain were tasked with running them.

"And?"

Callum exhaled loudly. "You're not going to like this."

CHAPTER 4

*C*assie dragged in a long breath. Rays of light played over her eyelids, indicating it was morning.

That smell—woodsy and masculine. Even in the depths of sleep, it permeated the air, slipping deep into her chest.

Aidan. Was she dreaming about his scent now too? Did she miss him that much? She always dreamed about the man's eyes. His touch. But never his scent.

Mm. She didn't mind. In fact, she welcomed it. She might not be able to have him right now, but in her dreams, she could have as much of him as her heart desired.

She rolled onto her back, trying to tug herself back to sleep, needing the escape it offered from reality. She lay there for a few long minutes, then blew out a resigned breath. Nope. It wasn't happening. Dang it.

She rubbed her arms, then stopped. She was wearing long sleeves. That couldn't be right. She always slept in her pale pink silk gown. She'd had it since she'd been with Aidan, and wearing it, especially on the toughest nights, made her feel just that bit better.

Her eyes flew open.

Instead of seeing the crystal chandelier that centered the ceiling of her bedroom, there was a fan with a light in the center. And not only that, but the roof was made from wooden beams.

What the heck was going—

Suddenly, her last memory rushed back to her. The noise in the bedroom. The open window. And the man grabbing her.

Her breaths started to whoosh in and out. Something else poked at her memory. Something important about the man who'd taken her...

"How are you feeling, Cassie?"

The voice shot right into her chest, piercing her heart. She turned her head, and her world slowed. For a moment, she drowned in her memories. Memories of him. Of them. Of the life they'd built and lived together. The life she thought she'd always have.

A long silence filled the room.

"You're not real," she finally whispered, pushing up into a seated position.

He couldn't be. He lived in Cradle Mountain, with the seven other men who'd also escaped Project Arma. He ran a security business. He was living his life without her, just like she was without him. She knew that because every chance she got, she'd done research on him to learn as much as she could.

He shuffled his chair forward, and she didn't know if she wanted to pull back or throw herself into his arms. If she convinced herself he was real, but he wasn't, it would destroy her.

"I am." That voice, that deep rumble. "Are you okay?"

Okay? Was a person okay when they had to relearn how to breathe? When they questioned their very sanity?

Furious tears pricked the backs of her eyes, and her hands clenched the sheets so tightly, her fists ached. "I can't... I don't..." She shook her head.

She watched him in silence for long moments, swearing at

each inhale that she'd wake up. That she'd be back in her home with Damien. That Aidan would be far away, out of reach.

When she didn't wake up, when the realness of her world began to consume her, she straightened. "You're really here."

"I am."

"But if you're really here, then I'm really not home."

His expression didn't change. He gave nothing away. He was so different from the Aidan she remembered. The one who gave her all of himself and hid nothing.

"I own a security company with some guys in Cradle Mountain, Idaho," Aidan said slowly. "We got a call from your *husband* last week."

She flinched at the way he said "husband", like it took everything in him to get the word out. Then his words sank in. "Damien called you?"

He wouldn't have done that. Firstly, because Elijah tapped all their phones...unless he had a burner phone too? No. He would have told her if he had.

And secondly, because... Why?

Hang on... "You kidnapped me?"

"I did." His eyes held her captive. "Damien asked me to. He said if I didn't take you away and hide you somewhere safe, you'd be dead by the end of the week."

Her breath caught and tiny hairs rose on her arms. That wasn't true. It couldn't be. No one but Damien and Olive knew what she'd been planning. Unless... Did he know something she didn't?

She had a plan—a plan she'd worked damn hard to set into place. But she needed to be *home* to enact it. Damien knew all that. He wouldn't have stolen her away at such a critical moment.

"I don't believe you," she whispered.

There was a slight narrowing of Aidan's eyes. "It's true."

He shifted closer, and when he reached for a glass on the side table, the thick muscles in his biceps contracted.

Oh, holy Christ. The man hadn't lost a single muscle. If anything, he'd gotten bigger. Stronger. More...Aidan.

He lifted a glass of something orange. "Orange juice and water with a pinch of salt."

Her stomach fluttered. The man knew her so well. Salt and water were the best treatment after a fainting spell, and orange juice was the quickest sugar hit.

She hesitated. Was there a way she could take the glass without touching him? The idea of touching the man had fear catapulting through her. Because she remembered exactly what his touch did to her.

Probably not.

Slowly, she reached out and slipped it from his hand. It was unavoidable. She grazed his skin, and that heat... It whipped through her body.

This still didn't feel real. It felt like one of those dreams that had plagued her sleep. The ones where he whisked her away from everything, took her somewhere safe where it was just the two of them, and they could forget about the world.

She took a massive gulp of the juice. She wasn't looking at him, but she felt his gaze. That's all it had ever taken. One look and she was lost.

"Who were the men watching your house last night?" he asked quietly.

He was asking her questions about her life now? "What men?" Her mind scrambled to keep up with this situation.

"There were men in cars watching your house last night. There are also cameras in and outside your house."

Of course he saw them. The ones inside were tiny and hidden, but if she'd eventually found them, Aidan would spot them immediately.

She set the glass back on the side table and took a moment before looking at him.

Real. This was real. Aidan was here, and she was no longer at home.

She steeled her spine before speaking words her heart begged her not to say. "Aidan, I can't stay here. I need to go home."

Again. No change in his features. So unlike the Aidan she remembered. "I'm not letting you leave, Cassie. Not until I know you're safe."

Her heart thudded.

No. No, no, no. This was not happening! As much as she wanted to stay with Aidan, as much as she craved it with every fiber of her being, she couldn't. Olive was already skittish. If word got out that Cassie had been kidnapped, the woman would pull out. And then there was the detective. He'd show up at the diner, but neither she nor Olive would be there.

"No, Aidan. I need to get home. *Now!*"

She threw the sheets back and shifted her legs to the side of the bed. Her mouth still felt dry and her limbs heavy, but she ignored both. She pushed to her feet. Aidan immediately did the same.

Her tummy did a little flip. God, he was tall. And broad. And why the heck did he have to smell so good?

Her fingers twitched to touch him. To run along his jawline. Through his hair.

No. Stop, Cassie.

She tried to step to the side but her knees wobbled. Even as Aidan reached for her, she swung away. She could not let the man touch her again. His touch would make her forget why she needed to get back. What she was working so hard to achieve.

He'd make her forget her reason.

~

CASSIE DODGED AIDAN'S TOUCH. He almost growled when she swayed.

Goddammit.

"No." She shook her head. "I can't... You can't touch me right now."

"Tell me what's going on, Cass."

She shook her head.

He ground his jaw. "Why not?"

"Because if I tell you, you won't let me go back."

He took a small step toward her. All he wanted to do was touch her. Cup her cheek. Pull her into him. She seemed like the same Cassie he remembered, but she also seemed...different. "Why do you think I won't let you go back?"

She swallowed. "Because you always thought I was made of glass and I'd break at the slightest bump. You tried to shield me from everything. If I tell you why I have to go, you'll think I'm not strong enough to do what I need to do."

It had been his job to protect her. And standing here with her right now, he just wanted to shield her from all the danger in the world again. "I never questioned your strength." Not for a damn second. He knew the woman was made of steel. "Why do you think that?"

"Because you always wanted to fight my battles for me. Whenever a guy got too familiar at a bar. Whenever I got upset about literally anything."

"Because you were mine to protect." Were. Not are. God, it sounded wrong. "What's going on, Cassie?" He'd continue to ask until he got an answer.

Her voice quieted again. "I'm not yours to protect anymore."

The words were like a dagger to his gut. He'd just thought the same thing, but fuck, it hurt more hearing them out loud. "You'll always *feel* like you're mine."

Then, because he was weak and couldn't stop himself, he reached up and cupped her cheek. She didn't pull away this time, and for a moment, her features softened and she leaned into him.

His breath stalled. This. This was everything he'd been missing. This inexplicable connection they'd always shared. For a split second, it was like they were back where they used to be.

Then she blinked—a single, slow blink—before stepping to the side, away from his touch. It hurt like hell.

She started a slow backward walk toward the door, never taking her eyes from him. "I have to go."

"No."

Frustration contorted her features. "Yes, Aidan."

"I'm not letting you go, Cassie. You won't win this one."

"You can't make me stay."

He heard the lie in her voice. He could, and she knew it. Not just because he was faster and stronger than he should be after Project Arma. He was also former Special Forces.

She spun around and had only taken one step when he spoke.

"I know about the cult."

Her feet slammed to a halt, and he heard her heartbeat speed up. When she turned back to him, it was a slow movement. "How?"

"My team ran the plates of the cars outside your house last night. We know the leader of Paragons of Hope was there, as well as his brothers."

Color drained from her face.

He stepped closer, not entirely sure she wouldn't pass out on him. "Then we did some more digging. Found that you spent a chunk of your childhood living on their compound. That your mother got you and your sister out on your tenth birthday, just before she died."

It had been like a bucket of ice water on his head when Callum had shared the intel. Cassie hadn't told him. *Any* of it. And it killed him. Had she not trusted him enough to tell him?

Another step closer. He thought she'd move back, but she almost looked rooted to the spot. "Why didn't you tell me?"

"I didn't see the point in rehashing my past."

"It was a pretty big omission. I always thought you didn't

want to talk about your childhood because losing your mom and going into foster care was too painful." She was silent. "Did you rejoin because of Damien?" Fuck, he hated saying the guy's name. "Because he was part of the cult?"

According to their research, the man had never left. Another little fact Aidan hadn't been aware of. Cassie had hung out with him regularly while she and Aidan were together, but he'd always gone to her house, never the other way around. Now Aidan knew why.

She swallowed. "I joined because I had to."

"Not an answer to my question, Cass. Why do you need to get back so desperately?"

"Because there's something I have to do."

"Not enough detail."

She took a big step back, and some of the uncertainty turned to anger. "No. You don't get to do that."

He frowned. "Do what?"

Her lips thinned and sealed shut.

"Cassie—"

She ran out of the bedroom and beelined for the front door. When she turned the knob and it didn't work, a loud huff slipped from her lips. She turned and scanned the room.

He moved forward and leaned his shoulder against the door-frame. "That's the only door."

Her jaw ticked and she moved to the window, trying to shove it open.

"Bolted."

She tried another window.

"They're all bolted, Cassie."

She spun around. "I'm not even allowed to breathe fresh air?"

"Tell me you won't try to escape and if I believe you, I'll open one."

"I won't try to escape."

Interesting. She'd gotten better at lying. Not good enough to lie to *him*, though. He could spot a lie on anyone. Little things gave people away. The dilation of the eyes. A shift in breathing. And the big one—the change in heart rate.

"You used to be a terrible liar. What happened?"

She crossed her arms. It pulled his attention to her chest and had his body hardening. "A lot of things happened."

He almost growled, because he wanted to know everything.

She turned back to the window and started pulling at it again. "I can't believe Damien did this!" she protested, almost to herself. "He knows how close I am."

"Close to what?"

She ignored him. Her tugs on the window grew more aggressive. "After everything we've been through, he'd contact *you* to kidnap me? What the hell is wrong with him?" Another tug. "What the hell's wrong with *everyone?*"

On her next try, he moved across the room and grabbed her wrists, halting her movements. She sucked in a sharp breath.

"Stop before you hurt yourself," he said quietly in her ear. "You're not going to get it open."

She did stop. And he became immediately aware of her heat pressed against him. Of her shortened breaths and her heart soaring. Her reaction to his nearness set off a trail of fire inside him. One he hadn't felt in far too long.

CHAPTER 5

*H*e surrounded her. His front pressed to her back. His long fingers circled her wrists.

It was suffocating, but at the same time, it sparked something to life inside her. Something she hadn't felt in so long she'd almost wondered if it had perished.

She closed her eyes. His touch was like being thrust back to a time when her life was simple and made sense. A time when she had love and happiness and security. A time when smiles were easy. God, that felt like a lifetime ago.

His touch lightened from a hold to a graze. Her eyes opened as his thumbs brushed the insides of her wrists. It set fire racing across her skin. A fire that moved through her body, ravaging her heart.

Those strong, familiar fingers moved up her forearms, and even though the material of the dress was between his touch and her skin, it burned her like he was touching skin.

She swallowed hard, trying to bring herself back to sanity. Trying to remind herself why she needed to distance herself from this man. But instead of creating distance, instead of stepping away like she knew she should, she leaned back into him.

Oh, his body... It was as achingly familiar as the rest of him. She swore she could feel his heart beat into her back. A heart that once beat for her.

As those fingers stroked their way back down to her hands, she felt paralyzed. Unable to look away from his touch. Unable to step out of his warmth and the sanctuary his closeness provided. Because that's what he was. What he'd always been. Her sanctuary. Her refuge.

Step away, Cassie. Before he awakens parts of your soul that need to stay dormant.

The words were a scream in her head. A warning. And she almost listened. But then his warm exhale brushed her neck. Her heart stopped. A heavy stillness descended. Then those lips, lips she still tasted in her dreams, touched her sensitive skin. And the words disintegrated in her head. Everything disintegrated except him. Except what he made her feel.

Her breath became heavy. Her eyes wanted to close, but she couldn't stop watching his hands move and graze.

His lips caressed up her neck. She couldn't speak. She could barely think. His mouth did something to her that nothing else in the world ever could. It made her feel things that no one and nothing else ever had.

He paused behind her ear at a place only Aidan knew about. When he sucked, she moaned, tilting her head and giving him better access.

A fog of red ravaged her mind. A fog of desire and yearning and Aidan. All Aidan. It overwhelmed her. *He* overwhelmed her.

When he applied pressure to her hips, she turned, unable not to. For a moment, they just looked at each other. There were no words spoken, not out loud. But in that look, in the heavy silence, she felt everything. The lost time. The pain. The regret. But she also felt harmony. Because this was Aidan. Her Aidan. And he was here. Right in front of her.

She skimmed her hands up his chest before threading them through his hair.

God, he felt exactly the same. His heat and hardness were exactly as she remembered. How had she known this existed, *he* existed, and not run toward it? Not given up and sacrificed everything to have it?

"Aidan," she breathed.

His eyes never left her. "Cassie."

The moment felt so heavy, tears almost pressed to her eyes.

"I shouldn't touch you," he whispered. "But you make me weak."

Weak. That was a word she felt intimately familiar with in this moment. The man made every part of her that was supposed to be strong, that had hardened over the years, feel debilitatingly fragile.

"I missed you," she whispered, unable to stop the words from rolling out from somewhere deep inside her.

"Every day." His breath brushed her face.

Every minute of every day. He hadn't just been her partner. He'd been her entire world. Her everything.

Slowly, she drew his head down. She told herself she only planned to touch her forehead to his. Bring him close. But when his lips hovered over hers, she felt that thing. That undeniable pull. That certainty, that peace was a mere inch away.

So she tugged him that bit closer, and she pressed her lips to his.

Her world stopped, and she finally felt it. Peace. The kind that comes from deep inside you. The feeling that everything in the world is finally okay.

His hands tightened on her hips, and he pulled her close, his lips swiping across hers. This was the kiss she knew so well. The one she was supposed to have known every day for the rest of her life.

She leaned into him, and when her lips separated, his tongue slid inside her mouth. A sound slipped from her lips. Something between a groan and a whimper. Because, God, she wanted to drown in him. She wanted to let this moment capture them both. Keep them here for eternity.

"Aidan..." She breathed out his name once again, this time between swipes of their lips.

"My name sounds so right on your lips," he whispered.

Right. Yes. That was the word. He felt right. He *was* right. It was like they'd been made to fit together so perfectly that anything else just felt wrong.

She didn't know how long they stayed like that, tangled together. Refamiliarizing themselves. She could have stayed there forever. Nothing compared to this. Not a single thing in the entire world.

She was just skimming her hands down his neck when his lips tugged away from hers.

She wanted to pull him back. She wanted to seal herself to him. But then she met his gaze. And instead of love, instead of contentment and peace, she saw something else. It was like a cross between pain and frustration and agony.

The heat in her chest turned cold. She'd done that. She'd put those emotions there.

He stepped back. The cold, which had been building inside her, turned to ice.

He ran a hand through his hair. He didn't meet her eye, almost like he couldn't bear to look at her. "I need to do a perimeter check. I'll be back."

She opened her mouth, but before she could utter a word, he was already walking away from her. He unlocked the door quickly and pulled it closed behind him. The click of the lock was loud in the otherwise silent room.

Something splintered in her chest. Something that had only been put back together mere minutes ago.

WHAT THE HELL was wrong with him? He'd touched her. Kissed her. Made himself believe for a moment that she was his again.

Fuck. He shouldn't have done that. Any of it. The second he'd touched her, the second he'd heard the rise in her heartbeat and felt the heating of her skin, he'd lost himself.

And that kiss...

He closed his eyes. For a short moment in time, that kiss made him forget. About their time apart. About their history and how quickly she'd moved on from him. She'd felt like his again. The soft Cassie who treated him like he was her world. Like no length of time together would ever be enough.

But then he'd forced the haze to clear, and he'd remembered everything. Awareness had dropped like a boulder onto his chest, crushing him.

He hadn't had the words, so he'd left. Deserted her like she'd deserted them.

His gut twisted.

He sped up his steps, his feet sinking into the soft ground. For once, he wished the cold affected him like it used to. He wanted his skin to be as chilled as his heart right now.

He'd run out of the house because Cassie had been standing there, eyes hooded and glazed, and all he'd been able to think was —*mine.* But she wasn't his. She was married to someone else. Her heart *belonged* to someone else. While his was, and always would be, chained to her.

An all-consuming anger and devastation tried to swallow him, but he ignored it, quickening his steps again.

He needed more goddamn self-control around her. And he needed answers. Like why the hell had she rejoined that cult? Why was her life in danger? He could *not* kiss her again. Or touch her. Or do anything else to jeopardize his damn sanity. His heart was already in pieces.

Smoke tinged the air. He already knew it wasn't just smoke from their cabin. There were campers half a mile west. He'd seen them last night, and they hadn't moved any closer, but he'd keep an eye on them just in case.

He jogged to the border of the property, scanning every inch of his surroundings as he went. The time outside and away from her should be calming his body. It wasn't. Because she was still there, back at the house. And soon enough, he'd be returning to her.

Dammit.

He'd made it halfway around the perimeter when a call from Tyler came through. "Hey."

"Hey, brother. How's it going out there with Cassie?"

He blew out a breath. That was a loaded fucking question. "Fine."

There was a heavy pause. "What happened?"

God, you'd think he'd be better at keeping his emotions in check. But nope. He was a mess. "I kissed her."

He'd done more than that. He'd allowed emotions to pass between them that had no business passing. But his friend didn't need to know all the sordid details.

"And?" Tyler asked.

"And then I remembered she's married. That she gave up on us six months after I disappeared. That she won't tell me what the hell's going on."

"Shit. I'm sorry, man. If it's too much, we can send someone else—"

"No." The idea of someone else being alone with her in the cabin... *Hell no.* Not happening. Maybe he was a sucker for punishment. "I've got it." He just needed to remind the rest of himself of that.

"Okay. The offer stands, if anything changes."

"It won't, but I appreciate it."

"Have you gotten any more information from her?" Tyler

asked. "Like why she returned to the cult or who might want her dead?"

That. That's what he needed to focus on. "No. But I will. We've got time." Yeah, time for him to torture himself some more. "You guys keeping an eye on Damien?"

"Yep. And the compound, although it's like a fortress. Heavily guarded, with high walls around the perimeter and cameras everywhere."

Aidan wasn't surprised. "What are they trying to hide?"

"My thoughts exactly."

Before he could respond, a beeping sounded on his phone. His insides iced.

"Is that—"

"The silent alarm," Aidan finished for Tyler. "Someone breached the cabin."

Either that...or someone left.

CHAPTER 6

*C*assie's feet sank deep into the wet earth. It was cold. Really cold. The second Aidan left, she'd forced herself to move. To forget her devastation. To remember what she needed to do and the people who relied on her.

She'd dug around and found clothes. Her clothes. A lot of them. It confirmed her suspicion that he'd planned to keep her for a while.

There was no part of her that could allow him to do that.

She'd thrown on some pants and a top and layered it with a jacket and boots, but Jesus, they were doing little to keep her warm.

She wrapped her arms tighter around her waist and moved her feet faster. The outline of a knife pressed against her side from inside her jacket pocket. It was the same knife she'd used to pick the lock on the front door, something Aidan obviously had no idea she could do or he never would have left her alone.

Well, there was a lot he didn't know about her.

There had to be someone else nearby. Someone with a phone who could call a car. Someone who could help her get home. What she'd do or say once she got there, she had no idea.

One problem at a time, Cassie.

Her muscles tensed at the thought of Damien. He was supposed to be on her side. But he'd had her *kidnapped* when they were so close? And kidnapped by, of all people, Aidan? What the heck had he been thinking?

Maybe he *hadn't* been. Maybe Paragons of Hope was finally affecting him, leaching into his head, like it did to so many others. God knew it was a challenge not to let the place affect *her* some days.

On the next step, her boot sank deep into a muddy hole, and it took three pulls to tug her foot out. It must have stormed here recently. Maybe even last night. Every inch of ground was saturated.

As soon as the thought entered her mind, a speck of rain hit her nose. Oh, jeez. Now it was going to rain? Even the sky was against her.

A shiver rocked her, and she paused. Maybe this hadn't been such a good idea. But what was her alternative? Stay? Let him keep her for an unknown length of time, miss her meeting with Olive and the detective, and allow everything she'd sacrificed over the last two years be for nothing?

Including Aidan. She'd sacrificed *him*. And he was everything. When memories of that kiss tried to return to her, she pushed them away. She couldn't think about that right now. It would have her turning around. Running back to him. Begging for forgiveness.

No. She needed to focus on getting back. On shutting down Elijah's organization and saving Mia.

At the thought of her sister, her heart clenched. She wished her sister could see the truth on her own. But she was in too deep.

She'd rejoined the organization for Sampson. They had met in town and begun a tentative acquaintance. Sampson claimed he was far too busy at the compound for much else. Until a few years ago. He'd reached out to Mia not long after Aidan had gone missing and started spending more time with her. Telling her about the "community" at Paragons of Hope, and just a few months later, Mia admitted she felt something. For both Sampson and the group.

Cassie had tried so hard to convince her sister not to move into the compound. There was a reason their mother had taken them away from that place. A reason she hadn't had a chance to tell them before she'd died.

As Mia got more and more involved with the cult, Cassie knew that if she didn't do something, she might lose her sister forever. It had been an all-consuming gut feeling inside her. In Cassie's head, Mia had become her responsibility the second their mother was gone.

She'd felt so broken. In a period of just a few months, she'd lost the two most important people in her life—Aidan and Mia.

She'd had a choice. Accept that both of them were gone for good or channel her energy into getting back the one person she had a shot at saving.

A gust of wind made her shiver, and she tugged her jacket tighter. The cold was better than heat. Heat and standing for too long were two of the biggest causes of her fainting. She allowed the cold to seep into her limbs and drive her forward. When thoughts of Aidan began to weave their way back into her mind, she gritted her teeth.

Do not look back, Cassie. You can return to him soon—if he'll have you. But not now.

The meeting with the detective was hopefully the beginning of the end. That's what kept her going.

A few steps later, she heard it. Voices. They were faint but there. Hope danced in her chest. There were people nearby. Hopefully, people with a phone and a way for her to get out of here.

The farther she walked, the louder the voices grew.

Finally, people came into view. She hesitated. Three men, sitting on logs around a fire. The men looked bulky even beneath the thick jackets, and they all had dark hair and short beards. One of them had a tattoo running onto the right side of his face.

Her gaze caught on the empty beer bottles scattered around the fire. Then the rifles stacked against the tent. Were they hunters?

She took a step back. A twig snapped. *Shit.* Her eyes shot up to see the closest man looking directly at her.

Double shit.

He rose to his feet. "Why, hello. Where'd you come from?"

The other two men glanced up, noticing her for the first time. Her skin tingled under the weight of their gazes, and not in a good way.

She tried for a smile. "Hi. My name's Cassie. I was hiking with my boyfriend and got a bit lost. I was wondering if you had a phone I could use?"

She threw the boyfriend comment in at the last second. Having these guys think she had someone in these woods looking for her made her feel a bit safer.

The men looked at one another, and the smiles that grew on their faces had unease slithering down her spine.

Okay, this was definitely a mistake.

"Chugs, why don't you go see if that phone in the tent is working," the guy on his feet said to the man closest to the tent. Then he looked back at her. "I'm Slim, by the way. That's Meathead and Chugs."

Interesting nicknames. "Hi."

Chugs rose from the log. She wrapped her arms around her waist, running her thumb over the outline of the knife inside her jacket.

"Come here. Sit by the fire, you look cold." Slim motioned to the log beside him. "I can get you a beer. It'll warm you right up."

Yeah right. Like she'd be accepting a drink from these guys. "No, that's okay. I don't need a beer. Just a phone to make a call."

Her gaze flicked to the tent Chugs had disappeared into, then to the guns. "You guys hunters?"

"We sure are."

"What do you hunt in Utah in winter?" She paused. Wait…was she even in Utah anymore? She had no idea where Aidan had brought her.

"There's plenty to hunt around here," Slim confirmed. "Mostly upland game birds. Also some of the best blue and ruffed grouse you can find."

She nodded. She glanced at the man still sitting on the log to see his gaze scanning her body from head to toe. He was the guy with all the tattoos. The fine hairs rose on her arms.

"You think your boyfriend's close by?" Slim was probably trying to come off as soothing, but God, his voice gave her the creeps. Suddenly, she was regretting all her decisions.

"I'm sure he's really close. Has your friend found a phone?"

One corner of his mouth lifted. Then, without taking his eyes off her, he called out to his friend. "Chugs…anything?"

His friend stepped out of the tent. He had a hand behind his back. "Sorry. No signal."

Okay. Time to go. "Thanks anyway."

She'd only taken a few steps when Slim was suddenly close enough to grab her arm. "Hey. Where you goin'? Let us warm you up."

She tried to tug her arm away, but his fingers dug into her flesh. "Let go."

"Come on, baby, stay." His voice deepened. "I insist."

Anger coursed through her veins at the way the man touched her. "*No*. Now take your hand off me before I hurt you."

All three men laughed. They actually *laughed*. And damn if that didn't make her angrier. The man who'd disappeared into the tent, Chugs, brought the hand behind his back forward.

Her heart thumped. Rope. The guy was holding freaking *rope*.

Slim pulled her harder, toward the group.

Nope. She was not going to stay and become some plaything for these assholes.

Before he realized what she was doing, she'd whipped the knife out of her jacket and slashed at his arm.

Slim cried out, releasing her to grab the cut on his forearm. The knife was so sharp it had sliced clean through his jacket and into his skin.

The smiles slipped from the men's faces.

Meathead rose and Chugs stepped forward.

Shit, shit, shit. Not good. The guys might be drunken assholes, but they were also big. And a knife wouldn't save her for long.

She turned and ran, pumping her legs as fast as they'd take her, forcing them out of the wet ground with each step.

"Come back here, you fucking bitch!"

Their words had her chest seizing and fear spiraling through her limbs. She rounded a tree and ran several more yards before a heavy weight landed on her shoulders, sending her to the ground. A piercing scream tore from her throat.

Strong, punishing fingers latched onto her hair and yanked her onto her back.

The man who'd remained on the log, Meathead, hovered over her. And he looked ready to kill.

COLD AIR WHIPPED across Aidan's face as he ran through the woods. Cassie's footprints made an easy trail, which was a good thing. He needed to get to her fast. It was too damn cold for her to be outside. But even if it wasn't, she didn't know these woods. There were wild animals. Predators. Hell, even damn hunters camping out here—which was the exact direction her prints were leading him.

He'd expected to find intruders at the cabin. A broken door, signs of a struggle. He didn't know if what he'd actually found was better or worse. The lock had been broken from the inside. Cassie had escaped him.

A loud scream pierced the air. Aidan's blood ran cold.

Cassie.

Fuck. He moved faster, whipping through the woods. Suddenly, he saw them. A man hovered over Cassie, his fingers tangled in her hair and a fist raised.

Fiery rage clouded his vision. He flew forward and grabbed the man by the shirt, tearing him off her moments before his fist landed. Then he threw a punch of his own, right into the guy's face. It was powerful enough to send him flying back into a tree.

Another man ran at him. He pivoted, grabbing the asshole by the neck and squeezing. The guy coughed and choked, but Aidan didn't let up. He squeezed hard enough to cut off the man's air.

When a third attacker ran toward him, knife in hand, Aidan finally released the second guy and let him drop to the ground. He spun and grabbed the third man by the wrist, holding the knife. He clenched so hard that there was an audible snapping of bone. The knife fell. The man cried out.

Aidan kneed him hard in the ribs, snapping another bone before tossing him to the ground.

The man he'd thrown into the tree finally rose, charging him. So he was an idiot, as well as an asshole.

Aidan grabbed him by the throat and slammed him against another tree. He squeezed, cutting off the guy's breath before leaning forward. "You and your friends are going to leave these woods today. If I return here and find a single fucking trace of you"—his voice lowered—"I'll cut out your throats."

Real fear widened the man's eyes. Aidan gave one final squeeze, then released him. The jerk tumbled to the ground, coughing and spluttering.

Anger had his chest rising and falling in quick succession. He turned slowly. Cassie was on her feet and looking at him with wide eyes. Her clothes were wet from the rain and the soaked ground.

He moved toward her. She took a quick step back, but that was as far as she got before he reached her. In one swift move, he lifted her off her feet and cradled her against him. He moved quickly through the rain, not sparing the hunters a backward glance.

When he felt the trembles racking her body, a new wave of fury washed through his limbs. Whether she was trembling from cold or fear, he didn't know. It didn't matter. She shouldn't be trembling at all.

"Did they hurt you?" he asked through gritted teeth.

If they had, he'd go back there and murder them.

"No," she said quietly. "You got there b-before they could d-do anything."

A small sliver of relief helped him breathe again. Then a gust of fierce wind lashed them, and she snuggled closer.

"How did you get out?" he asked.

"I p-picked the lock with a knife."

Yeah, he knew that part. "How do you know how to do that?"

More trembles raced throughout her body. "I t-taught myself. In case I ever needed to do it."

A frown marred his brows. "In case you were locked in a house?"

"In case I was l-locked *anywhere* and needed to get out."

Why the hell would this woman go through the effort of teaching herself how to escape a locked room? It made his blood fucking boil.

"You *will* tell me everything, Cassie," he said quietly. "Including every part of your life that you omitted when we were together." He was sick of this guessing game. "And if you ever try a stunt like this again, I'll cuff you to the damn bed."

ull-body shudders rocked Cassie's frame. Her skin felt like ice, her insides so frozen she could barely drag in breaths.

Every time a gust of wind blasted them, Aidan hunched over her, attempting to block the cold. But it wasn't enough. The rain had made her clothing frigid. That, in combination with the wind... It was hell. Pure. Freaking. Hell.

When the cabin came into view, she could have sighed. Or maybe she did sigh because a low growl was just audible from Aidan. The man wasn't happy. After telling her he'd cuff her to the bed if she tried to run again, he'd been stony silent.

As if her hand had a mind of its own, she trailed a finger down his jaw. "You're so much angrier than you used to be."

She wasn't talking about just this moment. Back in the cabin, there had been an unfamiliar thread of anger inside him. A new hard edge. A new *dangerous* rage. He'd always been big and strong, and scary to people who pissed him off. Now he was just...more. Hell, he'd beaten three large men without breaking a sweat.

Was the fury her fault? Had he become this hard and angry because of her?

She swallowed at the thought.

His gaze shot down. His brows twitched before he looked up again and carried her up the porch, shouldering open the cabin door.

Before he'd looked away, she'd seen a flash of something. A flash of softness. Of the gentle Aidan she remembered. She wanted more of those moments. Hell, she craved them.

He stopped in the bathroom and lowered her to the floor. Her knees almost caved, and she grabbed onto his thick biceps even as he clasped her arm.

He swore under his breath. "Dammit, Cassie, what the hell were you thinking?"

He held onto her with one hand and reached to turn the shower on with the other.

"That I had to g-get out." Christ, would this damn teeth-chattering stop? She could barely speak.

If the clenching of his jaw was anything to go by, he didn't like it any more than she did. "Why?"

The sound of water hitting tiles echoed throughout the small room.

She tugged her arm out of his hold. "Because I have an important meeting on W-Wednesday. And if I'm away too long, the person I'm meeting won't come."

And then the detective wouldn't have the testimony and evidence he needed to lock away Elijah and his brothers—men who were pure evil. She planned to shine a light on that evil.

His eyes turned questioning. "Who are you meeting?"

"Someone from the organization." She wrapped her arms so tightly around her waist they pinched into her ribs.

He took a small step forward. He was too close in this tiny bathroom, and he took up far too much space. "You're not very good at answering my questions. I remember a time when I thought we didn't have any secrets between us."

Thought. Past tense. That probably shouldn't hurt as much as it did.

"That was a long time ago," she whispered. "A lot's changed."

He grazed her cheek. "Yet I remember it like it was yesterday."

Me too. She wanted to fall into that heated stroke. She wanted to let the man take her in his arms.

Steam clouded the room. The next shiver to rock her body was more violent than the last.

His voice lowered. "Why'd you do it? Why'd you marry him?"

She tried to hide the flinch but failed. It sounded as strange when he said it as when she'd made the decision. She'd married someone else. It must have destroyed him.

When she didn't respond, he spoke again. "The Cassie I remembered would have waited for me. She wouldn't have forgotten we existed."

The man thought she'd forgotten him? Her next breath was a shudder. She'd never forgotten. That was like asking someone to forget how to breathe. When she remained silent, he sighed. His hand dropped and he tugged his sweatshirt over his head.

Her lips separated and her breath caught. Holy Christ, the man was bigger than she remembered. There wasn't an ounce of fat on him. It was muscle on muscle. He turned to the water, all but dismissing her.

"What about you?" she whispered, forcing her trembling lips to work and form the words she needed to speak. "You didn't come for me either, Aidan."

The muscles in his back rippled. "You were—"

"Married. I know. And I know I owe you an explanation for that. But you owe me an explanation too." Suddenly, she forgot about the cold. She forgot about everything as she spoke words that had been buried deep for years. "You never came and asked me why. Why I did what I did. Why I didn't wait for you. Didn't you want an answer?" If situations were reversed, she would have gone to him.

"I'm asking now."

She stepped closer, lifted her chin. "But would you have come and asked me if Damien hadn't hired you? Would you have demanded answers?"

It was unfair of her to ask. She knew it was. She was the person who'd married someone else. She'd broken them apart. But if their situations were reversed, she would have wondered what the hell had happened. What had driven him to marry someone six months after her disappearance. She would have wondered if something was infinitely wrong.

The last words were a whisper inside her soul.

He moved forward and opened his mouth, but then a full-body shudder rocked her again. His eyes softened. "Take off your clothes, Cass."

Her mouth opened and closed three times before she got words out. "I can shower alone." She balled her fists to try to stop the trembling.

"You think I've forgotten how susceptible you are to passing out in warm showers? And trust me, this shower won't be cool. It needs to be hot to chase away your chill." He took a step forward.

She retreated the same distance, her hip hitting the edge of the vanity.

"Cassie—"

"I can't shower with you." No. No way. It was too intimate. How would she return to her life when she'd felt all of him again?

He took off his boots and followed it up by tugging off his socks. When the pants were pushed down his legs, her stomach quivered. All power and sex. That part of him hadn't changed.

He tilted his head. "Underwear can stay on."

Did he think that would help?

His voice softened again. "Come on, Cassie."

Swallowing, she shot a look at the shower then back to him.

"Fine. But you need to get in first and face the other way while I undress."

Why that was important to her, she had no idea. They'd seen each other naked so many times—she knew every inch of the man, and he knew every inch of her.

His lips twitched, but he didn't argue. Instead, he stepped into the stream of water and faced the wall like she'd asked.

Blowing out a long breath, she started pulling off her clothes. *Jesus, Cassie, this is a bad idea.* But even as the words screamed inside her head, there was a trickle of something else. Something that made her stomach dip and her insides heat.

When she stood wearing just her bra and panties, she sucked in a quick breath and stepped into the shower. The second the water hit her, she gasped. It was like tiny pricks of ice on her chilled skin.

She turned her back to Aidan. His skin just touched hers. It was impossible *not* to touch him. The space was too small, and he was too big. She let the warmth from his body and the water filter into her and warm her insides.

When she felt him turn, and his stomach press to her back, her belly quivered.

There was a moment of silence. Silence so heavy it settled over her like a blanket. Then fingertips touched her neck.

No. Not her neck. Her necklace.

She scrunched her eyes shut. Crap. She hadn't taken it off. Because she *never* took it off.

"You still have this," he whispered.

Her heart kicked. "I do." It made her feel close to him. Some days, it was all that kept her going.

Another beat of silence. Then, big warm hands trailed down her shoulders to her waist.

"There have been moments when I've wondered if what we had was a lie," he said quietly, almost to himself.

"It was real," she whispered.

Why couldn't she breathe when he touched her? Why did he make her want to give up everything for him? For *them*? For what he made her feel?

His head brushed the side of her neck. She tilted her head to give him better access. "I didn't come to you because I couldn't stand to see you with another man. I couldn't see you *belong* to someone else, and for someone else to belong to you. The thought of you happy with a man who wasn't me, the thought of another man touching you... It annihilated me."

She bit back a groan. His words touched a place in her heart she thought had been boarded up long ago.

"He hasn't," she breathed, unable to keep the words to herself any longer.

Aidan's fingers tightened on her. "He hasn't what?"

Don't do this, Cass. Don't say it.

She ignored the whispered warning in her head and turned around. When she pressed her hands to his chest, the dull beat of his heart thumped beneath her touch. Then she said the words she knew would change everything.

"Damien hasn't touched me. No one has. Not since you. Our marriage is in name only."

She looked up to see something flare in his eyes. Something intense and carnal and possessive.

Then he moved.

His head dipped and he claimed her mouth. He swept her up in his arms as the chill from moments ago left her body, replaced by blazing heat. Her insides turned molten. One of his hands went to the back of her head, and the second she parted her lips, his tongue thrust inside.

Everything. The man made her feel *everything*. It was like a tornado of emotions and feelings and flutters at play inside her. And suddenly she knew—there was no walking away from him. There never was. No escaping him or his touch or his possession.

She belonged to him. It was like their hearts were chained together.

His tongue slid across hers, tormenting her while his hand cradled her head. When their lips finally separated, they were both gasping for breath. He touched his forehead to hers, and his fingers threaded through her wet hair.

"You're not going to let me go, are you?" she whispered. She wasn't just talking about this cabin. She was talking about *them*.

"No." His breath brushed her lips as he spoke the single word. "If you'd come to me and made it clear you weren't mine anymore, I would have. Even if it killed me. But that's not the case."

No. And it never would be the case.

"We need to talk about everything," he said.

It was always going to come to this. The second she'd opened her eyes to find him by her bed that morning, she'd known. She just hadn't wanted to admit it. "I will."

Her plans needed to change. She wasn't about to give up, she had too much to lose, but she'd have to pivot.

She was just closing her eyes when the heat of his body and the shower started to make her lightheaded. As if he read her mind, Aidan reached for the water and turned it off.

But he didn't lower her to her feet right away. Instead, he walked out with her still wrapped around him before grabbing a towel and draping it over her shoulders.

When he lowered her to her feet, she was about to walk away, but he gently grabbed her arm and turned her. She looked up to find that his eyes had blackened and he was staring at her hip.

"Jesus, Cassie. What the hell happened?"

She didn't need to look down to know what he was seeing. "I passed out last week." And her hip had made an unfortunate collision with the ground. His jaw clicked in that all too familiar way it did when he was angry. "I was at the compound. I've been a bit…stressed." God, that was an understatement.

Thank God Damien had been there to peel her off the floor.

Aidan growled. Whether he was growling at her passing out or being at the compound, she wasn't sure.

"You're sure as hell not going back there." Her spine straightened at his declaration. "Now, I need to feed you."

She watched the back of him as he grabbed a towel for himself and left the room.

The problem was, she *was* going back there. Not necessarily to the compound, but at least to speak to Olive. She just had to convince Aidan to let her go.

CHAPTER 8

He hasn't touched me. No one has since you.
The words had been on repeat in his head all day, tormenting him.

He hadn't asked any more questions. Instead, he'd wanted her to rest. She'd been attacked. His blood boiled at the memory. They'd spent the day puttering around the house. And they'd talked. Not about anything important, he'd kept the conversation light. Stories about past security clients. What had changed in Salt Lake City. The damn weather. When there was a break in the rain, they'd even taken a short walk outside. It had felt like old times.

He shot a look toward the bedroom door. It was evening. And now, he needed to know. Why marry someone if you weren't going to consummate that marriage? And more than that, how could any flesh-and-blood man marry Cassie and *not* touch her?

He spread pesto over a piece of bread, then topped it with sliced chicken.

If Cassie and Damien hadn't married for any kind of romantic connection, and it had been in name only, then why *had* they married?

59

He grabbed a tomato out of the fridge and sliced it.

His team had done more digging into the organization. Roughly half their members lived inside the compound, while the rest lived outside. All members living outside were married, with the men working and the women staying at home. Most had kids. The houses outside the compound, including Cassie and Damien's, were owned by Paragons of Hope. They were all expensive, with top-of-the-line security.

Another question—how the hell did the organization have so much money?

He lay the tomato over the chicken. He was just setting cheese on top when the bedroom door opened and Cassie strolled out. He stopped. She wore yoga pants that molded to her legs like a second skin and a long pale pink knit sweater. Her auburn hair lay thick over her shoulders. He'd always loved her hair. It reminded him of a river—flowy and shiny and fucking beautiful.

Her steps slowed. "Stop looking at me like that."

He played dumb. "Like what?"

"Like you're a stone's throw away from pinning me against the closest wall."

His dick twitched. He was definitely close to doing that. He set the second slice of bread on top of the cheese. "Come. Sit. I'm just making us some sandwiches for dinner."

She perched on a barstool. "You're making chicken pesto sandwiches?"

"They're your favorite. Or at least they were..." Had that changed too?

"They still are," she said quietly. "You always hated them, though. In fact, I distinctly remember you saying pesto was horse food."

A smile tugged at his lips as he set the sandwiches in the press. He *had* said that. "Maybe I've changed my mind."

He hadn't. Honestly, he'd stayed as far away from pesto as

possible the last few years. Just the sight of the stuff made him feel sick with thoughts of Cassie.

He grabbed the apple juice from the fridge and poured some into two glasses.

"Apple juice too. Another favorite of mine," she said.

"My team and I made sure the place was fully stocked before we arrived."

She tilted her head. "Your team as in the guys who run Blue Halo Security?"

He wasn't surprised she knew things about him. With the media coverage the way it had been, it would have been impossible not to. "Yep."

There was a small pause before she spoke again. "I'm sorry about what happened to you."

Not sorry enough to come find me when I returned. He swallowed the words. "I got out. My team and I are stronger than ever, and we're using what was done to us to help others."

It sounded like a silver lining, and it was. But he'd never get those stolen lost years back with Cassie. And he'd never get to say "I do" before another man.

She ran her finger along the edge of the counter. "I know you might not believe me, but I missed you."

He looked over to her. There was the hint of tears in her eyes. He hated that.

"A lot," she pressed. "Some days, I didn't know how I'd survive."

More shredding of his heart.

She shifted her finger to the rim of the plate in front of her. "Then just two months later, my sister went back to the cult. Even Felix died. I felt like I'd lost everyone I cared about."

His jaw ticked. Felix was technically her dog, but he'd really been both of theirs.

"And it was one of those moments," she continued. "Sink or swim. I had to decide if I was stronger than my circumstances."

He stepped around the counter and turned her stool so she faced him. "I'm sorry about Felix and your sister." And about him. If it had been her who'd gone missing, he would have been destroyed.

She swallowed. "Thank you. I never missed my mother so much as I did then."

He clenched his teeth. Her mother had died in a house fire when she was ten. Fucking heartbreaking.

"Why did Mia go back to them?"

"A man from the organization, Sampson... She met him one day in Salt Lake City." She lifted a shoulder. "They got close. He spoke a lot about the community, and she said she wanted to go back. I think part of it was because she'd fallen in love with Sampson, but another part was that maybe I wasn't enough. It's just been her and me since she was eight."

No chance. "You're more than enough."

She gave him a small smile but didn't say anything.

"You didn't think she was safe when she went back there?"

Her finger continued to move. "Mom took us away from there for a reason. She died too quickly after we left to tell me what that reason was, but I have a couple of vague memories of her speaking about Elijah before she died. There was real fear in her eyes. I remember it vividly. It was the only time I ever saw her scared. I knew it wasn't safe for Mia to be there."

Aidan's gut tightened. If it wasn't safe for Mia, it sure as hell wasn't safe for *her*. Something she had to be aware of.

"Why didn't you tell me about the cult?" he asked quietly.

Her brows twitched, and her voice quieted. "I didn't like to talk about any of my childhood. You had these beautiful parents, this beautiful home. While I was raised in a cult until I was ten, then went into foster care after Mom died." She lifted a shoulder. "I guess I was embarrassed."

Suddenly, she stood and moved around the counter. Without a word, she went to the sandwich press and opened it. She'd always been like that. Needed to keep busy when things got hard.

He waited until the sandwiches were on the plates and she returned to her seat. He watched as she took a bite of the sandwich and closed her eyes. A moan sounded in her throat.

Fuck. That sound... It did things to him he needed to push away. For the moment, at least.

"How do you make this sandwich taste so much better than anyone else's?" she asked. When she opened her eyes, they were soft. "Yours always taste the best. I missed them."

He'd missed *her*. All of her. He'd gotten good because he knew she liked them, and he'd do anything to hear that hum fall from her lips. "Talent."

She chuckled. And yep, even that soft, lyrical sound had every part of him hardening. "My housekeeper, Mrs. Alder, prepares most of our meals, and I swear she knows everything I hate and makes a point to prepare those dishes as much as possible." Her face screwed up when she said the woman's name.

"You don't like her?"

She scoffed. "The woman's the devil incarnate. She's basically a spy for Elijah. If it were my choice, she'd have been fired long ago. Heck, she'd never have been there to begin with. Elijah doesn't like married women to have jobs, so I just sit around and twiddle my thumbs most days. Basically, I'm brain dead."

Hardly. He stroked a hand up her thigh, reveling in her little shudder. "Are the cameras his too?"

"Yes. They're in every room except our bedroom and the bathrooms. Thank God. I think I would have murdered him myself if he put them in there."

Aidan lowered his own sandwich. "Why's he watching you?"

"He watches everyone. Especially those who don't live in the compound."

"Why?"

She laughed, but there was no humor behind it. "To make sure we're living according to his rules. No TV, music, pop culture or world news. Women have to wear conservative clothing and aren't allowed to work. Most children are homeschooled, except some of the boys who attend high school."

She shook her head. "Oh, and to make sure we're not asking questions we shouldn't be. It's all about control for Elijah. People refer to him as *Holy Leader*."

He sounded like a sick scumbag. "So what have you been doing, Cassie? Why do you need to return so badly?"

This was about more than getting her sister out. She'd said what she was doing was dangerous. Damien had said if she stayed, she'd die. Aidan needed to know why.

For a moment, her eyes remained on the window. But when she looked back at him, they were steely. "I'm making sure that asshole Elijah goes to jail. That he gets locked up and stays in prison until his body rots."

CASSIE WATCHED as Aidan's eyes darkened and his fists clenched.

"Why would he go to jail?" he asked quietly.

So many reasons. "Well, for starters, he puts sedatives in the wine during family gatherings to make members calmer and more pliable. I'm sure some people have realized, but no one ever says anything."

"How do you know?" Aidan asked. "You don't drink alcohol."

She didn't. Alcohol wasn't good for her hypotension. "I've worked hard the last couple years to develop relationships with people from the organization. I ask the right questions. Get close to the right members."

Cassie was also good at reading people. Always had been. She could see in a person's eyes when they knew something. That's when she'd pounce. She made people feel safe around her, secure enough to open up.

Aidan's hand stroked her thigh again, and God, it was torturous.

"That's not even the big stuff, though." It certainly wasn't something that would get him thrown into prison for long, if at all.

"What's the big stuff?"

"He makes every member take out life insurance."

"How's that—"

"*He's* the designated beneficiary on the policies."

Aidan leaned back in his seat. "He's benefiting off his members dying?"

"More than that. He's *killing* them. Or his men are, at least. Every time the organization is running a little low on funds, a member dies in some freak accident. I have a direct quote from a guy on the finance team to support that."

Another ticking of his jaw. "Anything else?"

Aidan wouldn't like this part. "After he laces the wine, he gets...*close* to the female members, and he often takes them to his room." Another huge reason she had to get Mia out.

This time, Aidan's eyes darkened to near black.

"Even if the drinks weren't laced," she continued, "the women often don't feel they can say no to him. Because of who he is and the pedestal they put him on. Not to mention he often chooses younger women."

So, to summarize, he was drugging women, then having sex with them. It was rape, pure and simple.

"Has he ever touched you?"

That hard, dangerous voice sent a shiver down Cassie's spine. "No. And I've wondered why. I thought maybe because I never drink the wine. Or maybe because he could sense that I didn't like him." She frowned. "One of the last things my mother said to me before she died was that Elijah thought I was special. I don't know exactly what she meant by that but...maybe that's why?"

Not that she would have allowed him to touch her anyway. Not without putting up one hell of a fight.

Aidan frowned. "Do you know why he thinks you're special?"

Wasn't that the golden question? "No. Not exactly. The night before my mother took me and my sister away, Elijah told her he had some sort of revelation from God about me."

If only her mother was still alive to tell her everything.

"You're not going back there," he almost growled.

This was why she hadn't told him everything the second she'd woken up. Why she'd never tried to reach out to him, always planning to contact him when it was finished. Because this man had been, and always would be, her shield from danger. Only, she didn't need a shield right now. She needed a sword.

"I have to. There's a member, Olive. She woke up after a Friday family night naked in Elijah's bed, with no recollection of the night before. And not long after, Elijah killed her brother." Her heart ached for the woman. "She's too scared to go to the police. She probably wouldn't make it to them anyway. Elijah watches her like a hawk. He also has a ton of former military guards. All of them are prepared to kill for him."

The veins in Aidan's neck stood out. "So what was your plan?"

She wet her lips. "She's meeting me at a café on Wednesday. Her guards will see me when she sits down, of course, but they always wait outside. I've been communicating with a detective who's been investigating Elijah for a while and have arranged for him to sit at a table nearby and record our conversation. Olive knows what's going on, and she's agreed to tell me, and him, her entire story. Allegedly, she has evidence of what he did."

She breathed in a long breath. "It's taken a long time to get her to agree, Aidan. She lives in the compound with her mother, who's basically bedridden, and she's terrified Elijah will hurt her mother to keep her silent. She needs Elijah arrested so she can get her mother out of there and get justice for her brother and herself."

Please God, say the woman still wants to meet. She was so skittish. Cassie had to get back, and she had to get back quickly.

Aidan leaned forward. "My team will come up with a plan to get him arrested for the crimes he's committed. We'll get the proof we need to shut them down."

Cassie stood, and immediately he rose too. "Your team can't achieve what I can achieve so quickly. I told you, it took years to get Olive to trust me. And not just that, but she doesn't trust men anymore. Even if you got close enough, there's no way she'd let you help." Elijah needed to be locked up, and he needed to be locked up now. *She* could do that.

He moved toward her, and she took a quick step back, holding up her hand. "Don't."

He raised a brow. "Don't what?"

"You know what. Don't come near me or touch me."

He took another step forward. "Why not?"

He knew damn well why not. "Because then my heart will beg me to agree to whatever you say, and it won't care that my mind knows I need to finish what I started. My sister and the members who feel stuck at Paragons of Hope *need* me."

"You're mine to protect, Cassie."

She shook her head, even though her heart agreed wholeheartedly. "I'm not." Why did her voice come out so low?

He almost looked like he wanted to laugh. "But you are. You admitted your marriage is just in name. That the man you married doesn't touch you. When *I* touch you, you melt for me, even after all this time. But even without the physical stuff, when you talk, my heart listens. And I know yours does the same." Her heart thudded. "You belong to me, just as much as you did three years ago. And I belong to you."

Oh, Lord, it was true.

He moved forward again.

"Aidan, I haven't forgotten how to lay your ass out." The man had taught her himself.

This time he *did* laugh. "I'm not the same man I was, honey."

"And I'm not the same woman."

"Why didn't you have sex with Damien?"

Her breath caught at the abrupt question. She'd known it was coming, but here? Now? When he was making her entire body tingle with a single look?

"Because I don't feel for him what I feel for you, and he doesn't feel it for me either." They were friends. Best friends. But that was as far as their feelings went. "I found him again when I aged out of foster care and after he'd started working in finance." It was like no time had passed. That's how good of a friend he was before she and her family had fled the compound.

On her next step, the backs of her legs hit the couch. She was out of room.

He stepped forward and both her hands rose. They were supposed to stop him, but the second the traitorous things touched him, they smoothed over his hard edges.

He lowered his head, his breath brushing her ear. "Did he ever try to sleep with you?"

Her eyes closed. She had to push him away. Or at least, she told herself she did. Then his lips touched her neck.

A shuddering sigh slipped from her lips, and words she hadn't meant to speak slipped out with it. "He's not interested in women...and he's already seeing someone else in secret."

Every second of the long pause that followed dragged against her nerve endings.

"It's one of the reasons Damien also needs to get out," she continued. "At Paragons of Hope, homosexuality is a sin. We married in name only so we could live away from the compound. He had more freedom after we wed. He fell in love with Dean, a beautiful man he works with, while the two of us have been working on a way to get the place shut down."

"How does Dean feel about all of this?"

Her skin tingled. "He helps where he can. He found Detective Shaw for me. Got me a burner phone."

Another moment of pause, then those lips touched her neck again in light, tender kisses. "Everything finally makes sense. And now there's nothing to stand between you and me."

Wait…what? Yes, there was. "I'm still married, Aidan."

"On paper."

Finally, she pushed at him. He lifted his head.

"Aidan—"

"Do you love me?"

Her heart stopped at his question. It literally didn't beat for a moment. "Don't ask that." Not while she was weak and drowning beneath his touch.

He curved a hand around the back of her neck. *"Do you love me?"*

She kept her lips firmly closed. She needed the man to agree to send her back. Admitting anything would not help her cause.

"I love *you*," he whispered.

Her lungs seized, and something came alive inside her, a feeling she hadn't experienced in years. She hadn't heard those words in so long.

His fingers grazed her neck. "I never stopped loving you. I tell myself that I tried, but that was just a lie to keep me going. My love for you is like an obsession. It's something I was born to do, and I can't stop."

Her mouth opened and closed. Then she said the words she couldn't hold in any longer.

"I love you too."

His head lowered, and he took her lips.

CHAPTER 9

*K*issing Cassie was like fire. It was an explosion of desperate hunger. An obliteration of the world around him.

He grabbed her hips and tugged her body tighter against his. But she never felt close enough. When he slipped a hand beneath her shirt, and she gasped, he eased his tongue inside her mouth.

Christ, the woman tasted good. His. She tasted like she was *his*.

She kissed him back with the same need. As if the chance of separating meant they'd never find their way back to each other again. But then, he'd always needed her as much as she needed him. The inability to get enough of each other had been a frequent and welcome problem.

Those hands of hers, the ones that had been moving across his chest and tormenting him, ran up his shoulders, leaving a trail of fire.

He lowered his other hand to her ass and lifted her, then he swung them around, pressing her against the closest wall. Her sweet moan punctured his heart. It made him want to take her. Reclaim her as his.

He grazed a hand up her side beneath the sweater. No bra. Fuck, that made him harder. He cupped the small weight of her breast. Another hum from her throat, accompanied by another rippling of his chest.

He swiped a thumb over her hard peak, reveling in the shudder that rocked her spine. He swiped again. Same thing. She was so damn responsive to every little touch, just like he remembered.

He tugged his mouth free of hers and moved down her cheek before settling on her neck and sucking. Her head tossed to the side, giving him more access. With a hard, impatient yank, he tore the sweater over her head.

As if she needed to feel skin on skin as badly as he did, she grabbed the hem of his shirt and pulled. He helped, and when he finally pressed against her bare breasts, blood roared between his ears.

Cassie. *His* Cassie.

He reached down and unzipped her jeans. When he slipped his hand inside her panties, he strummed a finger across her clit. Her cry pierced the room, and her nails scratched his back.

He stroked again. The next sound was a whimper, and when he slipped a finger inside her, all her muscles tensed.

"You're so damn beautiful, Cass."

How had he survived these last few years, knowing this existed but was out of his reach?

"Aidan…" Her breathlessness as she said his name haunted him.

He trailed a line of wet kisses down her chest until he landed on her breast. Then he closed his lips around her sweet nipple and rolled his tongue over her.

She groaned and hummed, circling her hips against his finger and pressing her chest into his mouth.

He pushed a second finger inside, stretching her.

"Aidan!" Desperation. It fucking coated her voice. Those damn nails scraped down his skin. "I need you!"

And she'd have him. But first, he needed to feel her come apart in his arms.

In slow, deep motions, he thrust his fingers in and out, his tongue continuing to work her hard nipple. He absorbed every tremor until, finally, she came around his fingers. She screamed as her body pulsed.

He lifted his head and watched the array of emotions flicker across her face.

Perfect. She was *perfect*. And he wanted more. More of her. More of them. More of everything.

He captured her sounds with his mouth, his fingers still pumping inside her, and she kept grinding against his hand until the tremors finally stopped. Then he strode into the bedroom and lowered her to her feet, her harsh breathing and their pumping hearts the only sounds in the room.

CASSIE'S BODY rippled from the power of what Aidan had done to her. She was hot and tingly, and every part of her was in overdrive. Yet she wanted more. And she just knew nothing would ever be enough with him.

Slowly, she reached for his jeans, and with trembling fingers, she undid the buckle and pulled down the zipper. Then, with both hands, she pushed down his jeans and briefs.

Her breath caught at the sight of him, just as long and thick as she remembered. He stepped out of his jeans, and her gaze caught on a couple of scars on his stomach. Scars she remembered from his time serving. This body of his... She remembered it so well. Better than her own.

She stepped forward and lowered her head. Gently, she pressed a kiss to the first scar. Then the next.

It was on the third kiss when she reached down and stroked his length.

He sucked in a sharp breath. She'd always loved what her touch did to him. Loved that she could bring such a powerful man to his knees. His muscles tensed and clenched beneath her lips as she continued to graze and caress him. He grabbed her hips in a firm hold, and his chest moved rapidly as he began to suck in quick breaths.

She couldn't stop. She tightened her fingers around him, and a low growl rippled from his depths. A growl that made her heart flutter and her stomach fizz with little dips.

She moved her hand up and down his length, remembering everything he liked, rewarded with more primal sounds. He grew thicker in her hold, the fingers on her hips digging into her flesh.

She'd barely started exploring him when one strong hand gripped her wrist, halting her. Then his mouth crashed to hers again. Tasting. Sucking. Taking.

She pressed her hands to his chest, pushing him back onto the bed, then removed her leggings so that she stood in front of him wearing only black panties.

His eyes turned the darkest brown she'd ever seen. The way he looked at her...it was possessive. Like she belonged to him, and he to her, and that was simply how it would always be. Which was true. The man had owned her heart since the first day they'd met.

Her belly quivered at the way Aidan's eyes never left hers, even as she slid her panties down her thighs.

God, he looked big. All of him. Like a big, bronzed soldier. *Her* soldier. Slowly, she crawled up his body.

"This is a terrible idea," she whispered. But there was no conviction in her words. "I should keep my distance from you. Keep my focus on shutting down Paragons of Hope." But even as she said it, she knew the words were a waste of air. The man had already stolen her focus. One touch and she was lost.

He reached up to thrum her pebbled nipple again. Her eyes shuttered and a breathless moan escaped her throat.

"You and me are always a good idea, Cass. No one could ever love you like I love you."

Her brows tugged together. His words were like a fist around her heart, squeezing and forcing it to contract.

His other hand slid up her thigh. Her breath caught.

He swiped her clit. "Our love for each other is the same."

It was. Her love for him was so strong that losing him had almost meant losing herself.

"And I'm here," he whispered, almost reading her mind.

Here. The man she loved, the man she'd lost for a while, was here with her after years of forced absence.

"Take me."

At his whispered words, she lowered her head and kissed him. Her body dropped with her head, her chest against his, her core against his hardness. The need inside her was hot and aggressive, demanding she have him.

There was no hesitation in the way he kissed her back. In the way his fingers threaded through her hair, tugging her closer. His tongue tangled with hers, demanded more.

He flipped them over, and suddenly he was everywhere. His body surrounded her, making her feel small and fragile as he began a slow grind. Oh, God. She needed him inside her now. It was to the point she felt like she might die if she didn't.

"Aidan, now." As an extra nudge, she wrapped a leg around his hip, tugging him closer.

There. He was right there at her entrance.

One of those deep growls slipped from his lips. Then he abruptly rose. When he disappeared to a corner of the room, she could have cried. There was a crinkling sound. A second later, he was back on top of her.

When she felt him at her entrance once again, she touched his cheek. "I missed you."

The words were inadequate. What she'd felt was a deep ache inside her. One she'd managed to convince herself she could live with.

Not anymore.

His hand went to her thigh, lifting it to once again curve around his hip. "Never again will we go so long apart, Cass. Never."

Slowly, he sank all the way inside her, stretching her insides. Pleasure engulfed her.

"Never again," he whispered once he was seated all the way in.

She wanted to cry, and not just because he felt so damn good. But because this was Aidan, and his words held all the promise her heart and soul needed to hear.

He pulled out and eased back inside. Her fingers bit into his skin, and her whimper was silenced by his mouth against hers. He thrust in and out of her in deep succession, filling her so completely.

Soon, she began lifting her hips, meeting him thrust for thrust, tugging him back to her with her leg around his hip. Her limbs shook, her stomach molten.

With each thrust, her breasts bounced and grazed against his chest. God, she wouldn't last much longer. He reached between them and ran a thumb over her clit. She jolted against the sensation. Her entire body was alight, his hardness driving so deep, she swore she could feel him everywhere.

Her head tipped back, her eyes scrunching closed. "Aidan..." She didn't know if she'd whispered or cried his name. She could barely hear a thing through the blood rushing between her ears.

He nibbled behind her ear before whispering, "Come for me, Cassie."

Her back arched and she broke into a million tiny pieces. Pleasure pulsed throughout her body. He was still pumping, and she was still throbbing, when she opened her eyes to see a nearly pained look on his face.

She reached up and palmed his cheek, then she pulled his head down and kissed him, tangling her tongue with his. Finally, he broke. A growl rippled from him, but his lips never left her own.

He pulsed inside her. And when he finally tore his lips away, he pressed his head into the crook of her neck.

Her eyes closed again, and for a moment, she wondered how the hell she was supposed to leave this man, even for a week, and return to a life she'd built without him in it.

CHAPTER 10

$\mathcal{A}$idan watched the slight scrunching of Cassie's eyes. God, she was beautiful. Even while she slept, she was and always had been the most beautiful woman he'd ever laid eyes on.

It was early morning, but he'd been awake for hours. Listening to every little sound around the cabin. Watching her chest rise and fall as she breathed.

There was this throb inside him. It called him to touch her. Have her. For so long, their separation had torn him apart. Made him feel hollow. But here and now, being with her again, he could almost convince himself that no time had passed. The admission about her and Damien truly just being friends was everything. Just like last night was everything.

After she'd fallen asleep, he'd called his team and passed on what she'd told him. They were already working on a plan on how to move forward. She wasn't going back alone. He couldn't let her.

A soft murmur slipped from her lips. Then his name. "Aidan."

Fuck. That was the second time she'd said his name while she slept, and it had every territorial instinct roaring to life.

Slowly, she opened her eyes. And when their gazes met, a small frown marred her brow. "How long have you been watching me sleep?"

"Not long." Lie. Big lie. "Hang on."

He climbed out of bed and moved into the kitchen. A few moments later, he returned with a cupcake and a candle. "Happy thirtieth birthday, Cass."

With a gasp, her lips parted. "You remembered?"

"Of course. I couldn't forget."

Lord knew he'd tried. The last couple years, he'd done everything he could to forget. To distract himself on this day, in order to keep functioning.

She smiled and blew out the candle. When she took the cupcake from his hand, she swiped some icing and put her finger in her mouth.

He hardened. *Jesus Christ.* The woman was going to be the death of him.

Her eyes closed. "Oh my gosh. Chocolate hazelnut butter cream. I haven't had this in… Well, a long time."

It seemed she hadn't had a lot of her favorite foods in a long time.

She licked more icing off her finger, her gaze on the cupcake, but her brows pulled together like she was deep in thought. "They were throwing me a ball tonight in honor of my thirtieth birthday."

The heat in his stomach turned to acid at the mention of that damn cult. "Sounds extravagant. Do they do that for all birthdays?"

She shook her head. "Not all. Just some. Usually the big ones." She lifted a shoulder. "I guess thirty classifies as a big one."

She was five years younger than he was, though age had never been a factor in their relationship. They'd met at a baseball game. Both of them had gone with friends, each sitting on the outskirts of their respective groups, and had ended up next to each other.

He'd barely watched that game. At the end, he didn't even know who'd won. All he wanted to do was talk to her more. See her smile again.

He sat on the edge of the bed and ran a finger along her shoulder. She shuddered.

"Are you sad you're missing it?" he asked gently.

She scoffed. "No. I hate being around them. It's exhausting. I'll miss seeing Mia, though. And I'm worried about what Olive will think of my absence." Her gaze rose to his, and a new determination filled them. "I'm still going back, Aidan."

"No—"

"I *am*," she said quickly. "I have to. You can do whatever you need to do to make sure I'm safe. Put a listening device on me. Put your own cameras up in the house. But I need to finish this. I've put over two years of my life into getting close to people in Paragons of Hope. Learning what's really going on. Building relationships. Making plans. Dean risked his life to give me that phone and make contact with Detective Shaw. If Elijah finds out what he's done…" She paused. "Olive is the solution here. I can't lose her."

"And I can't lose *you*."

Her eyes softened. "You won't."

"Damien said you'd be dead if I didn't get you out of there." Even saying those words out loud made him feel sick to his gut.

Frustration washed over her face. "I don't know why. But I'm not going back in alone. You can figure out a way to keep me safe, and I'll find out from Damien what he knew."

He scrubbed a hand over his face. "Cassie—"

She touched his arm. "Please, Aidan. Trust me."

"I do trust you. It's other assholes I don't trust."

She swallowed, then her eyes misted. "I can't *not* do this. I can't give up. Mia's the only family I have left. She's not safe there. And neither is anyone else. Women are being raped. Innocent people are *dying*."

Fuck. He needed to say no. Hell, he should bundle the woman in bubble wrap and drag her back to his house with its state-of-the-art security. But if he said no, and his team couldn't shut the cult down, if something happened to her sister because he'd forced her to leave, Cassie would never forgive him.

He blew out a long breath. "I'll call my team today. I'm not making any promises, but we'll talk options."

She sighed and leaned her head into his chest. "Thank you."

"I don't need to be there for the call." Cassie tried to slip from the living room, but Aidan was suddenly grabbing her wrist. *Damn*, he was fast. He'd always been quick, but now... Well, now he could cross from the kitchen to the bedroom in literally the blink of an eye.

He frowned at her. "Why don't you want to be on the Zoom call with my team?"

Wasn't that obvious? "Because they're your best friends."

When he just kept looking at her with that "explain" expression on his face, she sighed. "Because we were dating. Not casually dating. Not on-and-off dating. In-love-forever dating. Then you disappeared, and six months later I married someone else. *You* don't hate me because you love me. But they love *you*, and they saw how much I hurt you." She tried to pull away, but his hold was unbreakable.

He pulled her into his chest, and his breath brushed against her ear. "They don't hate you. They've never hated you. In fact, almost every day since we got out, at least one of them has been on my ass about returning to you and getting the full story."

That had her pausing. She'd just assumed they'd all think the worst of her. "Really?"

He raised his head. "Really."

This time when he tugged her over, she moved hesitantly

along with him. She started to sit on a chair at the table, but he dropped into it first and tugged her onto his lap.

"Aidan." She pushed up, but the Zoom call came through on the laptop in front of them. Aidan leaned over and pressed a key. Suddenly, five broad-shouldered, well-muscled men appeared on the screen, all of them sitting around a long table. Even though Cassie had never met a single one of them, she knew each by name. When the media frenzy had occurred, she'd squirreled away every newspaper and magazine article she could get her hands on. She'd read and reread everything every chance she got, needing to know as much about Aidan and his life as she could.

"Hey, guys." Aidan's voice was as relaxed as she'd ever heard it, and there was real affection there. "This is Cassie. Cassie, this is Blake, Flynn, Tyler, Callum and Liam."

She received a series of nods and "heys". None of them seemed to blink an eye at seeing her on Aidan's lap. And more than that, none of them looked at her with any obvious hostility.

A breath she hadn't realized she'd been holding released from her chest. "Hi."

"Logan and Jason are currently watching the compound," Blake said. "How are you both holding up?"

"We're good," Aidan answered. "Had a little bit of trouble yesterday morning with a few local hunters."

Her heart thumped at the mention of the run-in with the campers. Aidan's fingers slipped beneath the hem of her top, and he gently rubbed her belly with his thumb. Her muscles relaxed.

The guys all seemed to tense. God, they were all replicas of Aidan.

"I handled it," he said quickly. "They've moved on. No sign of anyone else around. Anything on your end?"

"Damien called from his burner phone yesterday and left a message here at Blue Halo."

Cassie straightened at Flynn's words. "What did he say?"

"He told us he would call at ten p.m. to talk to us, but he never did."

Cassie frowned. If there was one thing true about Damien, it was that he was a man of his word. "What do you mean, he didn't call?"

This time it was Liam who answered. "We were here, waiting for the call, but it never came through."

"In fact," Callum added, "Jason had been watching Damien, but he went to the compound yesterday and hasn't left."

Unease coiled in her belly. Damien never stayed at the compound, certainly not overnight. He hated that place as much as she did. Probably more.

Feeling her tension, Aidan grazed her bare skin again. "I'm sure he's okay," he said quietly to her before looking at the screen. "What are the police doing about Cassie's disappearance?"

Tyler leaned back in his seat. "There have been no police reports filed."

Cassie scoffed. "Of course not. Elijah does everything he can to avoid drawing police attention."

"That's not to say Elijah isn't looking for you," Callum replied, his voice hard. "He's got guys out roaming the streets. Don't ask how I know this, but they've hacked into street cameras and airline databases. They have guards from the compound searching everywhere."

Sounded like Elijah. "He sees the members of Paragons of Hope as his property. When Aidan took me, he would have considered that theft, rather than kidnapping. And of course he wants his property back." God, she hated the man. She'd never hated anyone even half as much.

Aidan sighed. "Cassie wants to go back, *temporarily*, until after this meeting with Olive and Detective Shaw."

There was a heavy silence. She wanted to squirm. Hell, she wanted to get off Aidan's lap and pace. His hand tightened on her hip. The damn mind reader.

"You're okay with that?"

Blake's words had her back straightening. "I'm my own person."

"Never said you weren't."

"I *have* to go back," she said quickly. "Olive will only go if the meeting is with me, and if she thinks it's safe."

The expressions on the guys' faces barely changed.

"We made contact with this Detective Shaw," Blake finally said. "He indicated he needs the recorded confession from Olive and whatever evidence she has to be able to arrest the guy and keep him locked up, at least temporarily."

Exactly what he'd told her.

Finally, Tyler spoke. "We'd need to find a different location to make sure it can't be traced back to any of us. We have to make it look like Cassie was held there and escaped. Make up a story but keep as close to the truth as possible."

"Yeah, the asshole running the joint will definitely send people to investigate and back up her story," Liam added.

"In terms of when she gets home, I can ensure some of the houses around hers are empty so we can stay close," Callum said, tapping on the laptop in front of him. "At least the houses on either side and opposite. We can also give Cassie a listening device."

"Under no circumstances would you go into that compound," Aidan added quickly. "If I even suspect Elijah's taking you there, I'll be raiding that place, and to hell with consequences."

She gave a short nod even as her heart thudded. They were actually letting her do this. She was going to return to her home. To Paragons of Hope. To Elijah.

CHAPTER 11

"You need to make it tighter."

"Cassie—"

"No, don't 'Cassie' me." She shoved her hands under Aidan's nose. "You need to make it *tighter*. Elijah's lapdogs need to see bruises on my wrists." They both knew it was the small details that would get them through this.

He growled. "I am not bruising you."

Her voice gentled. "The alternative is worse, and you know it. If Elijah figures out I'm lying…"

Truthfully, she had no idea what he'd do. She didn't think he'd kill her. Lock her inside the compound, though? Probably. "Please."

There was another vibration of his chest, then he tightened the rope.

Relief filtered through her limbs. Good. The man had been picking fights with her since yesterday. Throughout the drive to this campsite, then on the walk from his car. He'd carried her most of the way, muttering profanities about letting her go back home with every step.

She studied the tent. "When exactly did your team set this up?"

"This morning." His fingers brushed her wrist as he worked the rope. "It'll be gone by the time Elijah's guys search here, but if they're as thorough as they should be, they'll check for indents in the ground from the stakes."

Her gaze scanned the saturated ground. There was a light mist of rain now, but nothing like earlier. It was early. Like six a.m. kind of early. She wished she was still in bed. She'd spent most of her thirtieth birthday there with the man in front of her, and it had been bliss.

"There," he finally said.

She gave her hands a tug. She couldn't get free. Aidan had tied it perfectly so that escape was impossible, but it wasn't tight enough to hurt her. Fine. She'd just work the ropes to create the marks she needed.

She rubbed her wrists against the rough material, quickly feeling the burn. That lasted for only a second before Aidan grabbed her wrists.

"Stop."

"Aidan—"

"It'll rub your wrists enough while you're running out of the woods." There was an edge to his voice. He clearly hated this.

She touched his chest. "I'll be okay."

He glanced down, first at her face, then her hands on him, and it was as if the sight of her bound wrists only put gas on the fire of his anger.

She dropped her hands. "Okay, so you need to tackle me, right? Make it look like I fought my attackers at some point while they held me. You also said it will be good training if I end up in a precarious position with Elijah or any of his men. Like a self-defense refresher."

His eyes tightened at the mention of her getting in a precarious position.

She leaned up onto her toes and pecked a kiss to his cheek. "Come on. This could even be fun. You'll get to roll around in the mud with me."

His lips twitched. That's what she wanted. The old Aidan back. The guy who smiled and laughed and was open with his emotions.

She walked over and stopped beside the tent. The story was that she snuck away while they slept, but Elijah knew she wasn't a doormat. He knew she'd have fought as hard as possible to get away. She wore the black dress and stockings again. She'd already rubbed them in dirt, but she needed to look even dirtier. And there had to be signs of a struggle.

She turned. "Okay, I'm ready. Tackle me."

She was sure she heard another quiet growl from the burly man. Then he lunged.

Her eyes widened. She expected a big hit. But his arms went around her waist, and when they dropped, she hit the ground so lightly she barely felt it.

Then he was caging her to the ground.

"Your turn. Fight me," he whispered.

She pushed at his chest and tried to turn them over, but he didn't move an inch.

His head lowered and he nipped her neck. "Come on, princess. You can do better than that."

Princess?

When his hand grazed her breast, she gasped and began pushing in earnest. She hit his big chest and tried to knee him. No movement. None.

Now he nipped a spot behind her ear. "Forgotten what I've taught you already?"

Aidan had taught her a lot about self-defense, but she hadn't used it in years.

Another nip.

With a low growl, she wrapped her bound hands around his

neck and tugged him to the side. At the same time, she wrapped a leg around his hip and put all her weight into rolling them over. She was fully aware the man allowed it all to happen, but she still ended up on top. She pressed another kiss to his cheek. "Done."

Almost immediately, he rolled them back over. "Again."

They continued to grapple, with Cassie fighting her way out of various positions while Aidan teased and nipped. She didn't know how much time had passed before he finally stood.

"Good job." He pulled her up from the ground.

"Maybe we should do more?" She was covered in mud, and there were light impressions in the ground, but was it enough?

He shook his head. "No. You still need to run out of here. I don't want you getting too tired."

She opened her mouth to argue, then closed it. He was right. She was already getting tired, and she'd have to be on her feet the entire run out of the woods. "How long's the run?"

They'd chosen this location specifically because it was close enough to run to the house of a Paragons of Hope member, but far enough that it was believable the kidnappers might stop here. She didn't want police brought into this, and she knew if she ran to a member's house, they'd call Elijah instead.

They'd set up tents in two other places, each a bit farther away from the outskirts of town than the last, to make it look like they'd been making their way somewhere. Her story was that, forced to walk under increasingly high stress, she'd slowed down her captors by frequently fainting due to her NMH. It was the best they had, and it would be up to Cassie to sell it.

"At least an hour." By the clenching of his jaw, he didn't like that. "I'll be with you right up until the end."

She frowned. "Won't they see your prints?"

"It'll be worse if they don't. They'll expect someone to have followed your tracks."

She nodded, turning toward the woods. "Okay. Point me in the right direction."

When Aidan didn't respond, she turned to glance at him, only to find him looking pained.

A sinking feeling churned in her gut. Nope. No. No. No. "We are not changing course, Aidan." She crossed to him, pressing her hands to his chest. Man, having bound wrists was annoying. All she wanted to do was hold him.

He gripped her hips tightly. "I just got you back, Cass."

"And once this is over, you'll get me back again. Not to mention, you'll be surrounding the house, and you'll hear everything."

"There are still too many risks."

Her voice softened. "We've been through this. I'll be okay. Having him *not* locked up is an even greater risk." And not just to her.

When footsteps sounded from behind her, Cassie started to step back, but Aidan didn't let her move an inch. She looked over her shoulder and recognized the guy immediately. Callum.

He stopped a few feet away. "Am I interrupting?"

"No." She tried to pull away again but, damn, Aidan's hold was like iron.

Callum's lips quirked. "Good to finally meet you in person, Cassie."

Her cheeks reddened. "You too, Callum."

"You got it?" Aidan asked, only looking away from her for a second.

Callum nodded and stepped forward, holding out his hand.

She frowned, squinting. "What's that?" It was so small, she almost couldn't see it.

Aidan grabbed it and pressed it behind her ear, close to her hairline. "This is the listening device. It's waterproof, so you never have to take it off. I'll hear everything." Once it was in place, he cupped her cheek. "You remember my number?"

"I do." It helped that the man had made her repeat it a

hundred and one times in the last couple hours. "And as soon as I'm home and have access to my burner phone, I'll text you."

He lowered his head, his mouth hovering over hers. "Doesn't matter. Either way, I'll be watching, and I'll be close. At the slightest hint of danger, I'm tearing down walls to get to you."

He kissed her, and even though Callum was watching, she couldn't pull away.

When they separated, his teammate stepped forward. "All right, let's get this show on the road."

"We're going to run behind you," Aidan said. "If you get tired—"

"Stop and rest. I know." She turned to Callum. "Which way?" She was more likely to get the information from him faster.

He pointed to a break in the trees. When she stepped out of Aidan's arms, there was a sudden trickle of doubt. The last time she'd walked away from him, she hadn't seen him again in close to three years.

No. She couldn't think like that. She needed to focus.

"Be careful," he said quietly.

The intensity in his gaze almost had her calling the whole thing off. "Always."

"I HATE THIS. I fucking *hate* this!"

They'd trailed Cassie all the way through the woods and right up until she reached a street. It was a quiet area, and the house she needed to get to wasn't much farther. But sending her back there... Every part of Aidan rebelled against it.

He listened to her breathing through the earpiece.

Callum squeezed his shoulder. "She'll be okay. We'll make sure of it."

Of course they would. They had to. Losing her wasn't an option.

In the distance, he could see Tyler. He'd be keeping eyes on her until Aidan and Callum were done at the campsite. It needed to be foolproof. It needed to be so well staged that if the best damn tracker in the world were to traipse through the area, they wouldn't see a single red flag.

Callum tilted his head back toward the direction they'd come. "Come on. We need to pack everything up and make it look like we left in a mad rush."

"We *are* going to leave in a mad rush, because I want her in my sights." The second everything was packed away, he was returning to wherever she was. He trusted his team with his life, but it wasn't the same. *He* needed to know she was okay. *He* needed to see her with his own eyes.

They raced back toward the campground. They were fast, and it wouldn't take them long to pack. When they reached the site and started on the tent, Aidan felt Callum's eyes on him before he spoke.

"What exactly happened between you two?"

Wasn't that obvious? "Everything happened. She's mine. And you sure as hell better bet that if anyone harms a hair on her head, I'll burn that fucking compound to the ground."

CHAPTER 12

Breathe, Cassie. Just breathe. It will all be fine.

Cassie had repeated those words inside her head about a hundred times since she'd knocked on Lydia and Henry's door. The couple had actually opened it together and looked like their eyes were about to bug out of their heads. But the second they recovered, they'd swept into action just as she'd known they would. They'd driven her home, called Elijah, and were now waiting with her.

She clenched the sofa cushions beneath her thighs. Elijah wasn't here yet, but he would be soon. Would he buy her story? He had to. She'd become a damn good liar, but today would be a true test of her skills.

Lydia sat beside her, rubbing her shoulder. "It will all be okay, dear."

Henry paced back and forth on the other side of the living room, a worried look on his face, while Mrs. Alder stayed busy in the kitchen making coffee. The old bat had probably loved having the house to herself. Hell, she probably didn't even care that Cassie had been kidnapped and Damien hadn't returned from the compound.

God, please be okay, Damien.

The man was like a brother to her, and he still wasn't home. She'd been hoping that they'd walk in here today and there he'd be. Nope.

Yes, she was angry he'd organized this crazy kidnapping plan with Aidan, but he was her oldest friend. He loved her as much as she loved him.

The door opened and her nails bit into the cushion.

Mia was the first person inside. She ran across the room. Lydia stood, and Mia dropped into her spot and threw her arms around Cassie's shoulders.

Some of the tension eased from her limbs. This was the biggest reason she'd had to come back. Because Mia was family, the only family she had left, and hugging her was everything.

She closed her eyes and tightened her hold on her sister.

"Are you okay?" Mia whispered. "I was so worried!"

"I'm okay."

Mia's arms began to loosen, and Cassie steeled her spine. She felt him in the room before she saw him. He always made the air feel thicker. Some days, she thought she'd choke in his presence.

She looked up, not surprised to see his brothers, Isaac and Joshua, on either side of him. Two of his guards were there also, Antwon and Sampson. She wasn't entirely sure if Sampson was there for Elijah or Mia. Maybe both.

Another shudder tried to rock her, but she refused to let it. The brothers and Antwon had eyes as cold as Elijah's. Sampson was the only person she semi-liked.

Elijah perched on the edge of an armchair near the couch. "Cassie, my child, how are you?"

His gaze held hers. He'd always been good at eye contact. At giving someone one hundred percent of his attention. It made so many people feel heard and seen. But for Cassie, it just made her skin crawl.

"I'm okay. Rattled, but uninjured." Her voice shook just the right amount.

"Can you tell me what happened?"

Deep breath, Cassie. You can do this. "I don't remember much from the night I was taken. I was on my feet most of the evening, and you know how that affects me. I passed out almost immediately when the guy grabbed me in my guest room."

He nodded. Yeah, he already knew that part. He'd probably watched the surveillance video of her being taken a million times.

She wet her lips. "When I woke up, I was somewhere in the woods. My hands were bound, and there were two men with me. They'd set up camp. We hiked short distances both Saturday and Sunday, but I slowed them down a lot because I kept passing out. They didn't know about my hypotension. When we stopped Sunday evening, they said they were waiting for their boss to come get me."

"What did they look like?" Elijah asked.

She recited what she'd practiced with Aidan. "Both were over six feet tall. Fit. Day-old beards. One guy's hair was dark brown, the other a lighter brown. Both Caucasian." So basically, they were as ordinary and common-looking as possible.

"Names?"

"I assume they used nicknames. They referred to each other as Truck and Ace."

Frustration weighed on Elijah's face. "Why did they take you?"

This was the big question. "Because I'm a member of Paragons of Hope. They called us a...a cult." They were, of course. But Elijah would never use that word. "They were talking about us having a lot of money. I can only guess they were eventually going to contact you, maybe ask for money in exchange for me."

As lies went, it wasn't terrible. People who knew about Paragons of Hope also knew they had money. And there had been attacks on the organization before.

Mia's arms wrapped around Cassie's shoulders again. "Oh, C! You must have been terrified."

Cassie leaned into her sister. Elijah was still watching her closely, like the psychopath he was.

He leaned forward. "Can I see your wrists, child?"

She knew he'd ask. Knew he'd need some sort of proof. Because seeing her kidnapping on video wasn't enough.

Man, she was glad she'd rubbed her wrists against those ropes. Slowly, she rolled up the sleeves of her black dress and held out her wrists.

The second Elijah touched her, she had to grit her teeth to keep from pulling away. But even if she did flinch, he'd probably mistake her reaction for pain. Because who would flinch at their *Holy Leader's* touch?

His thumb swiped over the abrasion on her left wrist. "You said they didn't hurt you?"

His gaze ran down her body.

She hated his eyes on her. "I fought them to get away a couple of times but quickly realized there was no point. I wasn't going to win."

"How did you get away, then?"

She took a breath. "The guy on night watch fell asleep. When I woke up and saw him, I ran. When I got out of the woods, I recognized the street I was on."

Lydia took a small step forward. "She was still bound when she knocked on our door."

Elijah nodded, finally releasing her. It took everything in her not to scrub every spot he'd touched. "I'm sorry about what you went through." There was a small pause. "I think it's best you let Paragons take care of this from here. Involving the police will just make it messy."

Yep, she'd known that was coming. She gave a small nod. "I understand, Elijah. I trust you to find out who did this."

"And I think it also would be best you move to the compound for a while."

Her heart thumped. "No."

Mia stiffened beside her.

Shit. No one said no to Elijah.

She shook her head. "I'm sorry, I'm just in such a state. It's been a tremendously traumatic few days." She rubbed her eyes like she was exhausted. Which she was. Exhausted from sitting here talking to *him.* "I really would like to be around my things right now. Be in my own space. I think it will help me heal."

Mia rubbed her back. "Maybe I can stay with you?"

Oh sweet, innocent Mia. Her gaze turned to her sister. "I would love that." So freaking much. When she looked at Elijah hopefully, there was a fleeting expression of frustration. He was going to say no. She could see it in his eyes.

She added an extra tremble to her voice. "To be able to rest in my own bed would be such a blessing for my mental health. Not to mention having Mrs. Alder here to take care of me."

Another clenching of his jaw. His gaze rose to Mrs. Alder, and she was almost certain she saw something pass between them.

When he looked back at her, his smooth mask had returned. "Very well. Mia, you may stay for a week. Mrs. Alder will look after you."

Look after her? Ha. He meant *watch* her. She was sure he'd have words with the old woman before he left. He'd also, no doubt, keep a very close eye on the cameras in her house.

Mia rubbed Cassie's arm, giving her a smile.

"We've replaced the locks on your doors and windows and upgraded the security," Elijah continued. "I'll also put a guard outside your house."

"I can do that, sir," Sampson said.

That would make Mia happy.

Elijah looked like he was going to stand but then stopped. "We had to cancel your ball last night, of course, but we'll reschedule when you're feeling better."

Her back straightened at the mention of the ball. The second she'd gotten home, she'd snuck upstairs and texted Olive, but the woman hadn't replied. Maybe she would later, but if she didn't, she needed a way to see her.

How quickly could a party be arranged?

"Actually, a celebration might be the perfect thing to take my mind off everything." Cassie smiled timidly. "Maybe tomorrow night? A ball would be too difficult to arrange on short notice, but maybe just a small get-together with Paragon family members?"

His brows rose. But it was Mia who answered.

"Great idea. It will be a great distraction for you. I can take care of all the arrangements."

Some of the tightness in her chest loosened. It was Monday. If she could talk to Olive Tuesday night, it would be perfect timing for Wednesday.

When Elijah nodded and rose, turning toward the door, Cassie stood as well. "Elijah, do you know where Damien is? He wasn't home when we got here, and Mrs. Alder said she didn't know when he'd be back."

She'd been waiting for him to bring it up. Actually, she'd been hoping Damien would be *with* Elijah when he arrived.

He stopped. A full second passed. That small hesitation had dread knotting in Cassie's belly. When he finally looked at her, his smile was as fake as the rest of him. "He was so worried about you that I sent him away on a little trip. To take his mind off things."

Cassie frowned. "A trip?"

"He's doing some aid work for one of our charities. I'll inform him of your return and let him know he can come home."

Her dread intensified. "Can I call him? He must be so anxious."

Elijah was already out the door. It was Joshua who answered. "Leave that to us."

Then they were gone.

Equal parts fear and fury pumped through her veins. Lying dirtbags! She wanted Damien back, and she wanted him back *now*.

Lydia moved forward and wrapped her arms around Cassie's shoulders. When she pulled back, she kept hold of her briefly. "Call if you need anything. Okay?"

Cassie nodded and watched as the couple left.

Mia said, "I'll go home, pack a bag, and I'll be right back. Are you going to be okay while I'm gone?"

She nodded. "I have Mrs. Alder. Please don't take too long."

At least she didn't need to fake the worry in her voice. She worried all day, every day about Mia being at the compound.

Her sister slid some hair away from Cassie's face. "I won't. Promise."

She watched her sister right until the door closed behind her. She always hated goodbyes with Mia. Because every time, worst-case scenarios played out in her head. Of what could happen to her. What Elijah might do.

She exhaled loudly and moved toward the stairs.

"I'm making fried chicken for lunch."

She stopped at the sound of Mrs. Alder's voice. Fried chicken was a favorite of Cassie's. She eyed the housekeeper, trying to keep her dubious expression at bay. "Really?"

Mrs. Alder didn't look up. "Really. It will be ready by the time Mia returns."

Fried chicken with her sister. The day was looking up. Still made her suspicious as hell, though. "Sounds good. Thank you."

She trudged up the stairs and into the bedroom. The first thing she did was check every spot a camera could be placed. It had become somewhat of a ritual for her. If Elijah was ever going to put a camera in her bedroom, it was now.

She'd gotten close to the IT guy at the compound. And one night, when he'd had far too many of the spiked drinks, Cassie had questioned him about hidden camera placements in the members' houses. He'd told her each and every spot. Since then, she'd become an expert at checking those spots inconspicuously.

She scanned the entire room. And it wasn't until she surreptitiously glanced at the air vent that she saw it.

Son of a bitch. A freaking camera!

A fresh wave of anger swamped her. She was careful not to show it, but man, all she wanted to do was run outside, chase the asshole down, and murder him with her bare hands. The gall of him!

She stepped into the connecting bathroom and closed the door. Softly. No matter how badly she wanted to slam it. Then she went through a similar process in the bathroom, checking every little nook and cranny of the small space. When she didn't spot anything, she blew out a long breath.

Well, at least that was something.

Walking over to the shower, she turned it on, but instead of getting straight in, she moved back to the vanity and opened a drawer. She reached for the Tampax box and took out the small burner phone.

Her heart dropped. Still no response from Olive. It was fine. She might respond later. And if she didn't, hopefully she'd see the woman tomorrow night.

She thumbed in a new number. Excitement trilled in her veins. Excitement that she was about to text Aidan. Have contact with him.

Cassie: Hey. I made it home safely. I spoke to Elijah and he seemed to buy everything, but I guess you heard that anyway.

The response came almost immediately.

Aidan: I'm in the house to the right. Tyler's to the left and Callum's across the street. You're safe. Are you okay?

So they'd actually managed to empty the houses. The one

across from her had been vacant, but not those on either side. She had no idea how they'd pulled that off so quickly. They'd said something about the homeowners winning sudden trips, but she didn't care. The point was, they were there, and they made her feel safe.

Cassie: I'm angry. He's lying about Damien, and he put a camera in my bedroom.

Aidan: Son of a bitch.

She almost smiled. That had been her response too, only in her head.

Aidan: It will be over soon. I promise. X

Cassie: I miss you already.

There was a small pause.

Aidan: When you write things like that, I just want to get into that house and kidnap you again.

How she'd love for him to do just that. But he couldn't.

Cassie: Soon. Then I'm all yours.

Aidan: Forever.

She smiled.

Cassie: Forever x

CHAPTER 13

assie fixed the last pin into her hair. Somehow, Mia had pulled off a miracle. She'd moved all the plans for the missed ball to tonight.

It wasn't ideal. The last thing she felt like doing was standing on her feet for hours with every single member of Paragons of Hope. Not to mention, Aidan hated the idea. After Mia had announced it earlier this morning, she'd found about five messages on her phone from the man. But the ball wasn't at the compound and she'd be taking her own car, so everything would be okay. It had to be. Plus, she had no doubt Aidan and his team would surround the place and listen in.

The more she thought about it, the more she realized it wasn't really much of a surprise that the ball had been rescheduled on such short notice. Elijah had a lot of people working for him, so a lot of resources and manpower. Just one of the things that made him so dangerous.

Her mind flicked to the message from Dean. He'd asked if she knew where Damien was and when she'd told him what was going on. He'd been so worried.

Poor Dean. The man loved Damien so much.

Tonight. She needed to get to the bottom of where he was *tonight.*

She blew out a breath as she ran her fingers down the satin ball gown. As always, it was long-sleeved and high-necked, allowing very little skin to show. But unlike most clothing items she'd worn over the last couple of years, she liked this one, because Mia had chosen it for her, claiming the green shade made her jade eyes pop. And when could she ever say no to her little sister?

At the thought of Mia, her belly did a little dip. Her sister had been in and out of the house most of the day, setting things up for the party. She'd gone back and forth on whether to tell Mia everything. Ultimately, she knew she couldn't. Not right now. Her sister was too indoctrinated. By Sampson. Elijah. It made her sick to her stomach.

She lifted her mascara wand and applied a final coat.

There was a knock on the bathroom door.

"You're due to leave in ten minutes," Mrs. Alder called.

Cassie rolled her eyes. The woman had been worse than usual since her return. Cassie had barely gotten a second to herself with Mrs. Alder's obsessive need to check in on every little thing she was doing. Between Mrs. Alder and Sampson in his car on the street and the new security system... Yeah, Elijah was making sure she wasn't going anywhere.

"Thank you. I'll be out soon."

A moment passed, then she heard the heavy footsteps of her keeper moving away. Good. When she saw the back of that woman, it wouldn't be soon enough.

She closed her eyes. *Please, Olive, be okay for tomorrow. This all depends on you.*

When she opened her eyes, it was to see the back of a dark figure in the small bathroom as he closed the door. She opened her mouth to scream, but before a word came out, he turned.

The air rushed out of her.

Aidan.

Her lips separated to ask what he was doing here, but he quickly stepped behind her and covered her mouth, his lips brushing her ear. "Mrs. Alder is close by, so we have to be quiet."

His hand shifted.

"What about the cameras? And Sampson?" she asked quietly, her gaze shooting to the door and back.

"Callum hacked the system and set up a loop for the cameras while I'm in here. And Sampson's downstairs talking to Mia."

A loop? He could do that?

Aidan's mouth lowered to her neck. Her eyes closed again, but this time for a completely different reason.

"I like your dress," his voice rumbled, his hands skimming her hips.

"Thank you," she breathed.

Those hands rose to her ribs. Her heart skipped a beat as they shifted dangerously close to her breasts.

"I don't like the thought of other people seeing you in it, though. It's very figure-hugging."

Finally, he cupped her breasts. She leaned against him, and his thumbs found her hard nipples through the material. A quiet whimper slipped from her lips.

She watched in the mirror as he stood behind her, dwarfing her, his fingers on her breasts. Even his hands were sexy and muscular.

A dull ache began to throb in her core. "Aidan..." she whispered.

His thumbs alternated between thrumming her nipple and circular swipes. It was causing her belly to do strange little somersaults.

"I don't want anyone touching you tonight," he said quietly.

"No one's going to touch me."

A soft growl sounded from his chest. Did he not believe the men at the ball would keep their hands to themselves?

"My team and I will be close. You'll be heavily protected."

She wasn't worried about her safety tonight. Not in a roomful of people. She didn't plan to drink or eat anything. She was smarter than that.

She lifted her hands and set them on top of his. She intended to stop him. Halt the torturous fingers on her hard peaks. Or at least, she was pretty sure she meant to. But instead, her hands stilled as he continued to play with her nipples.

He suckled her neck. "I missed you last night."

A groan tried to slip from her throat, but she swallowed it. "I missed you too." She'd craved him. Wanted his arms around her. His front curled around her back. When she'd finally fallen asleep, he'd been all she could dream about. It had caused her to wake up and feel guilty as hell, because she shouldn't be thinking about that now. She should be worried about Damien's well-being. She should be focused on getting Elijah arrested.

A hand left her breast. He skirted down her ribs, then her thigh, when a knock came at the door.

She barely stifled a gasp.

"Cassie?" Mia called.

Aidan's lips went back to her ear. The whispered words were so low, she knew they'd only reach her ears. "Calm, Cassie."

"Yes, Mia?" Her voice was steady. Good.

"Just checking that you're okay? You've been in there for a while."

No, she wasn't okay. Her breasts were on fire and her body ached for more. More touches. Grazes. More tiny little kisses across her neck.

She swallowed. "Of course. I'm just putting on the last of my makeup."

"Okay. Great. The car's here. I'll wait for you downstairs."

Car? She'd thought she was driving...

Before she could respond, she heard the light pitter-patter of Mia's footsteps as she walked away. Cassie blew out a breath.

Aidan turned her to face him. She was still burning for him, but she pushed it down. She needed to focus. "I need to go. And so do you."

He reached down to his thigh and grabbed...a gun? He silently set the small weapon on the counter. Next, he unbuckled the holster from his thigh, then bent to one knee. His hands slid under her dress, touched her ankle, then slowly grazed up her leg, lifting the dress as he went. Her skin tingled, and her breath caught at the intimate touch.

He stopped midthigh, where he strapped the holster around her leg. "This is a holster designed to be worn under a dress and to keep the weapon concealed."

He reached for the gun and slipped it in, the slight weight settling on the inside of her thigh.

"You remember how to shoot?" he asked quietly.

Her mind was in overdrive. "Yes."

Slowly, he rose and cupped her face. "Good. Like I said, we'll be close, so I don't think you'll need it, but I want to be prepared for anything."

She opened her mouth to question him, but his mouth crashed onto hers, and the words disintegrated in her head as she melted into him.

His tongue slipped between her lips. Jesus, he tasted good. Of deep spice and all man. She clung to him, trying to anchor herself. His hands grazed along her back, warm and strong.

When he started to pull away, she latched onto his jacket. She didn't want him to go. That's when she realized what she'd missed until now.

He was wearing a tux.

"Why are you wearing that?"

A ghost of a smile played at his lips. "Remember, I'm close. And I'll always be listening."

"Wait—"

He bent down for one final kiss. Then he left, leaving the room as quickly as he'd entered.

Dammit. That man...

"Cassie?"

At Mia's shout from downstairs, she shook her head and left the bathroom. Once she slipped on her lacy heels, she grabbed her clutch and left the bedroom. The gun and holster rubbed occasionally on her opposite thigh, but she ignored it.

Mia stood near the door. She wore a simple red dress with long sleeves but an open neck. Beautiful. Her sister looked beautiful. But then, she was a natural beauty.

Mia's chest expanded on her inhale, and she rushed over to the bottom of the stairs. "Oh my gosh, Cassie. You look gorgeous!"

Cassie reached the bottom and took her sister's hands. "Me? That dress looks sexy as hell, Mia. Sampson must have had a heart attack when he saw it. Where is he?"

Mia's laugh floated through the air and her cheeks heated. "Thank you. He *did* seem quite taken by it. I can't wait to dance with the man. He's waiting in his car. He's going to follow us to the ball."

She gave her sister a little smile. She hoped Sampson was in the dark about what was really going on at the compound...for her sister's sake.

Cassie lifted her brows. "Ready?"

"Hang on. You're missing one thing."

Mia opened her own clutch and pulled out a small tube of lipstick. When she opened it, Cassie admired the deep red.

"This is your thirtieth birthday celebration," Mia said as she stepped forward and applied it to Cassie's lips. "I know your actual birthday wasn't the best." Mia's mouth turned down momentarily, but she quickly recovered. "We're going to make the most of tonight and really celebrate. Elijah's gone all out on this one."

"Do you know why?" Cassie asked before she could stop herself.

Mia pulled her arm back. "What do you mean?"

"Jenny Albot turned thirty last month, and she didn't get a grand ball."

The smile returned to Mia's mouth, and she did one more swipe of lipstick before capping the tube. "Jenny Albot is annoying. And not nearly as deserving as you."

The woman *was* annoying. But it didn't answer Cassie's question.

"You're special, Cass. Elijah's always told me he thinks you're special."

Cassie frowned. Her sister had never mentioned that before. It took her back in time to when their mother had said the same thing. "Why am I so special?"

She probably shouldn't be asking. Not with the cameras. But she couldn't stop herself.

Mia lifted a shoulder. "He said something once about a dream. That God came to him and told me you were important."

The fine hairs on Cassie's arms stood on end. She wanted to ask her sister more, but Mia dropped the lipstick back into her purse and tugged her toward the door. "And you *are* special. So, let's go celebrate your birthday!"

She linked her arm through Cassie's just as the doorbell rang.

Mia squealed. "That's our driver!"

"Our driver?"

"Yep. No boring old car for us tonight. I ordered a limo."

Oh, jeez.

Mia tugged the door open, and Cassie frowned. The guy looked familiar. He had a mustache and a bit of a belly, but he was tall and looked muscular beneath the tux...

She stared at him for a full second before recognition hit. It was Callum. He'd padded his clothes and wore fake facial hair and contacts.

Callum smiled at them. "Good evening, ladies. My name's Tony and I'll be your driver tonight."

Aidan. What are you doing?

CHAPTER 14

*A*idan balanced a tray of drinks in one hand while he stood to the side of the ballroom. Callum had somehow gotten them on the list to work the ball. He didn't know how, but he wasn't asking questions.

He scanned the large room. The women wore conservative ball gowns, all of which covered their arms and shoulders, while the men wore black tuxes. All except one. Elijah, who wore a white suit jacket.

If anything, it made Aidan hate the man even more. Did he feel the need to wear something different to show he was above everyone else or something? It was taking every bit of his self-control not to walk over there, kill the asshole and be done with it. The guy was a murderer. A rapist. Jesus, he regularly drugged roomfuls of people.

Since Aidan had arrived, the guy had worked his way through the crowd and touched almost every woman in the room. With a hand to the lower back. A graze of the cheek. Fingers around the wrist. The guy was a damn creep.

Aidan caught Tyler's gaze. He also wore a tux and held a tray of champagne glasses. And just like Aidan, he wore a disguise.

Contact lenses to change his eye color. A wig to change his hair. There was no doubt Elijah and his guys had seen Aidan and his team on the news. Their faces had been plastered everywhere. But even if they hadn't, the guy had probably investigated every inch of Cassie's life in the years before she returned to the cult.

She and Mia had yet to arrive. Aidan had instructed Callum to take the long route, possibly even create an "emergency" that required them to stop for a short while, if he could do so without making the guard following too suspicious. Not only did that give Aidan time to arrive first, it also meant less time for Cassie at the ball. He didn't want her here any longer than she had to be.

Mia's voice sounded from the earpiece. The woman had been talking nonstop throughout the drive. About flowers. Drinks. Music. That Sampson guy. He'd barely heard a word from Cassie.

He needed to stay away from Mia tonight. Even though he was in disguise, the woman might still recognize him from his time dating Cassie. He couldn't risk it.

"Pulling up now," Callum said quietly through the earpiece.

When Aidan spotted Elijah moving toward his brothers, who stood on the outskirts of the crowd, he crossed the room, offering drinks to people on the way. He stopped several feet away from the men. With the distance, an average man wouldn't be able to hear a word, particularly over the music. He wasn't average. And he heard every word they said.

"Is everything in place?" Elijah asked.

"Yes," Joshua answered. "Cars are ready. It will take a while to get there, but everything's good to go."

A while to get where? And *what* was ready to go?

"Good. We're already behind. We can't have any mistakes."

What the fuck were they talking about?

"Of course," Isaac said.

He looked up to see Elijah plaster that big, fake smile onto his face and walk away.

"Something's going on," Aidan said under his breath. "Tyler, if

Cassie's with her sister, I'll keep my distance, so I want you to stick to them like glue."

"Got it," his friend whispered under his breath.

"Liam and Blake, is it clear outside?"

"Guards on every exit, but no unusual activity," Blake answered.

Aidan was moving around the room again when the door opened and he saw her. Cassie stepped inside. And just like in her bathroom, she looked so damn beautiful, his chest ached. Every part of him wanted to go to the woman and drag her out of there.

"OH MY LORD, this place looks even better at night."

Cassie smiled at her sister's words. The place *was* beautiful. The ball was held in a big mansion that had a huge, historic-looking ballroom. With external catering and music, it was extravagant, and so over the top.

Elijah never spent this kind of money on a party. What the heck was going on?

She touched her sister's arm. "Mia, this is too much."

"Don't be silly! You deserve a big party."

They moved further into the room. Cassie scanned the crowd for Damien. Where was he? Elijah had assured her she'd see him tonight. She *needed* to see him. If she didn't, if Elijah made another poor excuse... Christ, she didn't know what she'd do. She couldn't do anything crazy before tomorrow, but she needed Damien to be okay.

A man holding a tray suddenly stood in front of them. "Champagne?"

She met the man's eyes. Yet again, she was filled with a feeling of familiarity.

"No, thank you." She said the words slowly, never moving her eyes from him. He held her gaze just as firmly.

Mia touched her arm. "Cassie, this is *your* party. You have to have a drink!"

She dragged her eyes away from the server and looked at her sister. "You know what alcohol does to me. I'm already going to be on my feet all night. I don't want to pass out on anyone." Thank God she could use her hypotension as an excuse.

Mia's eyes softened. "A few sips to celebrate won't hurt. And we'll get you a chair. Besides, everyone here is family. If, God forbid, anything happened, you'd be safe."

Yeah, right. She was about as safe here as in a pool full of sharks. Still, she smiled. "Okay. One drink."

She turned back to the man and went to reach for a glass, but he was already passing her one. Her hand grazed his, her gaze traveling up what looked to be a very muscular arm under his black jacket.

Hang on...

She met his stare again, her lips parting slightly. Tyler. Another one of the men on Aidan's team. Unbidden, her gaze shot around the room, looking for more. Aidan was here. He had to be. It was why he was wearing a tux earlier.

She continued to scan the room until finally, she found him, all million and one feet of him. Not only was he wearing a wig and contacts, he'd also donned a fake mustache like Callum. If circumstances were different, she may have laughed.

A warm hand pressed to her arm very briefly. Her gaze swung back to Tyler. "Enjoy your evening, ma'am."

Was that his gentle way of telling her not to stare? Definitely. Hell, it was stupid of her to look for even a moment.

Mia linked their arms. "Come on. Let's go have fun."

A large screen was mounted on the wall across from them. It was flicking through photos of her. Of both her years at the compound, and the many years out of it.

She swung her gaze back to Mia. Her sister was watching her with a massive grin. "I scrounged up every photo I could find. It helped that Elijah kept a whole bunch at the compound from when we were kids."

The smile almost slipped from her lips. It took a lot to keep it there. "Thank you. For all of this."

"Of course."

They spent the next hour moving around the room. Talking. Laughing. In her case, holding a fake smile that made her cheeks ache.

When they stopped at a tall bar table with Lydia, Olive, and a woman named Jodie, Cassie's heart thumped. She tried to meet Olive's gaze, but the woman kept her eyes firmly on a glass of what looked like water in front of her.

"Happy birthday!" Lydia moved around the table and hugged her. Jodie did the same.

Olive remained where she was, offering a tight smile. "Happy birthday."

She swallowed. "Thank you, ladies. This party is... Well, it's something else."

Jodie gushed. "I know. I can't believe how big this is!" She looked to Mia. "This is your doing, isn't it? You've always had a way of twisting our leader's arm."

Argh... she hated it when people called him that. He wasn't a leader. He was a dictator. An evil one.

Mia blushed. "I mean, I did a lot of the organizing, but it was all Elijah's idea. He wanted it big, so we made it big."

"How'd you pull it off so last minute?" Lydia asked.

Mia shrugged. "Elijah spoke to some people. It helped that it was a weekday, so nothing was booked."

Lydia's gaze went to Cassie. "And how are you doing?"

She gave a small nod. "After lots of rest, I'm starting to feel like myself again." Less so due to the rest, and more so due to the tall, dark and handsome man who'd made her feel human for the first time in years.

Cassie scanned the room one more time. "I haven't seen

Damien yet." She'd been searching for him since arriving, but so far, nothing. Maybe these ladies knew something more?

"I haven't seen him since I was at the compound on Saturday morning," Jodie murmured. "Is he still away doing aid work?"

Her heart sank. She gave what she hoped came across as a warm smile. "Elijah said he'd probably be here tonight. I haven't had a chance to talk to him yet, but when I do, I'll ask him." And he'd better materialize the man.

"Aid work?" Lydia made a face, as if to say that didn't make sense. Yeah, it didn't make sense to her, either. Elijah hadn't put much thought into this lie. No one would question him, though. Not to his face.

"Oh, I almost forgot." Mia pulled out a small card from her purse. "Here's your birthday card from all of us."

Cassie gave another tight smile and took the card. God, her cheeks hurt from all these forced smiles. She was about to slip it into her purse when Mia shook her head.

"No, open it now! I want to see what Elijah wrote."

She almost groaned. She didn't care about the note. She cared about tugging Olive away and talking to her privately. But she tore open the envelope. Inside was the usual check to a charity. It was the same charity she always chose, for fire victims.

Next, her gaze skittered over the card. Elijah always wrote in them on behalf of everyone. People loved it. That their *leader* would put time into writing a card and hand-selecting a Bible verse.

Happy thirtieth birthday, my child. May these words fill you with comfort.

"He reached down from on high and took hold of me; he drew me out of deep water." Samuel 22:17.

Mia leaned over her shoulder and sighed. "Oh, what a beautiful verse. And just what you need."

Really? She felt like she needed the card as much as she needed a kick in the head. "It's very thoughtful."

Suddenly, she caught sight of Aidan walking toward them from her peripheral vision. Not directly toward them. On a path that would take him behind her. When he passed, his arm lightly brushed her back. She swallowed, and her back tingled and heated.

She hadn't thought she needed him or his team here. But now, she felt so much safer and couldn't imagine being alone.

She glanced back to the group just as Olive pushed away from the table. "If you'll excuse me, I just need to go to the ladies'."

The knot in Cassie's stomach tightened. "I think I'll go too. I'll be back in a second."

She left her untouched glass and the card on the table and moved through the crowd. Only, while Olive slipped through undisrupted, Cassie was stopped at every step. With touches to her arms. Hugs and "happy birthdays".

By the time she made it to the bathroom, Olive was already drying her hands.

Quickly, Cassie scanned the stalls—all open and empty. Good.

She stepped beside Olive and lowered her voice. "You haven't responded to my messages. I wanted to check that we're still on for tomorrow."

Olive's bottom lip disappeared between her lips, and the sinking feeling that had been gnawing at Cassie's gut expanded.

"I'm sorry, Cassie. I can't."

Bile crawled up her throat. She grabbed the woman's arms. "Olive, please! Don't pull out on me now. It's all set up. You just need to sit with me and talk like nothing's going on. No one will know."

Olive's voice lowered and an almost desperate look came over her face. "You were *kidnapped*, Cass. There are extra eyes on you now. If I meet you, there'll be extra eyes on *me*, and we run the risk of being caught. I can't do that. I already lost my brother—I won't put my mom at risk."

"You'll be *saving* her. Saving others from losing their brothers. Saving women from becoming Elijah's victims."

She shook her head, fear like a dark cloud in her eyes. "I-I can't."

"Do it for your brother, Olive. He deserves justice."

She swallowed, and guilt warred with the fear in her eyes. "I just... I can't tomorrow. Maybe once all this stuff settles."

No! She didn't have time. Aidan would never let her stay longer. And even if he did, she'd drown if she had to keep living this lie. "Olive, it needs to be *now*."

The woman stepped back. Her words were so quiet, they almost didn't reach Cassie's ears. "I'm sorry."

She'd just touched the door when Cassie spoke. "If you change your mind, text me."

There was a glimmer of tears in the woman's eyes, but she quickly blinked them away. "I won't, Cass. Not for tomorrow's meeting."

Then she was gone, along with Cassie's hope.

CHAPTER 15

Cassie's face was pale—had been pale since she stepped out of the bathroom. Fuck. She obviously hadn't gotten the answer she wanted from Olive. Only thirty minutes had passed since then, but Aidan was done. It was time to go.

"I'm getting her out of here," he said under his breath to his team.

"This place is heavily guarded," Liam said softly.

"There are also three cars out back," Blake added. "They're idling near a door like they're waiting for someone."

His gut tightened.

"We need to be smart," Callum said quietly. "I'll be at the front door with the limo the second you tell me to be, but we can't bring unwanted attention to ourselves. There are too many guns and way too many innocent civilians."

He watched Cassie closely, and when she finally met his gaze, he tilted his head toward the door. It was subtle, and the second she saw it, he looked away. But not before he caught the flash of relief in her eyes. She wanted out as badly as he did. And he sure as hell didn't want to know what Elijah had planned with those cars. Not before he could get Cassie out.

He moved into the kitchen and set down the tray of drinks. That's when he heard Cassie's voice.

"Hi, Elijah."

His insides went cold. He knew she'd have to talk to him, but damn he hated it.

"Cassie, dear. I haven't had a chance to speak with you yet. How have you found your birthday celebration?"

There was a small pause. "It's been lovely, but I was wondering if you had an update on Damien. You mentioned he might be here tonight, but I haven't seen him."

Aidan started moving back toward the ballroom.

"Come with me, dear."

Don't even think about it, Cass.

"I'd prefer to discuss it here."

"I'm afraid this conversation needs to take place in private." His voice lowered. "And it's safer for everyone."

Was that a threat?

Aidan walked faster. He entered the ballroom in time to see Cassie moving out of the room with Elijah's hand on the small of her back, and his brothers trailing not too far behind.

No... Ice raced down Aidan's spine.

"I want everyone listening to their conversation," Aidan growled under his breath. "Tyler, I want you as close as possible and at any sign of trouble, get the hell in there and get her out."

They had a plan for this but hadn't wanted to use it.

CASSIE ALMOST SAGGED at Aidan's subtle nod toward the door. She was exhausted, and all she wanted to do was roll into a ball and pass out. But there was still something she hadn't done yet.

Casually, she moved across the room to Elijah, her heels clicking against the marble floor. The second he looked up, his gaze caught hers, and her stomach did that little sickly flip it always did in his presence.

She straightened. She would not let the man intimidate her. She was almost done with him. Yes, Olive's decision was a setback, but she'd figure this out. Aidan had said he'd find a way to help her bring him down, and she believed him.

"Hi, Elijah." She stopped in front of him.

He stepped forward and touched her elbows before pressing a kiss to her cheek. The only thing worse than his hands touching her was his mouth. Argh.

"Cassie, dear. I haven't had a chance to talk to you yet. How have you found your birthday celebration?"

Exhausting. Over the top. Strange. "It's been lovely, but I was wondering if you had an update on Damien. You mentioned he might be here tonight, but I haven't seen him."

A solemn look came over Elijah's face. Her stomach dropped.

"Come with me, dear."

He put his hand on the small of her back, but she hesitated. "I'd prefer to discuss it here."

"I'm afraid this conversation needs to take place in private." He leaned closer. "And it's safer for everyone."

His gaze stopped on something or someone across the room. She followed it to Mia—and her heart stalled. When his hand pressed harder against her back, the mixture of fear and uncertainty propelled her forward.

He ushered her into a hallway to one side of the ballroom, then into a much smaller room. There was barely any furniture in the space—a chaise and a small side table. That was it.

But there was also a second door. Did it lead outside?

He stepped inside, leaving his brothers at the door, and clicked it shut behind him.

She swallowed the nervous tension and straightened her spine. "Where's Damien?"

"Did you know your mother gave birth to you inside the compound?"

She paused. Where had that come from? "What?"

"Your mother never told you?"

"No."

She knew her mother had joined while she'd been pregnant. She'd been on her own at the time and just about homeless after Cassie's biological father had left her.

Elijah linked his hands behind his back as he slowly moved across the room. "She came to us, nine months pregnant, begging for shelter. It was raining that night. She was wearing a long white dress that stuck to her body. Her hair was down, and so blonde it was almost white. She looked like an angel."

He spoke like he was talking about a fond memory, not one of a heavily pregnant woman who was desperate for shelter and probably on the verge of hypothermia.

"We gave her a room, and a day later, you were born. You came so quickly, we couldn't even get your mother into a car. We called the paramedics, but you were born before they could get there." A slow smile spread across his face. "I knew then that you were a gift from God, and you were meant for great things."

Unease began to fester inside her belly. What the hell was he talking about?

Some of the joy left his face. "Then on your tenth birthday, your mother took you." He shook his head. For a moment, he seemed to be caught up in another memory, this one less pleasant. Then he recovered. "Snuck you away in the middle of the night. Tried to hide you from me."

Tried? "Where's Damien, Elijah?"

Another small smile stretched his lips. The man moved across the room toward her. "Did your mother tell you about my dream?"

"No." Not what the dream was about, at least. She wished she had. Was it the same dream Mia had mentioned tonight? Surely.

He stopped less than a foot away from her and raised a hand. She took a big step back. Nope. She may have to pretend she was all in with these people but letting him touch her face... There was a line, and that was crossing it.

He erased the space she'd created. "God came to me. Showed me just how special you are. When Mia returned, I was hoping you'd follow. And I was so glad when you did."

"She's the only family I have left," Cassie said quietly.

She took another step back and hit the wall behind her.

"I have big plans for you, Cassie."

Her heart thumped against her ribs. "What plans?"

He reached for her necklace and lifted it, inspecting the piece. When had that slipped outside her dress? He dropped the pendant and looked at her. "Come. Walk outside with me." He indicated the back door with a nod.

Ah, that was a big fat no. And not just because Aidan would murder her if she followed him.

"I'm not feeling great. I'm going home now."

She tried to step to the side, but his hand hit the wall beside her head, blocking her way. "I insist, Cassie."

A rapid chill swept over her skin. Aidan and his guys would be hearing this, but would they be able to get in? Well, of course they could get in, but without causing a scene? This place was crawling with security.

"Elijah—"

"Don't fight me on this, Cassie." His fingers wrapped around her forearm so tightly, pain shot up her arm. He gave her a hard tug toward the outer door.

That's when the interior door flew open. Her next breath caught in her throat.

Tyler.

Anger contorted Elijah's face. "Who the hell are you? And where are my brothers? They're supposed to be on the door."

"I'm working the function, sir. There's an issue with some of your guests."

"So why are *you* in here?"

Tyler moved further into the room. His eyes narrowed when he briefly glanced at the hand on her arm. "I was sent because I was told you're in charge. You're needed."

A loud scream sounded from the ballroom. Cassie frowned. What the heck was going on?

Elijah released her, and the relief was like a huge weight lifted from her chest. He quickly skirted around Tyler and left the room. Almost immediately, Tyler crossed the distance and pressed a hand to her back. He did it in exactly the same way Elijah had, but where Elijah's touch made her skin crawl, Tyler's was warm and reassuring.

They left the room and beelined for the front entrance. She tried to see what was going on in the ballroom, but Tyler blocked the view with his body.

Did she smell smoke?

The second they stepped outside, a cold breeze brushed over her skin. Tyler's arm wrapped around her shoulder, heating her.

"What happened in there?" she asked quietly.

"There was a little issue with the Baked Alaska. The flames caught on a tablecloth, and a couple guards got too close."

She shot a look behind her, even though she couldn't see inside the building anymore. "Baked Alaska?"

"It was a last-minute addition to the menu."

A car suddenly pulled up in front of them, only this time, it wasn't Callum in the driver's seat. It was Aidan. And he looked *pissed*. His face was set into angry lines, and when he got out and took her into his arms, his muscles were vibrating.

"Thanks, Ty. I've got it from here." He opened the passenger door, but when he tried to tug her in, she pulled back.

"I can't leave Mia here."

"We have her. She's in the limousine."

Cassie's eyes widened. "You do?"

"We weren't going to leave her with Elijah. The man's a killer."

She blew out a long breath. Snatching Mia from the party was *not* going to go well. Despite that, she was grateful her sister was safe. She slipped inside the car. "Where are we going?" she asked when he was behind the wheel.

"To a hotel a bit out of town. Then tomorrow, you're coming to Cradle Mountain with me." He tore off his wig and fake mustache. His gaze zipped to her before shooting back to the road. "Did he touch you?"

She frowned. "What?"

"Did he touch you?"

She hesitated.

His jaw clicked. "Where?"

"It was nothing. He just grabbed my arm."

He took his eyes off the road again and scanned her arms. Even though it was dark, she knew he could see everything. With one hand, he tugged up the material of her sleeve. His gaze narrowed when he saw the part of her arm that Elijah had grabbed. He grazed her skin lightly. Yeah, it was red and already bruising.

She cupped his cheek and kept her voice soft. "I'm okay. In fact, I was a step away from nailing the man in the balls."

Well, she was pretty sure she had been.

The smallest hint of a smile appeared on his lips. "Were you now?"

"Yeah. Go for their soft areas. You taught me that."

A smile was teasing her lips when Aidan touched something on his ear and frowned.

Her heart thumped. "What is it?"

"Mia's freaking out."

Of course she was. Strangers had snatched her away from people she considered family. Cassie opened her mouth to tell Aidan to take her to her sister when he suddenly pulled off into an alley. She saw the limousine stopping in front of them, having pulled in from the opposite end. The back door opened, and her sister all but fell out. She held her hands up, warding off Callum when he got out after her.

The car had barely stopped when Cassie leapt out. She heard Aidan's curse but ignored it, running over to her sister. The second Mia saw her, she dodged forward, frantically clutching Cassie.

"Oh God, Cassie, they took you too? They grabbed me from the ball and forced me into the limo! Are these the guys who kidnapped you?"

"Mia—I need you to calm down."

She frowned. *"Calm down?* Do you understand what's happening? We've been kidnapped!"

When Aidan's door snapped shut, Mia's gaze flew toward the sound. She paused before she tilted her head. "Wait...is that...?"

Her gasp cut through the quiet night air.

Cassie grabbed her sister's hands and waited until the woman looked at her. "I need to tell you some stuff—big stuff—but I need you to stay calm." She paused. "Elijah isn't the man you think he is."

Mia went very still, and her voice went oddly flat. "What are you talking about?"

"You know those mysterious deaths that keep happening to people in the organization? Those deaths aren't accidents, Mia. Elijah orchestrated each and every one of them because the members had life insurance policies—and he's the designated beneficiary of those policies."

Mia shook her head slowly. "No. I mean, yes, he's the beneficiary, but that's because he puts the money back into the church like his members want."

"You knew about the policies?"

"Of course!"

Oh, Mia. She swallowed, taking a small step closer. "Mia, those deaths were not accidental."

She snatched her hands from Cassie's hold. "No. Don't do that. Don't stain Elijah's image. He's a good man. He's our leader—"

"He's a murderer."

Mia flinched. "Stop it, Cassie."

"There's more. He puts sedatives in the drinks at our gatherings, then he sexually assaults the female members."

"Stop!"

"He's done it to so many women. He's a dangerous, terrible person, and he needs to be locked up."

"*Stop!*" Mia's voice was almost a shout.

"Has he touched you, Mia?"

She looked disgusted. "No! Of course he hasn't. He wouldn't do that."

Oh, he would. "We're leaving him. You and me. Tonight. Aidan and his team are getting us out of here."

"*You* did this?" Mia looked around at Aidan, then Callum, then back to Cassie. "You organized for me to be kidnapped?"

"We'll be protected."

"Protected from what?"

"From *Elijah!*" Was the woman not listening? "From what he's done. From what he *continues* to do."

Mia took two deep breaths, shaking her head, obviously struggling with everything Cassie had told her. But she'd known she would. It was a lot. And Mia had gotten in so deep. She lived and breathed the organization.

"Cassie. You need to take me back right now. I'm going to keep everything you've said to me tonight between us, because you're my sister and I love you, and I hope that you'll come back too. But you need to *stop*."

Had the woman heard the part about Elijah murdering innocent people? Drugging and raping women? "I'm *not* going to stop, Mia. I'm going to get that asshole sent to prison!"

Behind Mia, Callum touched his earpiece.

Aidan cursed, and when she turned her head, he was doing the same thing. He moved behind her and wrapped an arm around her waist. "They're on their way. We have to go."

Her insides chilled. "Who?"

"Several of Elijah's men, including the guy who was outside your house."

"Sampson," Mia breathed.

Hope lit her sister's eyes...and the hope in her belly dropped like a weight. Still, she stepped forward and tried one last time. "Come with us, Mia. *Please*. Choose me. Choose to trust what I'm telling you. You're not safe there."

Mia took a step back.

Cassie's heart cracked right through the center.

She wasn't going to come. The impact of that certainty was like being hit by a boulder.

"I can't," Mia whispered.

Broken. Those words made her feel broken. She spoke quietly, even though she wanted to scream. After everything Cassie had told her, she was choosing to stay? "But why—"

"Because he's my *father*, Cassie."

Her entire world ground to a halt.

No, she couldn't... She didn't mean...?

"Elijah is my biological father. I won't leave him," Mia continued quietly. "He's the only parent I have left."

CHAPTER 16

*A*idan looked at Cassie in the passenger seat. She'd barely said two words since they got into the car. The silence was deafening.

When he saw a tremble in her fingers, he bit back a curse. He turned up the heater before reaching over and taking her hand. "I'm sorry."

There was a small catch in her breath and a flinch at his touch. "You don't need to be sorry."

He felt like he needed to say and do a whole lot more. Everything about her screamed at his need to offer comfort. There was something inside him demanding he soothe her pain even though he had no idea how.

He glanced into his rearview mirror, spotting Tyler behind them. Mia had remained in Salt Lake City, refusing to leave no matter how much Cassie begged. She'd walked to the street at one end of the alley, and Callum had stayed behind, covertly watching to make sure Mia stayed safe until Sampson reached her.

Everything that had happened tonight made Aidan see red.

He pulled into the parking lot in front of the hotel. They'd driven an hour out and used a different name so they could avoid any unwanted visitors. Blake was already here and had checked into their rooms for them.

It was late, or early morning, whichever way he wanted to see it. Cassie needed rest.

He climbed out and moved around the car. Cassie's door was already open. He helped her stand. He'd given her his jacket, and under that she still wore the gown.

A visible shudder rocked her small frame. Aidan cursed, tugging her closer.

He'd made it halfway across the lot when Tyler and Blake were there, walking beside them.

"Hi, Cassie, I'm Blake," he said quietly to her.

She gave him a small smile. Aidan tightened his grip on her.

Blake nodded toward the side of the building. "We'll go through the back."

They bypassed the back door for guests, stopping at an entrance used by staff, and Blake keyed in a code. Aidan had no idea how he'd gotten it, and he didn't ask.

Once inside, they followed Blake up a set of stairs, then another. Finally, his friend stopped at a door. He swiped a card through the reader. After a click, it opened.

"We're right next door if you need us," Tyler said.

Aidan nodded. "Thanks."

He stepped inside and closed the door behind him. Cassie moved to the bed and perched on the edge. He crouched in front of her. "Cassie—"

She immediately stood. "I'm going to have a shower."

She stepped around him, but he touched her arm to stop her. "Want some company?"

A quick shake of her head, then she was gone, disappearing into the connected bathroom and closing the door with a resounding click of the lock.

CASSIE STRIPPED off her clothes before reaching across the shower and turning on the water. Usually, she kept her showers luke-warm. It was something she'd become used to for her hypotension, so the heat didn't affect her blood pressure. But tonight, she made it hot. So hot that steam immediately billowed in the room.

She didn't care about her hypotension right now. She didn't care about what she should or shouldn't do, or right or wrong. She was filled with shock. Sick with dismay. And all she wanted to do was forget what Mia had told her, the choice her sister had made.

She stepped under the stream. The scorching water burned her skin.

Father. Elijah was Mia's *father*. How was that possible? The man was pure evil. Whereas Mia was sweet and kind and had a pure heart...at least, that's how she'd always seen her sister. But tonight... Tonight she'd chosen *him* over Cassie. Tonight, she'd made the conscious decision to stand by a man whom Cassie had just revealed was responsible for despicable, heinous crimes.

She scrunched her eyes closed, dipping her head beneath the stream. The burn felt good on her skin. It took her attention away from the other pain in her body. The one rippling inside her chest, tearing her heart in two.

How long had Mia known the man was her father? And why hadn't she told Cassie?

Her sister's words repeated in her head.

I won't leave him. He's the only parent I have left.

She pressed her hands against the wall as light-headedness started to fog her mind.

But *she* was the only *sibling* Mia had. Hell, she'd basically raised Mia after their mother had died and they'd been shuffled around the foster care system. Didn't that count for anything? All the love and care and sacrifices she'd made, willingly putting Mia first at every turn?

And she wasn't the devil incarnate like Elijah.

More dots in her vision. She should turn the heat down. No, she should turn the water off and step out, but her feet felt rooted to the spot. Like if she switched it off and got out, she'd have to step back into the real world.

Her heart thumped in her chest and her vision hazed.

A knock sounded at the door, then a voice. She barely heard it as she focused on breathing.

Mia stayed. She'd told her everything...yet she'd stayed. She wasn't going to get her sister back. In every scenario she'd played out in her head over the years, it had never ended this way. Because her sister had never been *that* person in her mind, the kind who could willingly let others suffer.

Her knees buckled but before she could hit the tiles, strong arms latched around her waist and lifted her. She glanced up to see Aidan. He was also naked, his brows tugged together. He looked worried.

"I heard your heartbeat slowing. The water's too hot for you, Cassie."

He turned to step out, but she shook her head. "Just another few minutes. I just need this bubble for a bit longer..."

Something flickered through his eyes. A combination of anger and torment and pain.

For a moment, she thought he'd step out anyway. Then he reached for the faucet and turned the hot water down before positioning his body so that the spray hit his bare shoulders. She closed her eyes and wrapped her legs around his lean waist, resting her head on his chest.

"I locked the door," she whispered.

"I broke it."

Of course he did. They'd been separated for years, and now

they'd found each other. There was probably no lock in existence that could keep them apart.

He took away a bit of the pain in her chest. His steadily beating heart beneath her ear almost made her feel whole.

He kissed her head. "Talk to me. What's going on in that beautiful head?"

So much. So many words and feelings and emotions that she had no idea how to navigate. She traced a finger across his wet skin. "I missed you so much. I missed talking to you. Kissing you goodbye in the morning. I missed the goofy little notes you used to leave for me to find around the house when you went on your missions." She paused. "Some nights, I would lay there with my eyes closed and hope that when I opened them, it was all a lie. That you never disappeared. That Mia never returned to Elijah."

His sigh was heavy.

"It was so hard to stay away," she continued, deviating her finger to his shoulder and drawing circles. "When I saw you on the news, I almost left. I almost walked away from everything. Damien. My sister. I actually went upstairs to pack my bag. Then Damien got home, and he told me about Olive's brother."

A shudder worked its way through her body. Aidan's arms tightened.

"She and I were friends, and she'd already given me hints about what Elijah had done to her. I knew what happened to her brother might break her. I knew I needed to help, and that in turn, she could be the key to helping everyone else. So I made a promise to myself. That I'd work harder and smarter to get Elijah sent away. Then I'd return to you."

Aidan started a slow stroke down her back. "I'm sorry she wouldn't go with you," he whispered against her ear.

Her heart squeezed at his tender tone...and then a spark of something other than desolation rose in her chest.

She leaned back and looked at him. "I'm angry, Aidan. I'm *so* furious, and so hurt. Even if he *is* her father, he's a terrible, disgusting person. How could she listen to everything I said, know about all the things he did, and still want to stay?"

"Love blinds us," he said quietly.

Love? Mia loved Elijah? The thought made her sick to her stomach.

"Even if she does...is her love for him stronger than her love for me? He hasn't been there her entire life like I have, yet tonight, she chose *him*." Frustrated tears pressed to the back of her eyes, but she blinked them away.

He pushed a wet lock of hair from her face. "She made a mistake tonight. I hope one day soon, she realizes."

"Me too." She swallowed. "It's not just Mia. I'm worried about Damien."

"We'll find him."

There was so much conviction and promise in Aidan's words. She touched her head to his. "Thank you. For everything."

CHAPTER 17

*A*idan's eyes flew across the screen. The room was dark, and Cassie was still sleeping. He didn't plan to wake her, not after the night she'd had. God, seeing her so torn apart had killed him.

He'd gotten about an hour of sleep. That's all he wanted. All he needed. Now he was reading background information on members of Paragons of Hope. Elijah, his two brothers, and dozens of others.

He'd been wondering how Elijah had gotten so much manpower behind his organization. There were a lot of members who were former military. According to their background checks, most of them had some sort of PTSD and trauma in their military files.

Had Elijah gotten that information somehow and preyed on it? Offered them salvation and peace, then taken advantage of their training?

Aidan leaned back in his seat, his mind flicking back to what he'd read about Elijah. The man's father had been the leader of the organization before he'd died in a car accident when Elijah was twenty. That's when he'd come into power. That was also when the high walls had been built around the compound. The uncommonly high number of *accidental* deaths started shortly thereafter.

Aidan had read those reports as well. On the surface, they seemed like unfortunate events. A couple of car accidents. Fire victims. One man had even fallen from a six-story building.

At the rustling of sheets from the bed, his gaze lifted to see a pair of beautiful jade-green eyes looking at him.

A slow smile curved Cassie's lips. "Hey."

Thank God. He really needed to see that smile today after the night she'd had. "Morning, beautiful."

He sat the laptop on the sofa cushion beside him and was about to get up, but she was already climbing out of bed. He stopped, his dick twitching, not only at the sight of those long legs on full display but at the sight of her wearing *his* shirt. It reached halfway down her thighs, and it had every part of him screaming *mine*.

The second she was within reaching distance, he curved an arm around her waist and pulled her onto his lap.

He cupped her cheek and turned her face. Then he kissed her. Fuck, she tasted good.

When she pulled back, she was still smiling. Then she looked at the screen. The smile slipped. "Sampson and Antwon. Two of Elijah's main guards."

He stroked a hand up her thigh, enjoying the little shiver that trilled down her back. "Do you remember living there when you were younger?"

She sank back into him. "I actually remember liking it. There were lots of kids around. Everyone was always friendly and happy, especially my mom. The only time I remember her being unhappy was the night we left."

He heard her heart speed up a notch.

He stroked her leg again. "What happened?"

"A neighbor looked after me and Mia while my mom was out.

When she returned, I was already in bed, but I could hear her. Her frantic breathing and the sound of her rushing around. At the time, I didn't really understand, but now I think she was having a panic attack."

He frowned but remained silent, knowing there was more of the story to come.

"I got out of bed and went out to see her. She was a mess. Shaking and crying. I'd never seen her so out of sorts before. She was packing a bag and told me we were leaving. That she was taking us somewhere safe." She shook her head. "I didn't get it, because I thought we *were* safe. She was so strong to do what she did."

He pressed a kiss to her shoulder.

"I *remember* her strength. She was firm but kind. She never minced words, and she was the kind of mother who would do anything for her kids. Including sneak both Mia and me out of that compound." She swallowed. "I wish she was here for Mia now."

"And for you," he said quietly.

"And for me." She traced a finger on his chest. "If she hadn't died so quickly, she could have told me what happened that night."

"It certainly would have taken away the guessing game now."

She nibbled her bottom lip as she stroked his shoulder. "Anyway, what's the plan today?"

He smiled. "Today, I'm taking you to my home in Cradle Mountain."

There was a flash of something in her eyes. Fear? Uncertainty? "Will we still be able to take Elijah down from Idaho?"

"Blake and Liam are going to stay, and we're discussing various plans. We need to do our research first, on Elijah and his guards, and also a few of his most trusted members."

"Detective Shaw was pretty certain he needed Olive's testimony." She straightened. "With everything that happened last night, I never told him the meeting was off."

"We can do that." He studied her face as he said the next part. "I should also let you know that my team is already planning a covert search-and-rescue op at the compound…for Damien. And we're not telling the detective until it's done."

Their marriage might only be on paper, but the man was important to Cassie.

For a moment, she was silent. Her heart sped up, and she studied him as if wondering whether or not to believe him. Then she threw her arms around his neck and hugged him tightly. It was everything.

"Thank you," she whispered.

They remained like that for a few minutes. When she pulled away, her eyes were shiny with tears. She blinked them away. "I can help. I can go with you and show you where Elijah might be holding him."

The idea had fear sweeping through him. "Cassie—"

"I know that compound inside out. If he's in there, I know where he'd be."

"We can draw up blueprints and you can show us. You don't need to be there."

She blew out a huff of breath. "You know that won't be as effective."

"What I know is that you're safest away from that place." There was no way in hell she was getting anywhere near the compound. He tugged out his phone and called up a number he'd recently saved.

"You have Detective Shaw's number?"

Thank God they were off the topic of her entering the compound. "I do." He winked at her and pressed dial before putting the phone on speaker.

"Detective Shaw speaking."

"Hello, Shaw. This is Aidan Pratt."

"And Cassie...Webber."

She hesitated on the last name, looking at Aidan nervously. He squeezed her hip. Yeah, he hated that she had Damien's last name, but it didn't affect him like it used to. Not after knowing what he knew. And she wouldn't have it forever.

"Mr. Pratt, Mrs. Webber. My guys and I are ready to go today."

Cassie closed her eyes. "Olive's not coming."

There was a moment of pause. "Are we changing to a different date?"

"Not at the moment. She wants some...time to think about it."

The detective blew out a long breath. "All right. I knew she was a long shot to begin with. But *you* know there's nothing I can do without evidence. Elijah is a very connected man, and he keeps himself well protected at all times. If anything changes, let me know."

Aidan watched her shoulders sag. She was disappointed. God, he hated it.

"I will."

Aidan hung up. Cassie sighed again and leaned into his chest. He pressed a kiss to her head. "We'll get him."

She nodded almost absently. "Could we also call Dean?" There was sadness in her voice. "I need to update him on Damien."

"Do you have his number?"

She nodded and quickly typed it in. It rang three times before a guy answered.

"Hello?"

"Hi, Dean. It's Cassie."

"Cassie! Any news on Damien?" Aidan could hear the worry in the guy's voice.

"I'm sorry, but..."

There was a heavy pause. "That asshole still has him."

She nibbled her lip and looked at him, like she was asking permission to tell him about his upcoming op. He shook his head. She may trust Dean, but the information about the extraction was safer if it stayed within his group.

"We'll get him out soon, Dean," she said. "I have faith."

"Thank you for keeping me updated." He sounded defeated. Aidan didn't even know the guy and he felt for him. "Are you safe?"

"Yes, I'm safe."

They shared a couple more words before she hung up.

The next hour was spent showering, eating room service food, and getting ready to leave. He had Tyler bring Cassie new clothes, since all she had was the ball gown. He chuckled at the way her cheeks reddened when she found the underwear.

"Tyler probably got an employee to choose them." Or he better have.

When they got on the road, he immediately reached for her hand. Something told him any time *not* touching this woman would always be too long.

They traveled long stretches of open roads, talking about nothing and everything. It felt like it used to. It felt like he'd been sucked back in time and he was the Aidan who had never experienced Project Arma or lost the woman he loved.

When they started driving parallel to a river, Cassie sighed. "I love the water." She turned to look at him. "Remember our van? Every time you got home from a mission, we'd just hit the road."

"Of course. You always had the van packed and ready to go."

She laughed. It tightened his chest. "Yeah, I used to count down the days until you'd be home and I could be alone with you. When we'd just get lost in nature."

He squeezed her hand. "Maybe we can do it again soon." There was no maybe about it. They would. He'd make sure of it.

A wistful look crossed her face. "I would love that."

As a gas station came into view ahead, he glanced at the fuel level, noticing how low it was. He pulled into the station, and the second he stepped out, she did too.

She stretched, and his gaze zeroed in on the way the fabric of her shirt stretched against her chest, pulling up to reveal the creamy skin of her belly. His gaze shot away. He was going to get hard at a damn gas station.

She crossed over to him and pressed a kiss to his lips. "I'm just going to use the bathroom."

As she stepped past him, he snagged her wrist and tugged her back. "Don't stray."

"I won't. You may officially call me your shadow because you're stuck with me for the foreseeable future."

Didn't sound like a bad thing to him.

She pecked his cheek. She was walking away when she turned her head. "Can you get me some—"

"Sour worms?"

She stopped, her mouth pulling into a smile. "You remember."

"About your obsession with sour worms on road trips? Yeah, I remember." The woman had always had a thing for the candy. It had been a mandatory part of their trips in the van.

Her features softened before she turned and continued into the station.

He shot a look down the road just as Tyler pulled into the station, stopping at the pump behind Aidan's. Tyler had been shadowing them closely, while Callum was about forty-five minutes behind.

Once the car was filled, he stopped beside Tyler. "No tail?"

He shook his head. "Watched the entire way. Nothing."

Good. They were taking a longer, more meandering route home. They had no idea if Mia had told anyone that Aidan had taken Cassie. If Elijah wanted her badly enough, he could already have men waiting for them in Cradle Mountain.

"Callum says he's all clear too," Tyler added.

"We should be safe, then."

Once Tyler's car was filled, they walked across the lot and into the small store, stopping briefly inside to check out a car that pulled up to the pump opposite Aidan's. Two men exited the vehicle, talking to each other as they walked toward the store.

Tyler frowned when Aidan headed to the candy aisle. "You get a sudden sweet tooth?"

Hell no. He didn't eat this shit. "Sour worms for Cassie."

Tyler chuckled and moved to the counter.

When he scanned the shelves, his lips quirked. It felt like old times. She'd always sent him inside to get her candy. He grabbed the bag of gummies, then noticed the peanut butter M&Ms. Another favorite of Cassie's. He bent and snagged a bag of those too. When he straightened, his gaze shifted outside.

A van with tinted windows was turning in.

Tyler had paused at the counter, also looking at the vehicle.

Aidan frowned as a car pulled in—also with tinted windows.

His gut churned. Something wasn't right. His gaze flew to the bathroom door near the exit. He started toward it and glanced into a round mirror secured to the ceiling.

The man behind him was pulling something from under his arm, beneath his jacket.

In the next aisle, a guy was reaching for the small of his back.

The men who'd pulled into the station as Aidan and Tyler had entered the store.

Aidan dropped to the floor just as a bullet shot toward him.

CASSIE TURNED on the tap and washed her hands under the cool stream of water. When she caught herself in the mirror with a small smile, guilt slithered down her spine. She looked happy.

How could she be *happy* after what her sister had told her and the decision she'd made? God, how could she be happy when Damien was missing?

The smile melted away, and she blew out a breath. A part of her whispered that she'd been through so much in the last five days that it was okay to feel everything right now, including happiness. Despite the battle still ahead of them, she'd sacrificed a lot over the years and finally had the man she loved back.

But still, any happiness at all felt...wrong.

After drying her hands, she turned the lock and pulled open the door.

The loud bang of a bullet sounded, quickly followed by a second.

Panic was a lightning bolt inside her chest. She opened her mouth to scream, but suddenly Aidan rose from an aisle with a gun in his hands and shot a man. Tyler popped up near the counter and shot another.

When Aidan's eyes swung to her, fury marred his features. "Shut and lock the door!"

Before the words had finished coming out of his mouth, more guys with guns flew into the station, all aiming at Aidan and Tyler.

Her heart stopped and her limbs froze as Aidan shot one of them before dropping as a bullet flew over his head.

She snapped herself out of her shock and quickly stepped back. She went to shut the door, but a big hand grabbed it before she could and tugged it wider. When she saw the black ski mask and the dark eyes, fear exploded in her belly.

Because she didn't recognize those eyes. This wasn't one of Elijah's guards.

She pulled hard on the knob, but he snagged her wrist and threw the door open before yanking her forward. She fought, punching with one fist and kicking any part of him she could reach, all while tugging on her arm, but his strength was unbreakable. A few more men entered the shop, gunning for Aidan and Tyler.

She shot a final glance at Aidan before she was dragged outside.

They'd only made it a couple of steps before the guy abruptly threw her over his shoulder and ran toward a van.

Cassie swung her foot, connecting with his thigh with as much force as she could muster. When he growled and tugged her legs together, holding her tightly, she pounded his back. Too soon, the van door slid open, and she was thrown into a dark space. Before she could recover, the guy climbed in with her. The second he pulled the door closed, the van was moving.

The back of the vehicle was dim, but not fully dark. Her breathing was heavy as she looked at the man. "Let me go."

His silence was deafening.

God, she wanted to scream at him. "What do you want with me?"

Finally, those dark eyes settled on her. "Me? Nothing. I'm just a contractor. It's my job to deliver you to a location. So that's what I'm doing."

CHAPTER 18

*A*idan rose and shot scumbag number two in the head while Tyler had another drop to the floor. His heart stopped when he saw the open bathroom door but no Cassie. Before he could search for her, he crouched and rounded an aisle as more bullets flew at his head.

When he rose again, he swiftly shot two more men before scanning the area.

Then he saw her—outside, being thrown over a guy's shoulder.

Another bullet narrowly missed him. Rage tried to consume him, but he shoved it down like he'd been trained to do. He needed to end this and go after her.

There were three more men with weapons in the shop. They'd all die.

Quiet footsteps sounded in the next aisle. Some asshole was trying to sneak up on him. He saw the guy's foot before his body cleared the end of the aisle.

Aidan shot twice. The man cried out and fell to the floor. With a burst of speed, Aidan grabbed the man and held him against his body. The next bullet, a round aimed at Aidan, hit the guy in the chest.

He lifted his Glock and fired back, dropping the shooter easily, while Tyler took out the last man standing. He hadn't even hit the floor before Aidan dropped the asshole he was holding and ran.

The van was gone.

He squashed the sickening panic churning inside him and noticed an elderly man hiding behind his car. "Which way did they go?"

The man's eyes widened, and he pointed.

Aidan threw himself into his car and sped back the way he'd come. Tyler appeared in his rearview mirror, driving just as fast. He pressed a button on the wheel and a second later, Callum answered his phone.

"Hey, man. Everything okay?"

"They took her."

Callum's voice turned deadly. "Where are you?"

"We're following the van, but they left about two minutes before us." He gave Callum the location of the gas station. How the fuck Elijah's guys had found them, he had no idea, not when neither he nor Tyler identified a tail. But he'd sure as hell be finding out.

"I'm only twenty minutes away. If they're on the highway, they'll have to pass me," Callum said quickly. A car engine roared through the line. "I'll cut them off from the other direction."

"I'll let you know if I catch them first. White van with tinted windows."

"Got it."

"Thank you, brother."

They were coming at Cassie from both directions. This was going to work. It had to. He just had to hope like hell she wasn't harmed by her captors or the van didn't crash.

CASSIE TUGGED AT THE BINDINGS. The asshole had tied rope around her wrists, which were now bound together in front of her. To be fair, she *had* lunged at the guy.

She shot a death glare his way. "So you don't care that you're taking an innocent woman to her death?"

He hadn't admitted he was taking her to Elijah, but she knew he was. She had no idea what Elijah's plans were. It *could* be her death. Hell, she could be locked away in a dungeon for a decade or two. Who the hell knew how a crazy man's mind worked?

The guy remained quiet. He didn't even look at her. He'd been annoyingly silent through each and every question she'd asked.

She tilted her head. "Do you get a bonus for delivering me?"

"Stop talking."

At least he managed words this time. She probably shouldn't antagonize him, but she was angry, dammit. And scared. So scared for Aidan and Tyler that she had to distract herself. There had been so many men shooting at them. They were good, but were they good enough to survive a fight like that?

Her belly cramped.

"You know you're working for a cult leader, right?" she asked. "A man who has no problem ordering hits, and plenty of men on his team to execute his orders. You'll probably be a loose end after this."

A vein stood out on his neck.

"Is the risk to your life worth the money?"

"Lady, every job's a risk to my life. Now shut your mouth before I *tape* it shut."

Not a chance. "What's the going rate for performing a kidnapping and attempting to murder innocent men? Hope it's a lot."

Finally, a quirk of his lips. "Attempt? Your boyfriends are dead. I guarantee it. There was no surviving that."

Terror shot through her, but she was careful to mask her emotions. He didn't deserve the satisfaction. "Trust me. They're not."

Something flashed in the guy's eyes. Anger. And pure evil. "It's hard, isn't it? To accept how quickly and easily we can lose the ones we love. How every fucking thing we've ever done can be rendered pointless thanks to a single bullet."

She ground her teeth. "He's. Not. Dead."

He looked toward the back doors. "Don't worry. You'll probably be joining him soon. The people I'm hired to obtain are rarely seen again."

She barely had time to process that statement before the van violently swerved.

Cassie cried out as she flew into the side panel. Before she could recover, the van came to a crashing halt, and she was thrown to the floor. Pain ricocheted through her back, side and knees. With bound hands, she hadn't been able to cushion her fall.

She was pushing herself up when gunshots sounded. Oh, God. Someone was shooting at them! She sucked in a breath and looked around the back the vehicle. Her captor groaned from the floor.

More bullets, this time accompanied by angry voices.

Cassie didn't hesitate. She lifted her bound hands and lunged for the door. She'd just gotten it open when fingers bunched in her hair and yanked her head back.

She yelped in pain. Her back hit the floor of the van, and the guy leaned over her. "You're staying with me."

The hell she was.

She kneed him between the legs, throwing as much force as she could into the hit. Then she fisted her hands together and propelled them into his jaw.

He grunted and fell to the side. She rolled over and crawled around him. One leg was out of the van when a hard body hit her from behind.

She grunted and fell to the road, the air knocked from her chest, concrete scraping her side and her cheek. To her left, Callum ducked behind a car as bullets flew his way from the front of the van.

Her captor once again fisted her hair, and he yanked her to her feet. He used her body as a shield as he backed behind the van. She was tugging and twisting in his hold when she spotted the knife strapped to his thigh.

She didn't give herself time to think about what she was doing. She yanked it out, twisted and plunged it into his side.

He howled in pain and released her, dropping to the road. Bile rose in her throat at the blood spurting from the wound. She took a stumbling step back. Then another. He pressed his hands to the ground to stand—and when he glanced up, he looked ready to kill.

Cassie spun on her heels and ran down the small decline beside the road. The faint sound of water grew louder as she ran. It was the river she'd been admiring from the car on their drive. Jesus, that felt like a lifetime ago.

She was almost at the bottom when her foot slipped. With bound hands, she couldn't catch herself. She tumbled the rest of the way down the hill and landed on the bank of the river.

With a groan, she pushed to her feet. Then she heard sliding rocks from above. Her heart flew into her throat.

The guy was halfway down.

Shit, shit, shit!

Water pooled around her ankles, and the wind whipped across her face, but she ignored it, running down the bank. Aidan would be here soon, she had to believe that. And until he got here, she had to put as much distance between herself and this kidnapping asshole as possible.

When a bullet caused a small explosion of dirt close to her feet, she screamed and stumbled to her hands and knees.

"Stop, or the next bullet will be in the leg."

Her breath stuttered. Slowly, she rose to her feet and turned. She raised her hands as the man advanced on her, gun trained on her chest. "I'm sure your *boss* said he wants me alive."

"Exactly why the bullet would be in your leg."

She shook her head. "You should leave me and run. The guys driving the van are probably already dead. You'll be next."

He grabbed her roughly and shoved her forward, heading back the way they came. "My guys are good with a gun. I don't think I need to worry."

"Do you even know who you're dealing with?" she asked. "All those guys are former Special Forces—and they were all part of Project Arma. Each one is equivalent to ten of you."

"Yet none of them are bulletproof." He tugged her toward the hill.

They'd made it halfway up the incline when Cassie saw him. Aidan.

The tightness in her chest released. He was alive.

Their gazes met, his darkening before running down her body. Then he focused on the guy holding her.

Cassie knew the second her captor saw him, because the asshole swung her in front of him. He wrapped an arm tightly around her throat while he pointed the gun at Aidan.

"Try anything funny and you die," he whispered into her ear.

His words had anger exploding in her chest. Did he expect her to be a pathetic victim who allowed the man she loved to be shot in front of her?

Aidan lifted his gun and aimed at the guy. "Let her go, and I might hand you over to the police instead of shooting you in the fucking head."

The arm around her throat tightened. "Walk away, and I might not shoot *you* in front of her."

Yeah right. The second Aidan turned his back, he was dead.

"She's coming with me, dead or alive," the guy said quietly. His arm tightened further.

Screw him.

She stomped on the guy's foot and threw her elbow up into his gun arm. The second his grip on her neck loosened, she spun. Aidan shouted but she ignored him, kneeing the guy in the dick and giving him a big shove. The grade of the hill instantly had him falling backward.

He grabbed her arm at the last second, and the two of them rolled back down the hill.

When they reached the bottom, he dove on top of her. The gun fired—

No.

Two guns went off.

Her breath seized. A second later, Aidan was frantically pulling a dead guy off her body.

"What the hell did you do?" His hand tugged up her shirt, and cold blasted her skin. A sharp sting at her waist drew her gaze down. God, she'd been shot!

Holy heck, the bullet had nicked her. It was small, barely abrading her side, but still, a bullet. She hadn't even realized.

Aidan's head dipped to his chest, and he heaved a loud breath. "It's just a graze." He tugged her to a sitting position and cradled her face. "Don't *ever* do that again!"

"He was going to shoot you," she rasped.

"Let him. I would have either gotten out of his way or shot him first. You don't ever try to save me. It's my job to save *you*."

She would. If she thought he was at risk, and she could save him, she damn well would. But something on Aidan's face told her to keep that information to herself.

As if he heard her thoughts anyway, he growled and crushed her to his chest. His warmth filtered into her limbs.

"You scared me so damn bad, Cass."

She sank against him, needing his strength. "I was scared for *you.*"

No. She was terrified. But he was breathing, and that meant she could breathe too.

CHAPTER 19

*A*idan waited until the doctor and nurse stepped out of the room, then he was in front of her. Cassie sat without her shirt on, a small bandage on her side, her feet dangling off the hospital bed.

She wrapped her arms around his waist. "Like you said, just a graze."

He growled. "You shouldn't have been anywhere near a flying bullet."

"Well, lucky for us, it's barely a flesh wound. In fact, the doctor said the field dressing you did on the wound probably would have been enough until we got to Cradle Mountain, since it had already stopped bleeding."

"It could have been worse." A lot fucking worse. "I'm going to have nightmares about that bullet."

She cupped his cheek. "I'm okay."

He grabbed her hips and stepped closer, lowering his lips to hover over hers. "Thank God."

He kissed her. And when they separated, she sighed. "I'm ready to go home now."

His body tensed. "Home?"

She shook her head. "Sorry. I should have said your home."

His heart started beating again. "*Our* home." Honestly, home had never been a place for him. It was anywhere she was. That's why he'd been so lost these last few years. "We can go now."

The second the last man had fallen today—the man who shot Cassie—Aidan had called Detective Shaw. He'd shown up within the hour and taken charge of the scene, while also calling authorities he trusted and directing them to the gas station.

Elijah had been smart to use outside contractors—and it pissed Aidan off. He was still counting on there being some sort of money trail that led back to the cult leader. If there wasn't...

Fuck. He couldn't think about that.

Cassie had been offered an ambulance, but Aidan insisted on driving her. He wasn't letting her out of his sight.

He'd hated every second of the drive to the nearest hospital, watching his rearview the entire way. He still had no damn clue how the men had found them at the gas station. There'd been no trace of anyone following. And they were too well-trained not to spot a tail, even if it consisted of professionals.

A knock came at the door. Cassie quickly tugged on a top as Aidan called out.

The door opened and Tyler stepped in, followed by Callum, both looking far from happy. "We need to go. A car just pulled up at the front entrance—and they don't look friendly."

Aidan frowned. "Who?"

"Didn't recognize them as members of Paragons of Hope," Callum said. "Could be more outside contractors."

Goddammit! There was no way Aidan wanted to hang around and find out. Yes, he could take the assholes, but Cassie had been through enough. And who knew how many guns Elijah had hired. The guy seemed to have endless resources.

"Before we go, we need to figure out how they keep tracking us," Aidan said quietly. He turned to Cassie. "Do you have anything on you that Elijah gave to you?"

Her eyes widened and she shook her head. "No."

"Nothing that came from anyone at Paragons of Hope? Even Damien?" Callum asked.

"All I had was the ball gown, which I left at the hotel." She glanced down, touching the necklace on her chest. "Well, that and my necklace."

Aidan frowned, looking closely at the small pendant. "Did he touch it?"

"What?"

"He mentioned the necklace when he had you cornered in that room last night. Did he touch it?"

Before she could answer, he reached for the pendant and turned it over in his fingers.

Son of a bitch. On the back was a small, almost undetectable, tracking device.

He tore it off the back of the pendant and held it out to show the guys. They both cursed softly.

Cassie gasped. "Is that—"

"A tracking device." He crushed it between his fingers.

If situations were different, he would have attached the device to something to create some misdirection. But in this case, it didn't matter. Elijah knew where he was taking her. He knew the team lived in Cradle Mountain.

But *fuck*, he'd tagged her like a damn dog.

Tyler moved to the window and tugged it open. Good. They were on the ground floor. He climbed out first. "Clear."

Callum was next. Then Aidan looked at Cassie. "Your turn."

He helped her out of the window, while Callum grabbed her from the other side. Then they moved around the hospital, continuing to scan as they went.

They'd just reached Aidan's car when he heard it—heartbeats.

Two more than the four heartbeats that should have been present.

Where were they coming from? He scanned the lot. There were no people sitting in any cars.

His gaze narrowed on a large black SUV several cars over.

"Stay with Cassie," Aidan whispered to Callum. He maneuvered silently through the vehicles, Tyler right behind him.

The second Aidan rounded the car next to the SUV, a pistol fired.

Aidan dropped, the shot narrowly missing him. Then he raced forward faster than the eye could track, diving for the shooter and rolling him beneath him. He seized the hand holding the gun and smashed it against the ground hard enough that there was a loud snap of bone. The guy cried out, dropping the weapon to the concrete.

Aidan clutched his throat and squeezed. "Who hired you?"

The man choked and attempted to push Aidan off. "The client's anonymous! Paid us in cash!"

He watched the man's face and listened to his voice, his heart. Truth.

The asshole was telling the truth. *Fuck.*

They wouldn't be able to trace the attacks back to Elijah.

Aidan lowered his head, whispering into the guy's ear. "You come anywhere near her again, I'll kill you. Got it?" His fingers tightened. "Pass that on to your friends," he finished, before applying enough pressure that the man passed out. He looked beside him, noting Tyler's guy was also down for the count. He rose and returned to Cassie.

She was shaking a bit but looked steady otherwise. "Are you okay?" she asked.

He studied her body, making sure no bullets had caught her this time. "Yes. Let's go, before more assholes attack."

CASSIE'S EYES flashed open as she sucked in a gasping breath. Oh God, the dream... It had felt so real.

She'd been down at that river, her kidnapper's hand around her throat while he pointed a gun at Aidan. But instead of fighting, Cassie had just let the guy shoot Aidan right in front of her. She screamed and scrunched her eyes closed because she didn't want to see his lifeless body on the ground, and when she opened them again, she was in the hospital parking lot...and once again, Aidan was on the ground, bleeding out.

Not real. The dream wasn't real. Aidan's alive.

She let her gaze flick around the masculine bedroom. Aidan's bedroom. But no Aidan.

He'd driven them home the day before. Tyler had followed while Callum waited at the hospital for Detective Shaw.

Cassie had worried every second of that drive. Worried that more of Elijah's men would come after them. Worried that this time, Aidan wouldn't be able to dodge the bullet. It took her forever to fall asleep. Even having Aidan's arms wrapped around her last night hadn't made sleep come any easier.

Where was he? The curtains were still closed, but there was light bleeding around the edges. With a deep inhale, she glanced at the bedside clock.

Nine a.m. She'd slept in. Not a surprise after tossing and turning all night.

Carefully, she climbed out of bed. There was a small ache in her side from the bullet graze, but it was mild. Not that she'd be admitting that to Aidan. The guy was tormented enough as it was over her wound.

She moved to the dresser, and her gaze caught on a framed photo on top. It was of Aidan, his brother, and his parents.

Memories assaulted her. God, she hadn't seen them in years. Christmases and birthdays and other celebrations had always been fun with his family. She'd loved them, and they'd seemed to love her.

Not anymore, a voice whispered in her head.

They had to hate her after what she'd done. How could they not? She'd kept in contact with them, his mother in particular, for the first few months. They'd cried together. Been hopeful of his return together. Then Mia had returned to Elijah, and her plan to return to Paragons of Hope was set into motion...so she'd broken off contact. Aidan's family would have been leverage against her, and Elijah would have been a threat to their safety.

Sighing, she lifted the frame. The second it was off the table, something fell from the back. Her heart stuttered and a small gasp slipped from her lips.

A photo of her and Aidan.

She was sitting on his lap in the back of their van. She didn't know which road trip this was—there were so many. But she looked happy and carefree. Tears filled her eyes at the thought.

You had no idea what was to come, Cassie.

"I always loved that photo."

She jumped at Aidan's voice from the door. The framed photo almost fell from her grasp. "Oh my gosh! Aidan. You scared me."

He crossed the room and took hold of her hips from behind before kissing her neck. "Sorry."

Her insides warmed. She looked down at the photo of them. "I'm surprised you kept this." She'd assumed the man would have gotten rid of anything that reminded him of her.

Not just gotten rid of it. Burned it so it would never come back to haunt him.

"I needed it close, but at the same time, I couldn't look at it every day." His words sliced at her insides. "So I kept it behind the frame. And when I was feeling weak, or like the world was too heavy without you, I pulled it out."

She knew that feeling so well. "I wore the necklace for the same reason. It made me feel close to you, and that helped me get through the days without you."

His fingers tightened.

She placed the photo of his family back on the dresser. "How are your parents and brother?"

"They're good. I talk to them a couple times a week. They ask about you a lot."

That had her head shooting up, and she looked back at him. "They do?"

He turned her to face him. "Yep. Just like my team, they've been on my ass this entire time to go to you and find out what the hell was going on. My mom always insisted something wasn't right, and you wouldn't marry someone else without a damn good reason. Guess mothers really *do* know best."

She'd always loved that woman. "I didn't want to marry Damien." She'd already told him such, but it felt worth repeating. "But when I asked to return, it was either live inside the compound or marry. And I knew that if I lived there, my freedom would be gone. It would be harder to contact law enforcement and set things up. And I'd drown." Survival. A large part of her decision had been about survival. "I was already drowning with everything else." Without Aidan.

Aidan's hand continued to graze her side.

"I had no idea where you were. If you were dead or alive. I was mourning your loss and feeling so alone. So I just... I threw myself into doing everything I could to get Mia out. I knew if I asked Damien, he'd say yes to marrying me, because he wanted out of the compound too. He wanted freedom but had no idea how to obtain it. Elijah doesn't just let people leave the cult. In fact, I haven't seen anyone leave, ever."

Except her mother...

Aidan curved his arms around her waist. She didn't miss how careful he was to avoid her injury. "I'm meeting with the team at the office to plan our trip to the compound."

"I'll come and help."

He kissed her neck. "Good. I want you close. Always."

She hummed at the feel of his lips on her. "Will I get to meet the rest of your team in person?"

"Yeah."

A nervous trill rolled through her spine. The members she'd met so far had been friendly, but would everyone on the team be the same?

As if reading her thoughts, he whispered, "They'll love you."

CHAPTER 20

"We'll enter over the eastern wall," Aidan said, his eyes on the document in the center of the Blue Halo conference room table.

Cassie had drawn a diagram of the compound as best she could. It was rough, but it would have to be enough.

Cassie leaned forward. "Since it's at the back of the compound, and faces the backs of several buildings, they put fewer guards there. They assume the wall is enough."

And the wall *would* be enough. For normal men.

They still weren't alerting law enforcement of their plans. By the time Detective Shaw had authority to raid the compound, it might be too late for Damien. Hell, it might be too late already.

He couldn't think about that. It would hurt Cassie too much to see Damien gone. If he was there, and alive, they'd find him. But it needed to be a simple extraction. Something they'd all done plenty during their time in the military.

Cassie sat beside him, with Callum, Jason, Logan, Flynn and Tyler also at the table. Tyler would be staying home with Cassie during the op, but the man was still part of the planning process.

Blake and Liam were still in Salt Lake City, watching the compound.

Cassie nibbled her bottom lip. She was nervous. In fact, she'd gotten progressively more nervous throughout the meeting. When her fingernails dug into her thigh, Aidan reached over and set a hand on top of hers. "What is it?"

There was a beat of silence before she answered. "I was relieved when you told me about your plans to search the compound for Damien, and so grateful. But...there are cameras and guards *everywhere*. Elijah will already be furious that the contractors failed and the attention it's brought to him, even if there's nothing to prove he hired them. What if something happens?"

"Nothing will happen."

Her lips thinned. "What do you think he'll do when he sees you on camera?"

"We're going to hack into the system while we're in there," Callum said.

Her foot started a rapid tap on the floor. "Then he'll *definitely* know it's you."

"Good," Aidan said quietly. Her eyes flashed up at him. "The man sent people for you—*twice*. I *want* him to know it's me breaching his security. I want him to be painfully aware of who and what he's up against."

Because the man wouldn't win. And the sooner he figured that shit out, the better.

For a moment, she just watched him, an array of emotions flickering through her eyes. Then she sighed. "Okay. I trust you."

"Good." He squeezed her thigh.

She turned back to the diagram. "Saturday evening's probably the best time to go. Everyone in the compound does Bible study at the church, which is on the western side of the compound."

"And you think Damien is being held in the Great Hall?" Liam asked. According to Cassie, that's what members called the main building.

He heard the small elevation in her heart rate. She hated thinking about Damien being held there against his will. His fingers tightened around hers.

"Yes. There's a basement that runs the length of the meeting area," she said. "No one's allowed down there except for Elijah and his brothers. I've always suspected that bad things happen in that basement."

"If he's keeping Damien in the basement, he'll probably have the door guarded," Blake said.

Aidan stroked the back of Cassie's hand. "We'll knock them out but won't kill anyone unless necessary." He got several nods in return.

"I wonder..." Cassie paused.

When she looked at him, his stomach dipped, because he just *knew* he wasn't going to like what she said next.

"We still need Olive. I could go with you, talk to her one last time. Beg her for her testimony and evidence."

"No. Cassie, we've discussed this."

"We never actually finished the conversation."

Oh, they'd finished it. He didn't want Cassie anywhere near the place. "It would be too dangerous for you to come."

She cast pleading eyes on him. "Aidan—"

"There's also every chance that if Olive sees us, she'll alert others that we're there," he pressed. He didn't know this woman. He didn't want anyone in the organization seeing them. It was too much of a risk.

Cassie shook her head. "She wouldn't."

"She might," Aidan said quietly.

Tyler cleared his throat. "If we get Damien out of there and he can tell the police what happened to him, his experience will be evidence for a warrant."

Cassie's brows tugged together, but she eventually nodded.

She knew they were right, but *he* knew that she was desperate. Desperate to get Elijah locked up and her sister away from him. Desperate for him to go to jail, not just for kidnapping, but for murder and rape.

Distant tapping of feet on the stairs sounded, then the door to the Blue Halo office opening.

Based on the footfalls, four women had entered the building, and he already knew exactly who they were. A few seconds later, there was a knock on the door.

Jason grinned. "Come in."

The door slid open. Courtney was the first through. She held a tray of coffees in her hand and went straight over to Jason. He pushed his chair back, and she slid onto his lap.

Grace was next. Logan rose and took the woman into his arms.

Carina, Flynn's partner, entered the room, closely followed by Willow, Blake's woman. Both of them set more coffees onto the table, as well as cake.

"And what are *you* all doing here?" Tyler asked, leaning back in his chair. There was a smirk on his face because he already knew. They all did.

The women wanted to meet the infamous Cassie.

"Thought we'd bring you guys some treats," Courtney said, before looking at Cassie. "Hi, I'm Courtney. This is Willow, Grace, and Carina."

The women exchanged hellos.

"So…" Grace's eyes flashed to Aidan. "Any chance you boys are finished with Cassie?"

Aidan shook his head with a sigh. "If she wants to go with you, she's all yours."

Cassie's brows rose. "Uh…sure?"

She stood, and the women began to filter out of the room. Before Cassie left, she leaned down, pressing her lips to his ear. "The conversation about me going isn't over."

Then she was gone.

~

CASSIE SIPPED her coffee in the reception area of Blue Halo. It was good. Really good. And God, she needed it.

The four women sat around her. They'd spent the last ten minutes telling her everything there was to know about Cradle Mountain. So far, she'd learned that Courtney owned the coffee shop down the street, Grace was a therapist, Willow was finishing a teaching degree, and Carina worked as an in-home nurse for Flynn's mother. Oh, and they were all dating men from Blue Halo Security.

So far, the women seemed great. Funny. Kind. Friendly.

Courtney leaned forward. "So, enough about us. Tell me—what's going on with you and Aidan?"

"Courtney." Grace sighed before turning to Cassie. "You don't have to tell us anything. You've just met us."

Courtney frowned. "What are you talking about? We just told her our life stories. I'd say she knows us pretty well."

Cassie laughed. Yeah, she definitely liked these women. "Aidan and I are…back together."

There was an array of gasps and squeals.

"But aren't you married?" Carina asked. The question was gentle, but there was genuine confusion there. Which was fair.

"I am, but the marriage has only ever been on paper. My husband and I are best friends, and we married as a way to get each other out of a bad situation. In fact, he's been kind of seeing someone else." You couldn't really call it dating when they'd never gone on a date. But they loved each other.

Her heart hurt for Dean. The man was sick with worry. She'd called him again that morning, just to check in, and he wasn't doing well. She could hear it in his voice.

She wasn't sure if the women had been told about Paragons of

162

Hope and Elijah and the compound, but it was probably a bit much to share her entire messy life story on a first meeting.

"Damien's actually missing." Now *why* had she gone and said that?

When the women's brows rose, she continued. "That's what the team's doing right now. Planning an extraction."

"How does Aidan feel about Damien?" Willow asked.

"He's been really great about it since I told him everything. Aidan knows I love him. He also knows I love Damien as a friend, and that I need him to be okay."

"He missed you so much," Grace said.

Courtney nodded. "Anytime the guys brought up your name, his entire face would change and he would kind of just...shut down. Like it hurt too much to think about you."

Cassie sucked in a sharp breath. Those words were like an arrow to her chest. "I hate that. I wanted to come to him, but I was being watched. And I was so close to..."

Courtney was the one to finish for her. "Shutting down Paragons of Hope?"

Yep. Their men had told them. "You know."

Carina lifted a shoulder. "We weaseled the information out of them."

Grace's voice lowered. "How's your sister?"

Even the thought of Mia made her heart hurt. "I asked her to come with me. She chose to stay." That pretty much summed it up.

For a beat, the women were silent. Did they hear the pain in her voice?

"At the start, it was only about getting Mia out," Cassie continued. "I just knew she wasn't safe there. Then I learned the extent of what was going on. It was so much worse than I thought. Now it's become a personal mission to make sure Elijah goes away for a long time so he can't hurt anyone else."

Willow reached over and squeezed her hand. "The guys

163

specialize in protecting good people and taking down bad ones. If anyone can do it, it's them."

She was just nodding when Aidan stepped out of the hallway. At the solemn look on his face, her gut clenched. "What is it?"

"Mia's on the phone."

She shot to her feet. "What?"

"She just called through the Blue Halo line."

She moved forward. Aidan's arm slipped around her waist as he led her back to the conference room. Why was her sister calling? Where from? Did she want out? Was she calling because she needed help?

The second she stepped into the room, Callum handed her the phone. It wasn't on speaker, but she knew all the men would hear Mia clearly.

"Mia?"

A sigh gusted over the line. "Cass! Are you okay?"

Oh God, hearing her sister's voice... It was everything. "I'm okay. Are you?"

"Yes." There was hesitation in Mia's voice, and it had Cassie's stomach churning anew.

"What is it, Mia?"

"I've been so worried since the other night. I know you were going through a lot, and that's why you thought you had to leave. But I want you to come home now. Not home, to your house. Come *here*. To me. You'll be protected at the compound."

Cassie frowned. "What?"

"Elijah told me you were attacked at some gas station. And then a *hospital*? He's so stressed," Mia continued. "And the police were here!"

Hurt and disbelief were like razor blades on Cassie's insides. Her sister hadn't called because she wanted out. She'd called because she wanted Cassie back in. After everything she'd told her...it still shocked her to the core that Mia refused to believe her.

"You'll be safe here. I swear."

She swallowed the lump in her throat. "Yes, I was attacked, Mia. But I think you already know what I'm going to say. Elijah sent those men—"

"No," Mia interrupted. "If he sent men, it was to *save* you. To bring you home because he's worried sick!"

Cassie closed her eyes. Aidan touched her back. "Elijah hired professionals to *forcibly* kidnap me while I was with Aidan. The guy threw me into the back of his van, tied me up, and would have brought me back to Elijah against my will while basically confirming that the person who hired him, *Elijah*, was going to kill me!"

He hadn't said Elijah's name, but she knew it was him.

"No—"

"He also sent men to snatch me from the hospital." Anger and frustration weaved their way through her veins. "He's not a good man, Mia. I'm *never* returning to that place."

Mia's voice lowered. "None of that's true, Cassie. It can't be. Elijah *loves* you. You're like a daughter to him. Please...at least retract what you said to the police about suspecting he sent those men. You're ruining his good name!"

Her breath caught. Who was this woman? It wasn't the sister she thought she knew.

"No. He doesn't love me. And I'm not retracting anything. You're making the wrong choice, Mia."

Cassie hung up. She didn't want to hear anything else her sister had to say.

She loved Mia. She'd always love her. But right now, her sister's belief in that vile man cut so deep, she couldn't bear to hear another word.

CHAPTER 21

*A*idan scanned the wooded area. It was late, and other than the dim light from the moon, it was dark. It was also quiet. So quiet, a normal person wouldn't be able to hear the traffic from the road.

That's why Paragons of Hope had chosen this area for their compound. Because it was far away. Away from people. Stores. Workplaces. Well hidden.

Flynn, Logan, and Jason walked in front of them, while Callum was in contact via an earpiece. Cassie was at home with Tyler. Thank God she'd stopped arguing to go with them after her call from Mia. There was no way he would've risked her entering this compound with them. She was safer at home. And her safety was his priority.

He heard the heartbeats before he saw anyone. Two people outside the wall, somewhere to their left. Most likely perimeter guards.

He broke off from the group. Jason followed, while Logan and Flynn continued forward. They'd come at the men from both the left and right.

When the men came into view, chatting with each other,

Aidan shut down his emotions like he'd been trained to do. He waited until they turned their backs, each pacing in the opposite direction to patrol their section of the wall.

When they were a good few yards apart, he moved, racing to the man walking north and sweeping an arm around the asshole's neck. Logan did the same with the other guy.

The man clawed at Aidan's arm, but he didn't release him. He held on tightly until the guy went slack in his hold. Then he dropped him to the ground.

Logan's guy had just dropped when Callum's voice sounded in their ears. "Cameras on the east wall are now looped. There were no guards on the other side of the wall at your entry point."

Flynn nodded. "Going over the wall now."

Flynn was the first to take a few steps back, then he ran toward the wall, using his speed and momentum to propel him up and over. There was a soft, almost silent thud when he landed on the other side.

Logan went next, then Jason. Aidan was last. The second he was in, he shot his gaze around the area, taking in the cameras. His jaw clenched. This was where Cassie had been raised. It was like a damn prison, where the cells were nice little homes, lovingly landscaped and tended—but carefully watched.

They stuck close to the wall as they moved through the compound, closer to the Great Hall.

When the hall came into view, Jason moved away from the wall first, running across to the building too fast for most mortals to track. He stopped and waited. Listened for heartbeats. Breaths. Footsteps.

When he gave them a nod, Aidan, Logan and Flynn jogged over. Even though they couldn't hear anyone inside the hall, Jason again went in first to double check. The good thing about being behind such high walls—the building was left unlocked. Cassie had mentioned that nothing was locked here. No homes.

No common areas. Nothing except the basement under the Great Hall.

Jason stepped out and indicated it was clear.

"You guys doing okay?" Callum asked.

"So far, all good," Aidan responded.

He moved inside the hall. The space was massive, open and dark. There were chairs and tables stacked neatly on either side of the room. Aidan stopped and listened. He heard nothing. Not a breath or heartbeat that didn't belong to their group. Which either meant the basement was soundproof, Damien wasn't there, or he was…but he wasn't alive.

It needed to be the first option. For Cassie's sake.

Aidan and Flynn moved down the stairs, while Jason remained by the front entrance and Logan went to the kitchen, where there was a second exit. They'd be the eyes and ears while Aidan and Flynn checked for Damien.

Aidan was the first down the stairs and found the expected door at the bottom. He turned the knob. There was a small cracking sound of the lock breaking, then they moved inside.

The air was thick and musty. There were thick beams from the ceiling to the floor and boxes everywhere. It looked like a storage space. No light, just what filtered in from upstairs. Luckily, Aidan and his team didn't need light to see.

His gaze narrowed on a few specks of red on the floor. Blood. So *not* just a storage place. Damien's blood? Or maybe his, along with the blood of others?

Yet again, Aidan paused and listened.

From the back of the room, he heard a faint heartbeat.

"You hear that?" Aidan asked quietly.

Flynn nodded. "Yep."

Aidan moved one way while Flynn went the other. As they crept forward, Aidan's gaze zeroed in on the slumped man in the corner. He cursed under his breath.

Damien's hands were tied behind his back to one of the

beams. Bruises covered his face, as if someone had used him as a damn punching bag, and his head hung at an odd angle.

He quickly moved forward, touching Damien's skin. Cold. "His heartbeat's slow."

Flynn crouched on the other side of Damien and gave the ropes a tug. They broke easily. "We need to get him to a hospital."

Jason's voice sounded in his ear. "We've got company headed toward the main entrance. Joshua and Isaac. Get out. Now."

Fuck. Aidan lifted Damien while Flynn led the way up the stairs.

"I'm behind a table," Jason said. "You guys go out the kitchen exit. I'll catch up."

The second they made it to the top, Jason's voice sounded again. "Company stepping inside in five seconds. Four...three..."

Aidan cursed again and ran behind Flynn to the kitchen door.

Logan was waiting for them. He took a step toward the door —then stopped.

Everyone froze when they heard it.

Footsteps. And nowhere to hide.

Logan moved to one side of the door, ready to attack. It opened seconds later, and a woman walked through.

Aidan recognized her immediately. Along with intel on the guards, Callum had found all the information he could on her, as well as a picture.

Olive. She held an empty jug, and her gaze flew from him to Flynn. In that time, her chest moved up and down with three rapid breaths. On the fourth, her mouth opened.

Logan was behind her in a second. He slipped a hand over her mouth to silence her.

Aidan moved forward and kept his voice low. "We're not here to hurt you or anyone else. We're just here to get Damien out."

For the first time, her gaze fell to the unconscious man in his arms.

"He needs medical attention immediately."

Her focus remained on Damien, tears filling her eyes. When she looked up again, there was pain in her gaze.

"Will you alert anyone that we're here?"

She gave a small shake of her head.

Slowly, Logan removed his hand. If she gave any indication that she'd scream, Aidan knew he'd be back on her in a second.

"Elijah did this?" she whispered, her voice shaky.

"Him or his men. Damien was tied up in the basement. He's barely breathing."

Her jaw trembled and she sucked in more shallow breaths. "You're Aidan. Cassie's guy."

He gave a small nod. He was surprised that Cassie had trusted Olive enough to mention him. But it didn't matter. Not right now.

She shot one more look Damien's way before focusing on Aidan and stepping aside. "Go. Quickly. Bible study's finishing early. You have five minutes, max."

He held her gaze for another beat. "Thank you." Then they left.

∼

"COME ON, how can a young, charming, good-looking guy like you be single?"

Tyler grinned at Cassie as he rinsed a plate and put it into the dishwasher. "The lucky woman hasn't crossed my path yet."

She *would* be lucky. Tyler had been nothing but a gentleman since stepping into Aidan's house tonight. He'd helped her cook dinner, kept her from losing her mind over the dangerous op the men were on, and now he was cleaning up. Not to mention, he'd made her laugh so hard during dinner that her belly hurt. Oh, and he was sexy as hell.

"What kind of women do you date?"

He frowned. "I don't think I have a type."

"Everyone has a type." Hers was a big, burly man who loved her. Aidan.

"Nah, all the women I've dated have been very different. But I've always gotten the sense that I *had* to go out with them. Learn more about them. So for me, I guess it's less a type and more a feeling."

Oh God, he was too charming. The woman he eventually set his sights on didn't stand a chance.

"What I want in a partner, though? Someone kind. Honest. Tough."

Her smile grew. "I have a feeling you'll be finding her soon."

He chuckled—then quickly stopped, his eyes narrowing on the closed blinds.

The fine hairs on her arms stood. "Everything okay?" she asked quietly.

"Someone just parked out front."

This time, her tummy rolled—a big, panic-filled roll.

Tyler pulled a gun from the holster she hadn't even realized he'd been wearing and moved forward. On the way past her, he grabbed her hand and tugged her behind him.

Her heart pounded in her chest, and her breaths came too quickly. But she remained calm. Just.

When he reached the door, he stood to the side, ready to shoot. For a moment, there was silence.

Then his hold on her hand relaxed...and he smiled.

She frowned. "I hope you're smiling because we're safe and not because you're some secret adrenaline junkie who likes a good shoot-out."

His smile remained in place as he looked down at her. "I *do* love a good shoot-out, but only when assholes are on the receiving end of the bullets and women aren't around."

He holstered his gun and tugged the door open. Grace, Courtney, and Carina were walking up the path.

"You guys aren't supposed to be here," Tyler chastised as they passed him. Each of them hugged her on the way in.

"Cassie's probably crazy worried," Courtney retorted. "Of course we're supposed to be here."

Grace and Carina each held a bottle of wine, while Courtney had a bag of what looked like...candy?

Tyler shook his head and tugged his phone from his pocket before typing something.

"You're not texting them to tattle on us when they're on a mission, are you?" Carina asked.

"No, I'm texting Liam that I might need backup."

Liam and Blake had just driven back from Utah earlier today. She was sure they were exhausted from days of watching the compound.

The women set everything onto the counter, and Courtney started searching the cupboards for glasses.

Grace touched her shoulder. "You're okay with us being here?"

"I love that you're here. I don't really drink, but one glass shouldn't hurt."

"And Red Vines," Carina said, reaching into the bag and pulling out the candy. "Willow's home with her daughter, Mila, otherwise she'd be here too."

"She's very sad about missing this," Courtney said, setting six glasses onto the island.

Grace opened the first bottle of wine and filled each glass to the top.

The next two hours passed quickly, with the women sharing countless stories about their men.

"Flynn just upgraded the security on our house. *Again*," Carina said with a laugh.

"Well, your brush with danger was the most recent," Grace said.

"Um, mine feels like ages ago, but Jason upgraded the security just last week. He's also talking about higher fencing."

Cassie frowned. "You guys have been in danger?"

Tyler snorted. "Danger is putting it lightly."

"Yeah, we didn't tell you about that when we first met you," Carina said.

"We thought that was more of a second-date story," Courtney added, making everyone laugh.

Grace nodded. "We've all had our close calls. I ran from a very dangerous man for years, and he finally found me."

"I had a crazy-expensive item in my possession that some bad people wanted, and I didn't even realize it," Courtney said.

"And I had your typical stalker ex," Carina finished.

"Don't forget about Willow," Tyler added, leaning back in his seat. "She was almost blown up."

Cassie gaped at all of them.

"So we've each got a pretty good idea what you're going through," Grace said gently.

Courtney nodded, taking another sip of her wine. "Fortunately, you're in the best hands. These guys know what they're doing."

"Oh yeah. I'd be mincemeat without Flynn," Carina said.

They all laughed again. And it felt good. Because even though she'd been smiling all night, even though Tyler, and now the women, had engaged her in steady conversation, she was still worried. Worried about Aidan. About him being in that compound. And about what he'd find while there.

He'd promised they'd drive back tonight. The trip was over five hours, so she'd told him not to, but he'd insisted that he couldn't be away from her all night.

So having the women here was a great distraction...and she was sure they knew it.

CHAPTER 22

*C*assie stirred at the feel of warm lips on her neck. She hummed as they slid across her heated skin. A hand gripped her hip, tugging her back into a hard body. A body she knew so well. A body that, even in the dead of night and half-asleep, she recognized.

"Aidan," she breathed.

His lips moved down her shoulder, leaving a trail of fire. Burning her skin. "Cassie."

Even her name on his lips… It made her heart roar for him. It made her want to get completely and utterly lost. To leave the world and exist only for him.

She shifted her head to the side, giving him easier access.

The hand on her hip slid to her belly, then slipped inside her panties.

Her breath caught and her back arched. When he eased a finger across her slit, she cried out, grinding back against him. Everything he was, was everything she wanted. Everything she'd *always* wanted.

He stroked her clit. There was no urgency to the way he

touched her. The way his lips kissed and cherished her skin. He touched her like he had all the time in the world. Like they had a lifetime.

She reached behind her. She needed to touch him. Make him feel even a little of what she felt. He was naked, his skin hot. She wrapped her fingers around him and stroked his length.

He growled, low and deep, his teeth nuzzling her skin.

God, this was her place. The place where she wanted to bury herself alive. This vulnerable, bare moment of time with the man she'd loved for as long as she could remember.

Slowly, he turned her onto her back, then his weight pressed her to the mattress. She could only just see him in the dim light of the room, but there was something shining in his eyes. Some deep emotion.

And...fear?

She stroked a line down the side of his face. "Are you okay?"

"We got Damien out. He's in a hospital in Utah, with several of Shaw's men standing guard. Tomorrow, we'll arrange to have him transported to the Cradle Mountain Hospital so he can be near you, and we'll take over protection detail."

Hospital. Her heart squeezed at the thought. Wetness filled her eyes, but she forced the tears back. "We need to call Dean."

"I already did it on the way to the hospital."

God, she was grateful for this man.

"Thank you. For everything." She cupped his cheek, trying to memorize every inch of his face. "But you didn't answer my question. Are *you* okay?"

His breath was a warm whisp across her skin. There was another flash in his eyes. This time, she recognized it right away. Definitely fear. Maybe a bit of pain. "He's in a bad way, Cass. Those assholes beat him. If Damien hadn't called us when he did, that could have been you—"

She put her fingers over his lips. "It wasn't."

He kissed her fingers before taking her hand in his own. "I should have come for you. I should have swallowed the fear that I'd find you happy without me. I should have forced myself to go to you and ask the question I was too cowardly to ask."

"And I should have gone to *you*," she whispered. "I should have found a way. Trusted you to do what I've been trying to do. We both made mistakes."

"Never again." His words sounded like a whispered vow. A promise to both himself and her.

"Never again," she echoed.

He lowered his head and kissed her. Like his touches, the kiss was slow and gentle, but she felt the desperation and intensity behind it. When his tongue slipped into her mouth, tingling spread to every single part of her.

She groaned low in her throat, reveling in the feel of his hard, naked body against her. Those lips trailed down her jawline and neck, while his hands slipped beneath her. She arched and he removed her bra. The second her breasts were free, his lips closed around a hard nipple, and he sucked.

Her breaths turned shallow, and her heart stuttered in her chest, no longer her own.

Him. Her heart beat for *him*.

He switched to her other breast. She threaded her fingers through his hair, wanting to keep him right where he was forever.

While his lips remained on her breast, his hands went to her panties and pushed them down her thighs. She used her legs and feet to wriggle out of them. Then she felt all of him against all of her. And it was healing. What they had was so much more than physical. It was like their spirits knew each other. *Needed* each other.

Featherlight kisses made their way back up her chest as he nestled between her thighs. His weight was like an anchor. She exhaled a heavy breath when she felt him at her entrance.

He cupped her cheek and lowered his head. She looked into his eyes. The eyes of the man who owned her.

"God, I love you, Cassie."

She covered his hand with hers and turned her head to kiss his palm. "I love you too, Aidan. My love for you runs so deep that it's a vital part of me. Without it, I'm nothing."

"You're everything," he whispered.

Then, his head and his hips lowered together, and he slid into her.

She moaned, long and deep. He filled her so completely. When he was inside her, he made her feel whole. Like everything was exactly the way it was meant to be.

He didn't move right away, instead pressing another line of kisses down her jaw. She held his head close, running her fingers through his hair, knowing no moment could ever match this one.

Finally, he raised his hips before thrusting slowly. Her whimper cut through the quiet.

"I love that sound," he whispered.

He thrust again. Another whimper. She wrapped her legs around him, and every time he brought himself back to her, she held him tighter.

That wisp of fear inside her, the one she hadn't even realized she'd been holding onto, telling her that history could repeat itself and they could be torn apart again, suddenly settled. She let go of it, all of it, and just allowed herself to be with Aidan.

He nibbled on her neck, and his fingers found her nipple. He rolled her sensitive peak between his finger and thumb.

Her inhale was a sharp gasp. "Aidan!"

"Come for me, honey."

More thrusts, harder now, combined with suckling at her neck. Finally, she bowed off the bed and broke. She let the storm of sensations wash through her as she drowned in all that was Aidan.

Even as her body pulsed, he kept thrusting, until finally his body tightened and he growled. His mouth crashed back to hers as he shattered inside her.

She clenched her legs around him, holding him, never wanting to let go.

A beat of silence passed, then he pressed a kiss to her lips and rolled to the side. When he slid out of her, she wanted to cry at the loss. But then he pulled her close. She lay her head on his chest and let the steady thump of his heart lull her to sleep, knowing she was safe.

AIDAN HELD CASSIE CLOSE. The realization that he hadn't worn a condom probably should have made him nervous. But he wasn't. Cassie was his forever. He wanted to marry her. See her stomach swell with their kids.

He pulled her closer.

He'd been fine all night, until they'd brought Damien to the hospital. Then it had hit him. That could have been *her*. Christ, it could have been *worse* for her. If Damien had never called Blue Halo, if Aidan and his men hadn't been at the ball, he might have lost her forever. He might have never gotten his second chance.

He closed his eyes and let the strong beat of her heart calm the turmoil inside him.

He should have gone to her sooner. He should have swallowed his pride and fear and damn well gone to her a year ago, the second he was rescued. Yes, she'd made mistakes too, but he could forgive her. He couldn't forgive himself so easily.

He stroked her side. This woman was his world. Hell, she was more than his world, she was his everything. They had the kind of love that people wrote stories about. The kind that you didn't find twice. And tonight, he'd finally realized just how close he'd come to losing her.

God, a world without Cassie was like a world without air to breathe. A world without light and laughter. It was a world that didn't make sense. One he didn't want to live in.

"I'm not losing you, Cass...ever," he whispered. "I can't."

CHAPTER 23

*A*idan leaned against a wall in the hospital hallway. Cassie was in full view from the open door, the early afternoon sun casting rays of light over her face. She sat on one side of Damien's bed, holding his hand, while Dean sat on the other.

Shaw had organized for Damien to be safely transported to Cradle Mountain. The team had also reached out to their FBI contact, Steve. They should have brought him in the second Cassie crossed state lines. Elijah's crimes were no longer a small-town jurisdiction issue. The contractors had also crossed state lines to reach Cassie.

Her cheeks were still wet from the tears she'd shed upon seeing Damien, and there were dark circles under her eyes from stress.

He hated seeing her upset. *Hated* it. It was like shards of glass tearing up his insides.

Fuck Elijah. Fuck his entire organization. Elijah and his brothers needed to die. Now.

He scrubbed a hand over his face and was about to go in and check on her when he saw Logan, Grace, Blake, Willow and

Callum heading down the hall. They stopped in front of him, the women immediately peeking inside.

"I might go see if she's okay," Grace said quietly, before heading into the small room.

Willow nodded and followed Grace.

"How is he?" Blake asked.

Aidan shook his head, watching as the women pulled chairs closer to Cassie. "He has brain swelling from so many knocks to the head. Because of the trauma, he's been put into a medically induced coma. They're not sure how long he'll need to be under."

Logan and Callum both tensed, and Blake swore under his breath.

"Steve wasn't happy we entered the compound last night," Aidan continued. Hell, he wasn't happy they'd waited this long to contact him. "But he left it at that, said his team will take over from here, starting with trying to contact Olive."

He needed this entire fucking mess to be over. He'd only allowed himself a couple hours of sleep last night. He'd spent the rest of the time holding Cassie. Listening to her breathing. Her heartbeat.

Logan gripped his shoulder. "So our job is to keep Cassie and Damien safe."

They'd sure as hell do that.

"She wants Mia back." She hadn't said the words out loud, but he knew. Despite the younger woman's choices, despite her belief in Elijah, Cassie missed her, had always felt responsible for her, and now was no different.

"When they get Elijah—and they *will* get Elijah—she'll have her," Blake said.

"We'll keep a guy on Damien's hospital door at all times," Callum added.

Elijah would definitely know the man was gone by now. And there was a great chance he was putting every resource he had into locating Damien and ending him before he could tell anyone what they'd done.

The guys waited in the hall for another ten minutes, then Aidan made his way into the room. He ran a hand along Cassie's back. "You need a break and some fresh air, sweetheart. Let's go downstairs for a walk, then we can come back."

It would also give Dean a few moments alone with Damien.

She must have understood, because her gaze flicked to Dean, then she gave a small nod. She pressed a kiss to Damien's hand before standing. She hugged both the women, who left with Logan and Blake, then she rounded the bed and hugged Dean.

The guy seemed nice enough. Quiet. Aidan could see the love he had for Damien. And Damien's current condition was tearing him apart. Dean had driven down earlier that morning, the second he'd received the call from Aidan's team.

Callum remained by Damien's door, giving Aidan a nod as he slid an arm around Cassie's waist and led her down the hall. She was quiet as they left the hospital. He didn't press her to talk. It was after ten minutes of walking that he finally squeezed her waist.

"I'm sorry, Cass."

He'd said it a million times this morning, but it felt worth repeating. He was sorry she had to go through this. Sorry she had to feel the pain of knowing Damien was in a coma.

When she looked at him, he expected to see more tears. What he saw was anger. Cold, hard anger. "I *hate* Elijah. I hate him so much! I want him to pay for everything he's done. I *need* him to pay for this!"

Her fury was something he was intimately familiar with. The same thing he'd felt for so long for his own enemies.

"When we got taken by Hylar and the people from Project Arma, I had that same hatred," Aidan said quietly. "Then we got out, and all I wanted to do was destroy everyone who played a part in what happened. I wanted to tear them limb from limb so they'd feel a fraction of the pain they'd brought on me."

Hylar had been the commander who'd created Project Arma. He was the man responsible for Aidan being kidnapped, his DNA forever altered.

He felt Cassie's eyes on him. "I thought their deaths would somehow dim the pain of what we went through...and the pain of losing you."

Her muscles tightened.

"It didn't," he finished quietly. "I'm not telling you this because I don't think you should focus on bringing Elijah down. The asshole needs to be ten feet under, or at the very least, locked up for a long time. But I just don't want you to think it will instantly make everything better."

Their friends in Marble Falls, a group of former SEALs who had also been affected by Project Arma, had killed Hylar and destroyed most of what remained of the project. Yet that hole in his chest, the pain from lost years and being changed irrevocably... Yeah, that had gone nowhere.

She leaned into his side. "I'm sorry about Project Arma. I'm not sure I've said that yet. But I am."

He kissed the top of her head. "We still ended up back together."

The first smile of the day tugged at her lips. "Almost like we were meant to be."

"We *are* meant to be, Cass."

They were quiet for the rest of the walk, but it was more of a peaceful quiet now, something he knew they both needed.

When they returned to the hospital, they'd just walked through the doors into the waiting area when Cassie stopped. He followed her gaze to a woman standing in the center of the room, looking lost. When she turned, Aidan sucked in a breath.

Olive.

~

CASSIE'S EYES widened as Olive met her gaze. The woman rushed over to them.

"Olive, are you... I mean, what are you doing here?" God, she was so shocked she could barely speak.

"I'm so glad I found you. I remembered you telling me Aidan lived in Cradle Mountain, so I hoped this was where you'd make sure Damien got treatment." Her voice filled with pain at the mention of Damien. "I don't have long. I need to give you something, then I have to get back."

Cassie sucked in a breath. Was it the evidence?

"We should go to the police station," Aidan said, his hand tightening around her waist.

Olive shook her head. "I don't have time. I told them I had a specialist appointment in Wyoming for my diabetes. If I'm away too long, they'll get suspicious."

"You drove all the way here on your own?" Cassie asked quietly, concern for the other woman filling her voice.

"I had to. After I saw Damien last night..."

Olive had seen Damien? Her gaze shot to Aidan. He hadn't told her.

He might insist on taking Olive to the police, especially now that the FBI were involved. Technically, Blue Halo was no longer supposed to be involved in dismantling Elijah's organization. And going to the authorities was safer.

But then they ran the risk of Olive leaving. Of this evidence slipping through their fingers.

She trusted Olive. The woman wouldn't set them up. Cassie gave Aidan a beseeching look.

He sighed and tugged her toward the door. "There's a coffee shop next door."

The air whooshed from her chest.

Aidan led her out of the hospital, and Olive followed. His gaze shot around the area before he pulled his phone from his pocket and typed something. He was probably texting his team.

The shop was busy, and they took one of the last open tables near the back of the café.

"This won't take long," Olive whispered.

There was fear in her voice, but there was also something else. Relief? That she was finally helping?

"I'm so glad you came, Olive. Thank you." Cassie reached across the small table and covered the woman's hand with her own. Aidan was tense and quiet beside her.

Olive glanced at Aidan. "Record our conversation. Take it to the detective or whomever you're working with."

Aidan did as she asked. The front door opened, and she saw Logan and Blake enter. They sat at the small counter at the front of the shop.

There was a heavy moment of silence while Olive's gaze held Cassie's, as if she was the only person in the room. "I always suspected Elijah was dosing the drinks at our family nights. I'd always end the night feeling dizzy and tired, and I remembered very little about those evenings the next day. But I didn't question it because you don't do that at Paragons of Hope."

Olive paused, her fists clenching on the table.

"One night, Elijah paid me more attention than usual. He was by my side most of the evening. Talking to me. Always ensuring my glass was full." She shook her head. "I was naïve and stupid, felt special that our *Holy* Leader was paying me so much attention."

Disgust scrunched her features. "I drank more than my usual one glass. At the end of the evening, he asked me to come to his quarters."

It took a lot of self-restraint for Cassie not to scowl. To not show her absolute revulsion for the man. *Scumbag.*

Olive looked down at her fists. "Everything was a blur. I could barely walk. But he was our leader. I felt safe."

She paused. And even though Cassie knew what was coming, her chest ached with dread.

"I remember bits and pieces from that night. Elijah touching me. Kissing me. Lying naked under him."

Bile rose in Cassie's throat, and she felt Aidan stiffen beside her.

"I woke up in my bed the next morning, but I can't remember how I got there."

Elijah had raped her. Like he had countless others.

Once again, Cassie reached across the table and squeezed her arm. "I'm so sorry, Olive."

God, her words felt so inadequate. They *were* inadequate. There was nothing she could say that would ever heal this woman's pain.

Olive nodded, tears shimmering in her eyes. "I didn't know what to do after that night. It was almost like I couldn't figure out how to live with myself. The world had gone from vibrant colors to a dark gray. I knew what had happened. He *knew* what he'd done. And yet I was supposed to just...go on. To *exist* in a world where I saw him every day and act as if nothing was different, when my entire world had changed. I felt so confused and angry and lost."

The anguish was so distinct in her eyes, Cassie wanted to cry for her.

Olive paused and breathed deeply before she continued. "I just tried to survive in this fog after that. But it was a couple of weeks later when I had to know... I snuck away from a family night and went to the kitchen in the Great Hall. When I heard someone coming, I hid in the pantry and watched through the slats of the door. It was Joshua and Isaac. They were preparing more punch. They grabbed a small bottle from one of the top cupboards and poured something into the pitchers."

She paused again—and pulled something out of her pocket before sliding it across the table. "When they left, I found the bottle and poured some into a small container. I don't know why. Maybe I was hoping I could find someone to test it one day. Confirm that what happened to me didn't just happen because of my own poor decisions."

Aidan grabbed the small container and slipped it into his pocket.

"This is amazing, Olive," Cassie said. It wouldn't have been easy to take this. Or to sneak into the kitchen at all. Heck, it would have been terrifying.

Olive glanced at her, looking exhausted. "A month later, I missed my period. I bought a test. That's how I found out I was pregnant."

Cassie's mouth slipped open, her skin chilling. That was a part of the story she hadn't known.

"I didn't tell anyone," Olive continued. "I was *terrified*. You had to be married to... To partake in physical intimacy with a man, and there was no way Elijah would admit to what he'd done. So I stayed quiet. Three weeks after that, I..." Her eyes closed, and when she opened them, there was a glimmer of tears. "I miscarried."

Oh, God. "Olive..."

"Suddenly, sitting on my bathroom floor, looking at all the blood, something inside me just...flicked. The devastation turned into this blinding anger. I didn't think, I just acted. I went into Rodney's room, grabbed his work phone, hit voice record and went searching for Elijah."

Cassie's heart thumped. Had she actually recorded Elijah saying something she shouldn't have?

"Elijah was alone in his office. I marched in there and told him I knew what he'd done to me, and I wanted him to admit it to my face. To admit that he'd drugged me, then raped me." More clenching of her fists. "At first, he played dumb. But I kept pushing. I wanted his words. His admission of guilt. Then, finally, he said it. He admitted to having sex with me while I was passed out. Spewed some ridiculous bullshit about God's will."

Olive's face turned white.

Cassie's stomach jolted. She wasn't going to like what came next.

"I didn't know that Rodney had seen me heading for the office and followed me." She choked on a sob. "He stormed in, shouting that he was going to kill Elijah. And Elijah—he just lifted a gun and shot him in the head."

Jesus Christ. This poor woman.

"I hadn't even noticed the gun. And Elijah didn't hesitate for a second. I dropped beside Rodney and just screamed. His men came running at the sound of the shot, and they shut the door. Elijah looked me dead in the eye and told me if I ever breathed a word of that night or about Rodney to anyone, my mother was next."

Every part of Cassie hurt for Olive and what she'd been through. Tears pressed at her eyes, but she willed them away. "God, I'm so sorry, Olive." It was as if the grief never ended for this woman. And here Cassie had been, pushing her for months to spill her guts to a stranger.

"He made Rodney's death look like a suicide. And while everyone mourned at his funeral, Elijah sat beside my mother the entire time, his eyes on me. And I knew he meant what he'd said. My mother would never be safe unless I played by his rules."

She reached into her purse—and pulled out a phone.

"It's been turned off and hidden since that day, but the recording should still be there."

Aidan took the phone, but Olive only had eyes for Cassie. "Make him pay, Cass."

"I will." It was a promise to Olive, to herself, and to every other person Elijah had ever hurt.

"I need to get back." Olive stood, and Cassie followed. She

tugged the woman into her arms. All she wanted to do was keep her here in Cradle Mountain, shield her from further pain.

She was just pulling away from Olive when she saw something. A car. Driving fast and headed straight toward—

"Get down!"

The shout had barely left Logan's mouth from the front of the shop before Aidan dove onto both women as a car crashed through the café's window. Shouts and screams filled the space.

Cassie's gaze lifted just in time to see men with guns.

CHAPTER 24

*B*ullets flew throughout the coffee shop. Aidan rose from behind their table and shot at the driver. Cassie swallowed, scanning the room. Everyone was on the floor, trying not to get hit, fear etched on their faces.

Aidan dropped behind the table as bullets whizzed above their heads. She met his gaze. His eyes were dark and stormy. The man was ready to kill.

"Stay down."

She gave a quick nod before he rose again. Then she reached for Olive's hand. It was shaking.

"Hey. Are you okay?"

Olive's face was white, and fear had her eyes as wide as saucers. She opened and closed her mouth, but no words came out.

Cassie squeezed the other woman's fingers. Then a loud grunt sounded from the table beside them. Her stomach clenched when she saw a man on the ground, dark blood soaking into his shirt. He looked at Cassie, shock and fear and pain distorting his features. Time seemed to crawl...then his eyes closed.

Oh, God.

She couldn't let an innocent person die. Cassie snaked her body toward him, keeping as low as possible, until she was close enough to touch. Quickly, she whipped her sweater over her head and pressed it to his stomach. She put two fingers at his neck.

Come on! Where's the pulse?

She closed her eyes and tried to block out everything around her. Then she felt it. It was faint but there. *He's still—*

Punishing fingers wrapped around her upper arm and yanked her back against a hard chest. Then she was being dragged along the floor, toward a back hallway.

She shrieked and clawed at the man's fingers. He didn't release her. Instead, the fingers tightened, digging into her skin.

They were almost at the hall when a big body collided with the man's side.

Aidan.

She wrenched her aching arm free and rose to all fours as the two men fought. She was crawling back to the fallen man when someone else grabbed her around the waist and lifted, carrying her into the hall again. Before she could blink, she was thrown over a shoulder. When the man rushed through a door into the back alley, panic blasted in her chest.

She heard a car door opening.

No, no, no. If he got her into a car, her chances of escape decreased massively.

Desperate, she reached down and grabbed the belt loops of his pants. Using all her strength, she pulled herself forward while throwing her heels into the man's face.

It worked. He stumbled with a shout, then fell back, landing right on her when she fell to the ground. A jarring pain whipped through her body. The weight lifted. Gray haze danced over her vision, but when those strong hands took hold of her wrists and began to drag her, she blinked it away.

Survive now, feel the pain later.

Cassie yanked and writhed to get her arms free. She shot a look over her shoulder and shuddered when she spotted the dark blue vehicle with tinted windows. Her gaze brushed over the man pulling her, but he wore a mask. Then she saw who was standing beside the open back door of the car.

Joshua. The sight of him was the stuff nightmares were made of.

~

A MAN LIFTED a gun from the open car window. Aidan shot his hand, then his chest through the front windshield. Before he could shoot again, a man behind a nearby table pulled a gun from an IWB holster.

Aidan dropped behind a table just before the bullet passed.

Shooters were goddamn everywhere. Some had come from the car. Some from the street.

And at least two had been in the goddamn café with them.

His gaze honed in on Cassie. A man in a suit had taken a bullet, and she was pressing her hands to his chest. He was just focusing on another shooter when she cried out. His head swung around.

Fuck!

A man was trying to use Cassie as a shield even as he dragged her toward the back of the shop. She was covering too much of his body to risk shooting.

Aidan holstered his weapon and leapt at them, then pulled the guy off her.

He'd just gotten the asshole onto his back when the man pulled a knife. Aidan shifted out of the path of an unskilled swipe. He grabbed the guy's wrist, turned the knife and plunged it into his chest.

A bullet hit the table beside his head, and he rolled. Then his gaze went to where Cassie should have been—only she wasn't there anymore.

He scanned the floor of the café. Fear catapulted throughout his body, turning his skin to ice when he realized she wasn't in the shop.

He took off toward the back door, not paying attention to the bullets still flying around the room or bodies slamming into bodies. He had one goal—get to Cassie.

He flew outside.

There they were—a tall man wearing a ski mask, dragging Cassie toward a car as she struggled to get free. A second guy stood by the back door. Joshua.

Aidan shot forward so fast the man didn't see him coming. He wrenched the guy off Cassie and threw him into the side of the building hard enough to render him unconscious. Then he turned to Joshua.

Elijah's brother was madly tugging at a gun in his holster, his movements frantic and clumsy.

Aidan was on him in less than a second. He grabbed his wrist and squeezed. There was the audible cracking of bone and a shout of pain. He lowered his head, and when he spoke, his voice was lethal. "Why do you want Cassie?"

The guy's breathing was labored from pain, and there was an angry scowl on his face. "Fuck. You!"

Wrong answer. He clenched harder. More snapping. He was crushing the guy's bones. And he'd keep crushing until he gave Aidan an answer.

Joshua screamed.

Suddenly, Cassie was beside him. Aidan growled. "Get the hell back, Cassie!"

She didn't listen. Of course she didn't. Why the hell would he expect her to listen to him in the middle of a goddamn kidnapping attempt?

"Tell me what Elijah wants with me," Cassie demanded.

Aidan loosened his grip. And the guy took a moment to catch his breath, then, slowly, his gaze shifted over to Cassie. A smile curved his lips. It was a cruel smile. One meant to incite fear. It had more rage rushing through Aidan's blood.

"You're the chosen one, Cassie."

"What are you talking about?" she asked, her voice a notch quieter now.

The back door opened. He shot a quick look over his shoulder to see Logan stepping out, followed closely by Blake.

Joshua's gaze never left Cassie. "A long time ago, God came to Elijah. Told him a revelation. Told him what needed to happen when you turned thirty, for the salvation of everyone else."

Unease swirled in Aidan's gut.

Cassie inched close.

"Cassie. *Stay. Back!*" The words were low and guttural through Aidan's gritted teeth.

"What needs to happen?" she asked.

"Logan, take Cassie inside." She didn't need to hear the asshole spewing bullshit that would only scare her more than she already was.

Logan moved forward, but Cassie threw out her hands to stop him. "No! I deserve to know."

Logan stopped, and Aidan wanted to rage at the man.

"What needs to happen, Joshua?" she asked.

Another shit-eating grin. "Your death is going to save us all."

Cassie's breath stuttered.

"You're our sacrifice," Joshua added.

Fuck.

Cassie took a shaky step back.

"Logan, take him. Don't let him go until he's sitting in the back of a police car with cuffs around his wrists."

The second Logan had Joshua, Aidan tugged Cassie aside. The asshole was still watching her, so he blocked the guy's view. "Don't listen to him."

She nodded, but her face was a shade whiter than it had been.

Carefully, he cupped her cheeks, but when the back door opened again and police streamed out, Cassie shut down.

The next hour was a rush of talking to police, liaising with Steve and his team, and people being moved next door to the hospital. Cassie barely left Olive's side. The second guy, the masked man who'd taken Cassie from the shop, had been Antwon, Elijah's top guard.

Between Antwon's and Joshua's presence, and with the recording Olive had provided, the FBI had the evidence they needed to raid the compound and arrest Elijah. Olive had insisted on going with them, to be with her mother.

By the time Aidan and Cassie got to his car, it was late afternoon.

"Do you mind if I stop by the office to grab my laptop?" He'd left it there, planning to take her with him while he did some work tomorrow, but he wasn't asking her to go anywhere. Not now.

She shook her head, her gaze remaining on the window.

When he parked on the street alongside the Blue Halo building, she remained quiet, gaze still turned away from him.

He touched her leg. "Are you okay?"

She nodded. Her bottom lip was between her teeth, and a frown marred her brow. "Mom knew."

He frowned. "What?"

"Elijah told Mom he planned to kill me on my thirtieth birthday. He must have. That's why she risked her life to get us out of there, but she never got the chance to tell me."

He touched her hand. "Your mom was strong. She loved you and did what she could to keep you safe."

"I just can't imagine that kind of burden on her shoulders, being told an entire cult saw her daughter as their human sacrifice."

He squeezed her thigh. "It would have changed everything for her."

"Yeah." Cassie blew out a long breath and climbed out of the car. He did the same. Once he was by her side, he wrapped an arm around her waist.

They'd just reached the corner of the building when he heard rattling.

A locked door. Like someone was trying to get into the Blue Halo office.

He eased Cassie away from the corner of the building with one hand and took out his Glock with the other.

She gasped at the sight of the gun and opened her mouth to say something, but she closed it again at the shake of his head. Gently, he pressed her back to the wall. "Let me check first."

She gave a quick nod.

It was probably nothing, but after the day they'd had, he wasn't taking any chances.

He whipped around the corner. A woman several yards away, standing in front of the door to Blue Halo, screamed before pressing a hand to her chest.

Aidan lowered the gun. "Mia?"

CHAPTER 25

*C*assie studied Mia's face as she sat on the couch in Aidan's living room. He'd driven them straight here, but she hadn't missed the looks Aidan had been sending Mia's way.

She didn't blame him. Not after the choices Mia had made.

An internal war battled inside her. She wanted to trust Mia. After basically raising her since the day their mother had died, there was nothing she wanted more. But after everything that had happened, it was almost impossible.

She'd just finished telling her sister about what had happened at the coffee shop—minus the part about the phone Olive gave them. Elijah's recorded confession was too important to the investigation to share with anyone. Especially someone who might still be loyal to the man.

Mia's eyes filled with worry. "I'm really glad you're okay, Cass. And I'm so sorry you had to go through that."

Was she? Cassie had no idea what to make of this woman. For the first time in her life, Mia was almost a stranger to her. And that killed her.

Her gaze flicked to Aidan in the kitchen. He was making pasta for dinner. He was trying to give them space, but at the same time, she knew he was listening to every word.

She looked back to her sister and forced a smile to her face. "Thank you. At least Joshua and Antwon were arrested, and the police are on their way to arrest Elijah." The guy might even be behind bars already. She wondered if Aidan's FBI contact would call to let them know.

When she looked at her sister, she caught a flash of emotion. It came and went so quickly, Cassie couldn't quite place it.

"Well, I'm glad you're safe," Mia said quietly.

Aidan walked into the living room, three bowls of pasta in his hands. He handed one to Mia, another to Cassie, then sat on the single chair opposite the couch.

"How did you get away?" he asked.

Mia met his gaze. "I told the guards I was getting some things for church night. Ordered a car and then, instead of going to town, I directed him here."

That was a long drive in a hired car. Expensive too.

Mia looked back to Cassie. "You'd mentioned Aidan worked at a security company called Blue Halo, so I figured that would be the best place to start looking for you."

Cassie gave a slow nod before looking at Aidan. He was a human lie detector. If anything Mia said wasn't true, he'd know.

His eyes never left Mia. "Did Elijah see you leaving the compound?"

"Elijah wasn't there."

Didn't really answer his question. Not directly, anyway.

"What made you change your mind?" Cassie asked. There was another pause from Mia. It did nothing to ease the rock that sat heavy in Cassie's gut.

Mia looked at her, and her eyes softened. "I love you, and you're important to me. I want to make sure I'm doing everything in my power to keep the people I love safe."

People. Not Cassie, specifically. Did those "people" include Elijah?

Cassie leaned forward and squeezed Mia's hand. "Well, I'm glad you're here now." She just hoped and prayed that she was here for the right reasons. That she was choosing Cassie. That she regretted ever choosing Elijah over her.

When Aidan's phone rang from the kitchen, he rose, lowering his bowl to the coffee table before crossing the room.

"Hey, Ty. What've you got for me?"

Aidan's eyes narrowed as Tyler spoke to him. Her stomach dropped. It wasn't good news.

When Aidan spoke again, his voice was harder than it had been. "Thanks for letting me know, brother. Keep me updated."

"What did he say?" Cassie asked almost nervously.

This time, Aidan only had eyes for her. "Elijah, Isaac, and some other members were missing when they got to the compound. They don't know where they are."

No! This was supposed to be *over*, dammit. They'd given law enforcement what they needed to lock the man up. He should be behind bars!

"They're working on locating them."

She was sure Tyler had been a lot more specific about their strategies, but no way would Aidan reveal anything in front of Mia.

Her sister leaned forward and touched Cassie's hand. "I'm sorry."

She'd said that a lot. What she *hadn't* said was "I hope they find him" or "I hope he goes to jail."

Aidan moved over to Cassie, pressed a hand to her back and leaned down to kiss her head. Then he turned to Mia. "Do you know where he might have gone?"

She shook her head quickly but didn't say anything.

Cassie could tell he wanted to press. But she also knew he

wouldn't, for her sake. And she appreciated it. Today had been long and harrowing and awful.

Tomorrow, they'd ask Mia more questions. They'd find out if her intentions were good. If they weren't, it would hurt, but she'd deal with it.

∿

AIDAN LOOKED into his bathroom to see Cassie slipping a shirt over her head. *His* shirt.

A low growl slipped from his chest, and he moved behind her, curling his arms around her waist. "I like you in my shirt."

He pressed a line of kisses down her neck, and her sweet moan had his body hardening.

"I like that it smells like you," she whispered.

He looked up at their reflections, and his eyes narrowed at the bruise on her cheek. He hadn't missed the bruising down her body as she'd pulled on the shirt, either. "I hate that you got hurt."

Her brows twitched, and the calm left her eyes, replaced by turmoil. "I'm okay."

Her hesitation told him everything.

"I'm glad we got the evidence we needed to have Elijah arrested. I'm also glad Mia's not at the compound. But…"

"But you don't trust her."

Pain. It drowned her features. "I *want* to trust her. I want to be able to rely on her like I used to. I feel responsible—"

"No." He spun her around and lifted her to the counter. "Don't say it. You are *not* responsible for her. You have sacrificed for her your whole life. Even before this stuff with Elijah and his organization, you spent most of your childhood making sure she was okay in foster care. Any decisions she makes as an adult are on her."

She nibbled her bottom lip and nodded. He could almost see

her mind ticking. "I still can't believe the man wants to kill me as a *sacrifice*. That's just... God, it's sick."

Aidan could think of a lot of other words to describe it. The man was a fucking psychopath with a demented need to control people.

"He's not going to touch you," he whispered.

Her eyes dampened, then she leaned her head to his chest. "Thank you. Thank you for coming for me. For protecting me. For loving me."

He held her head to his chest, kissing the top of it. "You never need to thank me for any of that. Especially loving you. It's all I know how to do."

They remained like that for a moment, then he carried her to bed. Once she was beneath the covers, he pressed a featherlight kiss to the bruise on her cheek. "I'm going to make sure everything's locked up tight, then I'll be back."

She grabbed his arm before he could leave. "Don't be gone long."

"Never."

She gave his arm a squeeze before letting go.

He moved silently down the hall, his skin still heated where she'd touched him. It was always like that. Her touch penetrated his skin and went right into his heart.

He heard Mia before he saw her. She was in the kitchen. He slowed his steps, and when he reached the entrance, he watched her from the side as she stood by the sink, cup in hand, just looking out the window.

Her brows were tugged together, and she seemed to be deep in thought.

He'd never found Mia to be the most mature person. Where Cassie was selfless, Mia was the opposite. Taking what people gave her. Wanting whatever she could get without working for it. And when he and Cassie were together all those years ago, before he'd disappeared, there'd always been something about Mia that struck Aidan as…reckless? Maybe it was her act-first, think-later behavior. Or maybe it was her more immature way of seeing the world.

She was only staying in his house because Cassie wanted her sister close. Even though neither of them trusted her, she wanted to ensure Mia's safety.

Aidan had relented—but he still asked a couple of the guys to be on watch outside the house tonight, just to help keep Cassie safe.

"Everything okay?"

Her body jolted and she swung wide eyes toward him. "Aidan! Oh my gosh, you scared me."

He took slow steps toward her. "Just locking up. Do you need anything?"

She shook her head. "No. I got stuck in my thoughts for a moment."

"Thoughts of Elijah?"

He didn't know if she'd ignore his question, or maybe get annoyed by it. She turned back to the window, and he could tell she wasn't really seeing anything.

"Yes. And Paragons of Hope. And Cassie. It's a mess. A huge mess."

There was a thread of regret in her voice. "You never knew?"

"That my father planned to kill my sister? No." Truth. "It's like a nightmare I can't wake up from."

It was a nightmare *no one* could wake up from.

She shook her head. "Anyway. I should go to bed."

She tipped the rest of her water into the sink and set the cup in the dishwasher. Then she turned to him. "I'm really glad Cassie has you back. She loves you. She's *always* loved you. And when you disappeared…" She shook her head. "Anyway, I'm glad you two found each other."

Another truth. She was crossing the kitchen when he called out her name.

"Mia." She stopped and turned. "Cassie can trust you... Can't she?"

Her brows tugged together. "I would never hurt my sister."

Another truth. But not entirely an answer to his question.

CHAPTER 26

"*This* place looks fun."

Cassie smiled at her sister as they walked into The Grind. "It really does."

This was her first time in the coffee shop too. Courtney owned and ran the place, and Aidan raved about it. It had Courtney written all over it, with vibrant colors on the walls, and it was exactly what Cassie needed this morning.

They were only staying for a quick coffee before visiting Damien, but she had a feeling she'd be back often.

Aidan slid an arm around her waist and pressed a kiss to her cheek. "I'll go order some coffees at the counter."

She smiled at him, wanting to drown in those dark brown eyes. "Thank you."

He'd held her the entire night, and so much of the anxiety inside her dissipated with his touch. He was the only reason she'd been able to sleep at all.

They slid into the booth, and Cassie noticed Mia watching her closely.

"What is it?"

Mia blinked, like she regretted being caught staring. "Nothing."

Cassie wasn't buying it. "It's not nothing. You're looking at me like you want to say something. Say it."

Mia squirmed uncomfortably in the booth. "It's just... I'm happy that you and Aidan have found each other again. I know you've always loved him. But...you're still married to *Damien.*"

With everything they'd had going on, she hadn't had a chance to tell Mia the truth about her marriage. "Damien's gay, Mia."

Her mouth dropped open. "What?"

"I've known for years. Since we were teens. When I decided to rejoin Paragons of Hope, I knew I couldn't live outside the compound because I wasn't married. I also knew Damien wanted out, but he had no way to manage it. So, I approached him and suggested we marry in name only. I also told him from the beginning that I was trying to get the organization shut down." She lifted a shoulder. "We were close friends, so it worked for both of us. Our marriage is nothing more than a piece of paper, but it helped us both get through the last few years."

For a moment, Mia just stared at her. When she spoke, her voice was quiet. "Why didn't you tell me?"

Cassie swallowed. She'd been expecting that question. "Because Elijah is a huge threat, and if he'd found out about Damien and me, or suspected *you* knew, you could have been in danger. I didn't want to put you in a position where Elijah might hurt you to find out what you know."

And Mia was in deep with Paragons of Hope. She believed everything Elijah had ever spewed.

Mia turned to gaze out the window. It was impossible to figure out what her sister was thinking. It wasn't that long ago when Cassie had thought she could read her like a book.

She leaned forward and touched Mia's hand. "I wanted to keep you safe." That was all she'd *ever* wanted. "Maybe I should have told you," Cassie continued. "I was just so scared to lose you. After losing Aidan, I needed you to be okay."

Mia opened her mouth, but suddenly Courtney was at their table, setting down two mugs.

"Here you go, ladies."

Cassie smiled at the café owner. "Hi, Courtney. This is my sister, Mia. Mia, this is Courtney. She owns and runs The Grind."

The women smiled at each other, but Cassie didn't miss how much friendlier Courtney's smile was in comparison to Mia's.

"Well, hi," Courtney said. "Man, you guys have great genetics. Beauty runs in the family."

Cassie chuckled. "Says the beautiful woman with the exotic multicolored eyes." Courtney had one green eye and one brown. She was gorgeous.

Cassie lifted her coffee and sipped the hot liquid. *Wow.* It had to be the best coffee she'd ever had. "Courtney, this is amazing."

The woman beamed. "That would be the love I pour into it."

Cassie lowered the mug, but before she put it down, she noticed the writing on the side.

I want to ki_ _ you. Results may vary.

Cassie laughed. She'd heard about the funny mugs here. And not only was hers funny, it was also very fitting for her life right now. "This is awesome."

"Oh, I have better ones than that. But you need to keep coming if you want to read all of them."

Cassie looked across the table and noticed Mia hadn't tried hers. Then she remembered. "Oh, crap! Sorry, Courtney, could Mia get a juice? She doesn't drink coffee."

Mia shook her head. "Oh no, that's okay—"

"Don't be silly! Of course I'll get you some juice." Courtney lifted the mug. "Don't get me wrong, I think you're nuts and I have no idea how you survive without coffee—the stuff fuels me—but I'll oblige."

Courtney took the mug and headed back to the counter.

Cassie caught sight of Aidan at the counter talking to Jason. He winked at her, and her heart did that big thud-against-her-ribs thing it often did for him.

Cassie looked back to her sister. "Sorry."

She shook her head, looking away. "You don't need to apologize."

Cassie frowned. "Mia, are you okay?" She knew there was a lot going on, but her sister was being quiet in a way that just wasn't like her.

Mia squirmed in her seat. When she didn't reply, unease began to slide into Cassie's gut.

"Mia..." She touched her sister's hand again. Mia pulled it away.

Okay, Mia had *never* pulled away from her before.

Finally, her sister looked at her. "This is all just a lot, okay? A week ago, I had a father. A community. A home."

"I know. And I'm sorry, Mia. But I'm also your family. And my home can be your home."

Technically, it was Aidan's home. But he would let Mia stay. He knew how important she was to Cassie. She still didn't completely trust her sister, but they had time to work on their relationship. To get back to something that looked similar to where they'd come from.

Mia's gaze lowered to the table. When she looked up again, her expression was pleading. "Are you sure about all of this? Like, *really* sure?"

Cassie pulled back, confused. "Sure about what?"

"Are you sure Elijah did everything you said he did?" Mia leaned forward. "Elijah's never been anything but kind to me, Cass, and I've never seen him be anything but kind to *others*. He has a huge community of people who believe in him. How can so many people be wrong?"

After everything Cassie had endured in the last several days, how could her sister still be questioning her? How could she still be *defending* him?

"Because he's good at putting on a show and only letting people see what he wants them to see," Cassie said quietly. "Olive wouldn't lie about what happened to her and what she saw."

"I just... I'm sorry! I'm really struggling to believe it."

It was like a kick to the gut. Again.

Mia sighed heavily. "Elijah is—"

"A *phony*." She couldn't take it anymore. "Maybe the Elijah you know didn't touch you because he's your father." Damn, that still hurt to say. "He didn't murder you for your insurance money." Yet. "But he *raped* Olive and countless other women. He *murdered* Olive's brother right in front of her eyes. And I guarantee you, ninety-nine percent of the members who've died have *not* died by accident."

"Olive is still mourning her brother's death," her sister said quickly. "That does crazy things to a person. It could even make them lie for attention. Or create stories in their head."

Cassie blinked. A slow blink that was accompanied by a shuddered breath. "Elijah told you that, didn't he?"

"Yes." Mia's response was immediate. "He also told me—"

She stopped.

Cassie frowned. Dread filled her. "What?"

"He told me that *you're* the reason Mom left. That you couldn't handle life at the compound and you wanted out, and no matter how much convincing he did on his part, Mom wouldn't stay. So she pulled us away from our community. From my father. For *you*."

Cassie sucked in a sharp breath. "And you believed him?"

But she knew. Not only did her sister believe his bullshit—she also blamed Cassie for the entire trajectory of her life. She didn't have to say those words for Cassie to see it in her eyes. Did she blame her for their mother's death too? If they hadn't left the compound, their mother wouldn't have died in the apartment fire, so it seemed likely.

Pain tried to steal Cassie's breath, but she fought it. "So what are you doing here?" she asked quietly, trying to keep the anguish out of her voice. "Why aren't you with *him?*"

"I came to ask you to stop this, Cassie. Ask Olive to retract what she said and stop lying! Allow Elijah to come out of hiding and lead our people again."

Our people. Not his.

Before Cassie could say anything, Mia kept going. "I love you, Cassie. I do. And I know you believe all of this is the truth—but I don't. And it has the power to destroy Dad."

Cassie flinched. It was the first time she'd ever heard her sister call Elijah "dad." And it sounded wrong. So wrong. But then, this entire conversation was wrong. And she'd reached her breaking point.

"There's *evidence*, Mia. A recording with Elijah's confession of drugging and raping Olive, and the sound of *his* gun going off as he killed Rodney!"

Her sister narrowed her eyes. "Have you listened to the recording? Have you actually *heard* Elijah admit to anything?"

"The FBI have listened to it and confirmed it's exactly what Olive said it was. And unless you forgot, Damien's lying in a hospital, in a *coma*, after being beaten repeatedly by Elijah's men!"

But her words didn't matter. She could see in her sister's eyes that nothing would convince her. She was so indoctrinated that she couldn't accept the truth that was right in front of her.

And God, it hurt. Because yet again, Mia was choosing *him* over Cassie.

Mia leaned back and scrubbed her face with her hands. "I'm going to the bathroom. When I get back, we can visit Damien."

Cassie said nothing. She had no words. She watched her sister walk away.

A stranger. Her sister was a complete stranger to her.

It was too much. All of it. All these years, she'd been so focused on Elijah that she'd missed it. The unwavering belief her sister had in the man. The truth that her love and alliance with him ran so much deeper than her love for Cassie.

Suddenly, Aidan was kneeling beside her. "Hey. Are you okay?"

The man would have heard the entire conversation. She looked at him and shook her head. "I just don't understand her." Her heart didn't want to believe her sister could be so blind, but she knew she had to accept it.

He cupped her cheek. The warmth of his hand was the only heat in her entire body. "I know, baby. I'm sorry."

His phone rang, and she watched almost numbly as he tugged it from his pocket and answered. "Logan, what is it?"

She straightened. Logan was watching Damien's room at the hospital. Was he okay? Had something happened?

Aidan nodded. "Got it. Thanks. We'll be there in ten."

The second Aidan hung up, Cassie touched his arm. "What's wrong with Damien?"

"He's awake."

She sucked in a sharp breath. "Oh my gosh! We have to go see him."

Aidan helped her out of the booth.

She shot her gaze to the bathroom. She no longer wanted her sister anywhere near Damien, but they needed to keep her close. They had to keep an eye on her until Elijah was found.

She looked back at Aidan, and he pushed some hair from her face. "We'll take her, but I'll assign one of the guys to watch her."

She sighed. "How do you read my mind like that?"

He leaned in and his lips hovered over hers. "Magic."

The second Mia left the bathroom, they told her what was going on and left for the hospital. No one spoke on the drive, but Aidan's hand never left Cassie's leg. It was the only thing keeping her grounded in that moment.

When they reached the hospital, Cassie all but ran inside. She didn't stop until she reached Damien's room. When she saw him, his eyes were open and he was sitting up. Dean sat beside him, holding his hand.

Her feet slowed as she moved into the room, and tears filled her eyes. "Oh my gosh! Can I touch you?"

He chuckled. "Of course. Come here, Cass."

He lifted an arm, and she sat on the edge of the bed. When his arm closed around her, tears welled in her eyes. Hugging him was everything. The man was her best friend. For the last few years, he'd been her only ally. The only person who was truly on her side and understood her.

When she straightened, he frowned. Then he swiped a tear from her cheek. "Hey, why are you crying? You never cry."

"I was scared I was going to lose you." So scared, her heart had felt close to breaking.

One side of his mouth lifted. "Can't get rid of me that easily."

"Thank God for that," Dean added quietly, squeezing Damien's hand.

Damien's gaze shifted behind her. "Aidan. It's good to see you again."

"Good to see you awake, Damien."

"I'm guessing I have you to thank for me being here?" he asked.

Aidan shook his head. "Nope. You have Cass. She drew us a diagram and told us where you'd be."

His eyes softened as he looked back to Cassie. "Thank you."

Dean reached over and squeezed her arm. "Yes. Thank you so much, Cass."

Her smile was watery as hell, but it was the best she could do. He was alive and safe.

He looked toward the door, where her sister stood. "Hi, Mia."

"Hi, Damien. I'm glad you're awake."

When he glanced back at Cassie, the softness on his face disappeared and his features hardened. "Tell me it's over."

Oh, how she wished she could. "It's not. Not yet. The FBI has a recording of Olive's story. Olive *also* gave us a recording of Elijah's confession of what he did to her, and you can hear him shooting Rodney shortly after. When they went to arrest him, he was gone. They haven't been able to locate him. A bunch of members went into hiding as well. Joshua and Antwon are with the police, but they aren't talking."

Damien's eyes closed, and when he opened them, there was cold, hard anger. "They'll find him. I'm just glad you're safe and with Aidan." He studied her face. "Has he come after you?"

"Yes. More than once. How did you know he would?"

That was something she'd been wondering since Aidan had first told her Damien arranged her extraction from their home.

Damien blew out a breath. "I'd heard whispers that something big was approaching. Elijah had started talking to a few people about 'the end'. Saying it was coming. That we were running out of time. Kept saying he knew how to save everyone. That God had shown him the way."

"And I was the way?" she whispered. More accurately, her *death* was the way.

His chest rose and fell with a deep breath. "At one of the family gatherings in the Great Hall, you disappeared to talk to Olive. You were gone for a while, so I went looking for you. I heard voices in the office, and I stopped outside. That's when I heard Elijah, Joshua and Isaac." He paused to swallow. "Cassie... they were discussing the details of your thirtieth birthday, and how they'd take you during the party, through the back door, into a waiting car... They planned to drive you to some location and perform the 'sacrifice' that night."

The fine hairs on her arms stood on end. She'd suspected as much. But hearing it out loud just highlighted how much danger she would have been in if Aidan and his team hadn't been there.

"I got out of there before they saw me," Damien continued. "But after that night, I knew I had to get you to safety." His gaze rose to Aidan. "I knew she missed you. And I knew you'd never let harm come to her. That's why I contacted you."

Cassie looked up to see a dark expression on Aidan's face.

"Never." He squeezed her shoulder. "Why did Elijah beat you and keep you in his basement?"

Damien's eyes narrowed into slits. "On Saturday, the night after Cass was taken, he requested my presence at the compound. I thought it was to discuss your disappearance. His men immediately took me to the basement." He visibly shuddered. "They'd seen me on video surveillance, standing outside his office. They knew I'd overheard everything. Said they couldn't let me get in the way, but they couldn't have my death take place days before yours because it would look too suspicious."

Red-hot fury flowed through Cassie's blood.

She turned to look at Mia. She was now a few feet away from the bed, an expression of horror on her face as she listened to Damien, her nails digging into her arms.

This had to be it. This *had* to be the moment her sister realized she needed to choose. Cassie or Elijah. Because it couldn't be both.

CHAPTER 27

*A*idan held Cassie's shoulder. She'd been in deep conversation with Damien and Dean for the last hour. He'd stay all day if he had to. Whatever it took to make the smile return to Cassie's face.

Callum and Liam were in the room too, while Tyler waited in the hall.

Even with the steady conversation, he heard the noise. The vibration of a muted phone. It was quiet, almost silent.

His gaze zeroed in on Mia, standing at the back of the room.

Where the hell had she gotten a phone, and how long had she had it? According to Cassie, female members weren't supposed to have any electronics, and men only had them for their jobs.

Quietly, Mia slipped from the room. Callum followed closely behind. Cassie, Damien and Dean stopped talking, and everyone's gazes went to the door.

Mia moved away from Damien's room and her voice quieted, but not enough to escape Aidan. "Elijah, where are you?"

Every muscle in his body tensed.

"It's time, child."

"Time for what?" Mia hissed. "You still haven't told me what you're doing. All you said was that you needed Cassie, but you didn't tell me why." Her voice lowered again. "They're saying you want to kill her as some kind of *sacrifice*. But that's not true, is it? It can't be! Tell me it's not true, Father."

Aidan shot out of the room.

Cassie's quick footsteps sounded behind him. "Aidan!"

"Mia, sometimes sacrifices are required for the greater good," Elijah said.

Mia was halfway down the hall, facing away. Callum was already snatching the phone from her fingers, Tyler right behind him.

"Hey!" she cried out.

Callum handed the phone to Aidan. It took every ounce of his self-control not to crush the cell between his fingers. He pressed it to his ear. "Elijah."

"Who's this?"

"You should already know. It's Aidan Pratt."

Cassie stopped beside him and touched his arm.

A loud sigh sounded. "Aidan. There's nothing you can do to stop this. I've known that Cassie was the chosen one since she was ten years old. That means I've been planning this for over twenty years. You really think I haven't gone over every single scenario in my head during that time? Including you? I knew I'd be challenged by evil. You *are* that evil, my son."

Aidan met the gazes of his teammates. They were all alert, with their hands on their weapons.

"We're out of time," Elijah continued. "In order to save us all, this needs to happen. Now."

The phone went dead.

This time he *did* crush the phone in his hand. He didn't need to open it to know there was a tracking device inside. "They're here," he growled.

The words had barely left his mouth when he smelled gas. He shot a look to his team. They smelled it too. They all looked up.

"It's coming from the air vents," Callum said before Aidan could.

Shit. They were on the fourth floor.

He wrapped an arm around Cassie's waist. They didn't have much time. "Callum, find the source of the gas and stop it. Tyler, get Mia out and alert hospital authorities. Liam, look after Damien and Dean."

Cassie coughed. He swore under his breath before lifting her into his arms. Then he was running. Her inhalations had already changed to wheezing. Thank God it wasn't affecting him. Yet.

He turned a corner and sped down the corridor. Nurses and doctor were stopped in the hall. Many were holding their mouths and looking around, confused.

"Get out!" he yelled.

Callum would get the alarm sounding soon. And the rest of the team would alert the authorities and arrive soon to help get people out.

He wasn't taking Cassie out the main entrance—they were heading down a back stairwell. It was the closest exit, and time wasn't on their side. He had no idea what was blowing through those vents, though he guessed it wasn't lethal. Elijah wanted Cassie alive.

Still, Aidan couldn't risk her breathing in too much of it.

He rounded another corner, and the door to the back stairwell came into view. Less than a second later, he pushed through and moved toward the stairs.

He'd taken a single step when a shot sounded from below. *Dammit!*

He moved back and set Cassie gently onto the floor. Her eyes were half-closed and her breathing deep. He yanked his gun from his holster and moved to peek over the rail.

There was the sound of more bullets hitting stairs. He

frowned as something bounced off the underside of the stairs leading to the next floor, then landed beside him.

Not a bullet. A tranquilizer.

He took a moment to calm his breathing and listen to the movement from the stairwell. Four men. All heavy. Probably well-trained.

Going to his stomach, he aimed his weapon. The first guy came into view wearing a bulletproof vest and a gas mask. His pistol came up, but Aidan got a shot in first, hitting the guy in the neck. He fell down the stairs.

Before Aidan could focus on the next guy, a dart hit him in the shoulder.

Fuck! He rolled back and yanked it out. Unlike the gas, he immediately felt the effects of the dart. His arms went heavy and his vision fuzzed. Alarm blasted through him. A common tranquilizer should barely affect him. They were using something else. Something stronger.

Ignoring the heaviness in his limbs, he rolled and steadied his gun again. He shot and missed. He *never* missed.

He fired a third time, this time getting his target in the temple. The guy dropped.

He rolled to the side as more tranquilizers shot toward him. Took a breath. His vision grayed, but he forced his eyes to remain open.

Suddenly, two men rushed the landing.

Aidan kicked the first guy in the leg, sending him to the floor. Another dart hit him in the chest from guy number four. Aidan lifted his gun and shot him in the head, just as the man on the floor got him with a third dart in the neck.

The pistol slipped from Aidan's fingers.

"Aidan..." Cassie's voice was weak.

No. He had to stay awake. He couldn't allow her to be taken.

He reached for the Glock—but his vision blurred, then his world went black.

～

CASSIE TRIED to strike out at the hands reaching for her, but her limbs were too heavy. A hard shoulder hit her stomach, then the man was moving. When Aidan left her view, her insides filled with acid. Was he okay? Was he breathing?

The stairs below her eyes were a blur, the footsteps dull thuds. "No," she whispered. She had to get back to Aidan.

She swallowed, trying to ward off the darkness.

They stepped outside and moved to a waiting van at the back of the building.

She pushed at the man's back but barely applied any pressure. Every part of her felt weak and heavy.

The van door opened, and she was placed inside surprisingly gently.

"Aidan..." She needed to get to him. He'd been shot so many times! Her heart shattered at the possibility that he wouldn't make it. *She* shattered.

"They weren't bullets, Cassie."

At the sound of the familiar voice, she forced her eyes open. The van was now moving, and the interior was dark, but there was no mistaking him. Elijah.

"W-what?" *Come on, Cassie. Get your words out and stay awake.*

Elijah folded his hands in his lap. "I've heard the stories. That those men keep going, even after being hit with bullets. I couldn't risk that. So I acquired a very strong tranquilizer. It would kill a normal man. Maybe even a large animal. What I really love about it, though, is that it's fast-acting."

She choked at his words.

"He took three hits before he went down," the man beside her reported.

She frowned at another familiar voice and looked to the right. She blinked three times. The gas was still affecting her, but each second that passed had her feeling a little bit better. The guy took off his ski mask.

Sampson.

It shouldn't surprise her that he was involved. But a tiny part of her had been holding out hope that he hadn't known what was really going on. He was former military and often worked security for Elijah, but for Mia's sake, Cassie had hoped he was good.

"Aren't you upset that the other men died?" she asked Sampson quietly.

He turned to look at her. "Sometimes, sacrifice is required for the greater good."

Ice froze her blood. It was almost an echo of Joshua's words. It was all bullshit that Elijah spewed, but she'd have thought some people were too smart to believe it.

"You seemed so normal," she said almost absently, speaking her thoughts out loud. "And smarter."

He didn't look annoyed by her comment. "When I got out of the military, I wasn't in a good place. Elijah, and our community at Paragons of Hope, saved me. I owe them my life and will forever be loyal to them."

Elijah had preyed on this man. And he'd fallen right into the trap.

"Check her," Elijah said to Sampson. "Remove and dispose of all jewelry and electronics."

No!

Sampson's hands began to pat down her body. She attempted to swat him away, but he ignored her efforts. She had no phone and almost no jewelry, just her necklace.

He paused when he found the pendant. Then he pulled it from her neck and snapped the chain.

A cry fell from her lips. She tried to grab for it. "Please, no! That's important to me."

Sampson ignored her, rolling down the window and

throwing it out. Cool air whipped across her face. Then the window closed, and her last connection to Aidan disappeared.

She swallowed the pain before turning back to Elijah. "Where are you taking me?"

"To the location in my vision, Cassie."

Deep breaths. In and out. "This is why my mother left you, isn't it? You told her about your little *vision.*"

She couldn't help but sneer the word.

Elijah leaned back in his seat. "Yes. I told your mother about my dream. I told her that you were the chosen one, and that when you turned thirty, your death would save us all. I was very clear that without your sacrifice, we would lose everything. I thought she'd feel proud that you were chosen for such an important role."

He thought her mother would be pleased that they planned to murder her? This man needed help. Lock-him-up-and-throw-away-the-key kind of help. "You told her you were going to kill her daughter. Of course she wasn't happy."

"Your mother never could see the vision I had for our people. She was a lot like you, actually. It's why I had to kill her."

Cassie's world crashed to a screeching halt. Every part of her turned to ice. "You killed her?" The words were almost a whisper.

"Well, not me. My men, at my direction." He crossed his legs. "She took you from me. Tried to hide you. I couldn't let that happen. The second I found you, her fate was sealed. Then I just kept on eye on you as you went through the foster care system."

Pain and despair were tidal waves in her chest. This awful man in front of her, the man who she'd already known was as evil as they came, had killed her *mother*. Forced her and her sister into the foster care system, all because her mother wanted to protect her.

Tears pressed at her eyes. She wanted to drown in her devastation. She closed her eyes, trying to steady her breaths. When she opened them, it took everything in her not to leap across the van and tear the man to shreds.

"And Mia?" she asked through gritted teeth. "Is she really your daughter? Or is that just some bullshit you told her so she'd trust you?"

"She *is* my daughter. I was disappointed at first, that you were the chosen one and not her. After all, I'm the leader of our people. But I quickly understood that she was supposed to remain by my side. That's why I sent Sampson to her. Encouraged him to grow close to her, remind her all about our organization. And once she rejoined, I told her who I was to her, and that was that. She was in."

She turned to Sampson. "So he told you to go and suck this poor woman back into the organization so he could kill her sister, and off you went?"

"For the good of our people," Sampson said quietly.

God. There wasn't an ounce of shame on the man's face.

Her gaze lowered to the gun strapped to Sampson's thigh. Maybe if she lunged fast enough—

"I wouldn't if I were you," Elijah said quietly. "We both know Sampson was in the Special Forces. Don't make him hurt you."

Hurt her? Nothing could hurt her more than learning about her mother's murder...or leaving Aidan in a stairwell, hurt, possibly dead.

Anger and grief tried to swallow her, but she refused to allow it. She needed a plan. She couldn't take on a soldier and win, not while she was still weak from the gas. But she also couldn't allow these people to take her God knows where and kill her.

Elijah lifted a bag from the floor and pulled out a white dress. He held it out for her. "Put this on, Cassie."

Hell no.

She didn't reach for it. She didn't move so much as a muscle.

Another sigh from Elijah. "If you don't, I'll have Sampson put it on you."

Asshole. "No."

Another beat passed. Elijah nodded to Sampson.

He reached toward her and grabbed the hem of her top.

"Stop!" she shouted before he could lift it. "I'll do it! Just don't touch me."

God, she couldn't stand the feel of any of these psychopaths touching her. Sampson sat back and she yanked the dress from Elijah's hand.

With a deep breath, she tugged off her top. The dress was lace, but it was also high-necked and long-sleeved. There was a pocket section in the front, like something a housewife would put garden cuttings into.

Once the dress was on, she pulled off her shoes and jeans. She was just leaning down to put her shoes back on when Sampson whipped them out of her grasp.

"Hey!"

He ignored her.

"You won't need them," Elijah said.

She huffed. Probably to make it harder for her to run away.

She looked out the window, running over every escape plan she could think of in her head. She wasn't sure how much time passed. Maybe an hour. Maybe two. But eventually they turned into a wooded area before finally stopping.

Elijah clapped his hands. "Ah, we're here." He turned to Sampson. "Bind her hands."

She spun toward Sampson and immediately tried to fight him, but it was no use. He secured her wrists in one hand, his grip unbreakable. He tied rope around both wrists.

Her heart pounded, rage flowing through her veins.

Elijah pulled the door open. There was the distant sound of water. A waterfall, maybe? And there were cars. Lots of them. She recognized some. Members of Paragons of Hope were here.

Sampson started to step out. She rose to her feet and immediately tripped on her dress, falling into his side, throwing a hand to his leg to catch herself.

While she was down, she quickly slipped the knife from his leg sheath and shoved it into the pouch of her dress.

Sampson turned, and he reached to help her up. "You okay?" he asked.

That question was almost laughable. "Sure. I love being walked to my impending death."

CHAPTER 28

*T*he tapping of laptop keys drilled into Aidan's head. He scrunched his eyes tighter. Fuck, his head pounded and his mouth felt like sandpaper.

"Aidan?"

At the sound of Flynn calling his name, the fog disintegrated, and everything came back to him at once. The gas seeping through the hospital air vents. The run to the back stairwell. And Cassie...

His eyes shot open, and he sat up. He was on a couch—Callum's couch—with Flynn on his haunches beside him. His gaze shot across the room to the table, where Callum and Tyler sat with their laptops. Mia stood alone at the side of the room, her chest moving up and down with quick breaths.

"Where's Cassie?" Aidan ground out, his throat so dry his voice almost didn't work.

Flynn handed him a glass of water. "Don't know. But we're working on it."

Acid filled Aidan's gut. He forced the water down his throat as Callum started talking.

"I'm hacking into cameras outside the hospital to find what vehicle she was taken in."

Tyler shot a quick look at him over the laptop. "Damien's upstairs. Carina's looking after him, and Dean's up there too. Logan, Jason, Liam and Blake are helping at the hospital. The gas got turned off, but a lot of patients need moving until the facility is sterilized."

Aidan shot to his feet. His knees almost caved, but he locked them in place.

Flynn grabbed his arm. "Whoa, take it easy. You took a shit-load of tranquilizer. Carina should probably come down and take another look at you."

Screw that. "I'm not damn well resting while the woman I love is God knows where about to be murdered!"

Mia flinched at his words.

"How much time has passed?" he growled.

"Almost half an hour," Callum said quickly.

He shot a look to Mia. "What do you know?"

Her eyes widened. She was deathly pale. "I-I don't know anything. I didn't know he'd do something like this!"

He moved across the room, glad his legs were carrying him, and grabbed her shoulders tightly. "We always know more than we think we do. Did Elijah ever say anything? Any small detail could help."

Her mouth opened to respond, then a voice from upstairs sounded.

"No—Damien, *stop*. You need to stay in bed."

A second later, an angry-looking Carina and Dean, and a slow-moving Damien attached to an IV pole, appeared at the top of the stairs. Carina was holding his arm. Whether she was helping or trying to stop him, Aidan wasn't sure. Probably both.

"Water," Damien said quietly.

Carina looked anxious. "You need water?"

He shook his head, eyes only for Aidan. "In the conversation I overheard, Elijah quoted a verse from Revelation. "Then the angel showed me the river of water of life, as clear as crystal, flowing from the throne of God and of the Lamb.'"

Mia frowned. "He quotes that verse a lot. Always in regards to our salvation." She gasped. "And in her birthday card, he wrote something…"

Aidan's hands tightened. "What?"

"'He reached down from on high and took hold of me; he drew me out of deep waters.'" Her breathing became rapid. "I thought he was trying to comfort her with the verse. I thought he was talking about her recent kidnapping and how she'd be okay. I didn't realize—"

"He was going to murder her in water," Aidan finished.

He turned, running frustrated hands through his hair.

"Found the van," Callum said quickly, his fingers flying over the keys. "I've tracked it on a couple of different traffic cameras. It's heading north."

"North?" Aidan frowned, moving behind the laptop. "He's not heading back to Utah?"

"Nope." His fingers continued to fly, and he paused the footage on the screen. "This is the last image we have. After this, there are no more traffic cameras. It's all open road."

He turned back to Mia and Damien. "What's north?"

Damien shook his head, frustration on his face. "I don't know."

"I don't—" Mia stopped abruptly.

He stepped closer, his heart pounding. "What is it?"

"He has a picture in his office. It's of me and Cassie in the water when we were kids. I always found it strange that he had it displayed, because he has no other photos. Not even in his house. This one is large and framed, hanging on the wall right above his cross. I assumed it was because I was his daughter. But maybe…"

Maybe it was where he'd always planned to murder Cassie. "Do you know where it was taken?"

She swallowed. "I asked him once…and he said it was Lady Face Falls."

Callum typed on his laptop. "The falls are in line with where he's driving."

Aidan was moving before anyone could stop him. He snatched Callum's keys from the side table and ran outside. He'd just reached the car when Tyler slipped in front of him.

"No way are you driving in your current condition."

He didn't have time to argue, so he let Tyler take the keys and ran to the passenger side.

Callum and Flynn slid into Flynn's car, hauling a rucksack that he knew would be filled with weapons.

As they pulled away from the house, Mia and Damien stood on the porch, and Mia yelled something.

Save her.

CASSIE STUMBLED for what had to be the tenth time. She would have fallen on her face by now, but Sampson had one hand on her wrist and the other on her elbow.

"Almost there," he said quietly.

The guy had been gentle and soft-spoken the entire walk. It was annoying the hell out of her. What kind of murderer was gentle?

Wind rushed past them, and a shiver coursed up her spine. It was cold. Really cold. The dress was thin, and her feet felt like blocks of ice. Her bleeding and bloody feet, that was.

She was kind of grateful for the cold, really. It was the only thing keeping her upright. In the heat, this amount of walking would have had her passing out within minutes. She didn't want to pass out. She wanted to slow them down as much as she could, but she also wanted to be conscious to plunge the hidden knife into whichever unlucky soul tried to kill her.

And she would. She wasn't dying without a fight.

The first half of the trail had been almost completely flat and easy to traverse. This second half, though... Man, it was tough. The majority of the ground was jagged, wet and blocked by dozens of fallen trees. Which was actually a blessing, in terms of slowing them down. She had to have faith that Aidan was okay. That he and his team would find her. And the slower they moved, the more time it gave Aidan to work out where she'd been taken. If he managed to find her, it would take him a tenth of the time to navigate these woods.

She tripped over another root, and yet again, Sampson kept her upright. If only the guy would walk in front of her, she could pull the knife from the dress and stab him before running.

The sound of the waterfall grew louder.

"So," she finally said. "Can you tell me what the plan is now?"

"All will be revealed in good time," Elijah said from in front of them.

She ground her teeth. "Okay, well, how about you tell me where we are at least. If I'm not going to live to see tomorrow, surely that doesn't matter?"

For some reason, this all looked familiar, but she wasn't sure why.

Elijah lifted a branch, and she stepped through after him. "Your mother took me to this waterfall just before your tenth birthday. You and Mia were swimming in the water, and the sun was hitting you in just the right way that you looked like an angel sent down from God."

Her chest constricted at the mention of her mother. So the man planned to drown her in that same water?

The top of the falls came into view ahead.

"That night," Elijah continued, "was when the vision came to me in my dream."

She was still in disbelief that this psycho'd had *one* dream about her when she was a child, then spent the next twenty years planning her death.

"Every time I'm here, I feel God's presence."

"They're going to find you, you know," she said quietly. She probably shouldn't be angering the man, but she didn't care at this point. "They've got Joshua and Antwon. It won't be long before they find you and Isaac and everyone else involved."

"Let's not speak of such things at such an important time."

Elijah stopped beside the waterfall and looked down. She paused beside him, and when she followed his gaze, she gaped. Holy crap, that was a steep decline to the base of the waterfall.

And there, on the rocks surrounding the pool below, were dozens of members of Paragons of Hope. All the members who'd been missing during the police raid. All dressed in white and holding candles.

Her gaze brushed over each face, pausing for a moment on Mrs. Alder. Of course. She'd never liked the woman, so she shouldn't be surprised to see her there. Still, the housekeeper had lived with her and Damien, cooked for them, cleaned, for the last two years. Did she hate her so much that she wanted to watch Elijah kill her?

"Do they know what you're about to do?" she asked.

"Yes," Elijah said quietly. "This is my inner circle. Members who understand what I'm trying to achieve. Who understand sacrifice."

What sacrifice? They weren't sacrificing anything.

Elijah began to climb down the rough-hewn steps, and when Sampson gave Cassie a little push, her eyes widened. "You can't be serious. You want me to climb down there with bound hands?" She'd fall and break her goddamn neck.

"I won't let you fall. I promise."

He *promised*?

He tugged her down a step, then another. Her foot slid, and

she yelped, but Sampson's hand on her arm tightened, keeping her rooted to the spot.

Cassie's heart raced in her chest the entire way. Terrifying. It was absolutely terrifying. When they finally reached the bottom, she wanted to get down on her hands and knees and kiss the earth beneath her feet.

But she didn't. She couldn't with Sampson pulling her forward.

A member walked up to Elijah and handed him a bundle of clothing. He removed his top, then his shoes and pants, before sliding on the white outfit. For a moment, he looked at the water and closed his eyes, taking a deep breath.

Jesus Christ. This was it. The man was going to drown her.

Finally, he turned to her. "It's time."

Sweat broke out on her forehead. No. No freaking way. Did he just expect her to waltz into the water with him and let him kill her?

She shook her head, attempted a step back. "Elijah, you don't need to do this. Please…"

"But I do."

She spun around. Sampson was right there. "Don't make this hard, Cassie."

"You want me to make killing me *easy?*"

Elijah grabbed her arm and tugged her toward the water. She dug her heels into the dirt and tried to stay where she was, but his hands were like steel.

She gasped when the water lapped around her ankles. It was freaking freezing. So cold it felt like shards of ice stabbing at her skin.

Elijah kept tugging her with a strength she didn't even know he possessed until they stood in the center of the pool, halfway to the waterfall. The falls splashed onto them, and the water in the pool reached just below her chest. Her entire body now shook violently from the freezing water.

Elijah didn't seem bothered by the cold at all.

"The spirit of God hovers over the water," Elijah called out loudly. "And today, we finally put our Lord's vision into action. It has been years in the making. These last few weeks have diminished us, just as we knew they would if we didn't enact his vision on time."

No. Their *diminishing* was because he was a violent asshole who kept sending people to kidnap her.

She tugged at the bonds, not caring who saw her struggle. Elijah continued speaking to his people, but Cassie blocked him out.

She continued to struggle until she noticed the members raise the candles above their heads. Then she felt Elijah's eyes once again fall to her. "It is time for you to enter the Kingdom of God, child."

That was all the warning she got before his hands gripped her shoulders and he shoved her beneath the water.

She slammed her mouth shut just before water washed over her head. Icy cold enveloped her. She tried to shift, to pull away, but his hands were manacles. With bound hands, she reached into the pouch of her dress and grabbed the knife.

Then, using every ounce of strength she had left, she plunged it into Elijah's thigh.

The hands on her shoulders instantly released as a deep red bloomed through the water.

Her body tried to float up, but she used her arms to keep her below the surface. She held her breath and swam toward the waterfall as fast as her body allowed.

CHAPTER 29

$\mathcal{T}$he car had barely stopped when Aidan was jumping out. Dozens of vehicles were scattered around the parking lot, one of those being the van that had driven Cassie away in the CCTV footage.

His stomach contracted. He pushed himself to run down the trail faster than he'd ever run in his life. He'd studied the trail on his phone during the drive. For a normal man, the trail to the waterfall would take an hour or more of walking.

He leaped over a tree root. Tyler's feet pounded the ground behind him. He also heard the distant sound of another car pulling up. Of more feet hitting the path. Callum and Flynn.

Fear was a familiar ball in his gut. Fear that he'd be too late. Fear that he'd never hold Cassie in his arms again. Kiss her. Marry her and fill their home with their children.

Fuck. He wanted to do all that. He'd barely survived losing her the first time, and he'd only been able to do that because she'd been *alive*. She'd existed in this world, and he'd thought she was happy.

He moved faster, ignoring the branches that whipped his face and the way his feet sank into the dirt. The footprints in the ground had the unease inside him intensifying. The assholes had forced her to the waterfall. Every last one of them would pay.

When the top of the waterfall came into view, he shut off his emotions. All of them. The anxiety. The fear. The goddamn churning of his gut.

He stopped at the top of the falls and looked down just in time to see Elijah shove Cassie beneath the surface of the water.

Every muscle in his body went cold.

He pulled out his gun but before he could shoot, the man cried out and dropped below the water as well. *Shit!* He couldn't shoot at the water. Not while Cassie was under.

Shoving the gun back into the holster, he began the climb down.

Sampson stood near the pool. When he spotted Aidan, he lifted a gun. He only got it halfway up when a shot sounded from the top of the falls.

Tyler.

Sampson dropped to the ground, bullet to the chest.

Screams erupted and people started running. Not all of them, though. Some ran into the water—aiming straight for Cassie and Elijah. Whether they were trying to drown Cassie or save their leader, he had no idea.

HANDS GRABBED at Cassie's feet, but she kicked them away. The waterfall wasn't far from where they'd been standing. That was her goal. Get there, find something, anything, that she could use to save herself.

She felt the hard pelting of the waterfall. She gave two more kicks. Then, finally, she propelled herself up.

The second her head broke through the surface, she sucked in a lungful of air and grabbed on to the rocks. There was a gap of space between the falls and the water. The space was tiny, but it was something. A small sanctuary.

She scanned the rocks, almost crying out in frustration. There was nothing here. No hiding spaces. No objects to use as a weapon. Except...

She reached over and grabbed a medium-size rock.

That was it. All she had. Now she had to fight and hope like hell that help was coming. She was not going to give up, and she certainly wasn't going to remain docile while Elijah tried to drown her. She had too much to live for.

She was just turning back to the falls when Elijah rose from the water, a vicious sneer on his face.

He dove forward and shoved her under.

She narrowly avoided water flooding into her mouth. She kicked and pushed at him from beneath the water, the rock still in her hands. The man didn't budge.

Her limbs started to ice, and darkness tried to hedge her vision from the lack of oxygen, but she forced herself to keep fighting. To do anything and everything to get away. To survive.

Gripping the rock tightly, she flung a hand out of the water and hit him as hard as she could. She had no idea what part of him she connected with, but his hands slipped, and she rose up, sucking in big gulps of air. Her mind was going fuzzy, and she wasn't sure if it was the lack of air, the cold, or her hypotension. Maybe all three.

The water from the falls pummeled them both. She threw back her arm and slammed him in the head with the rock. Elijah cried out. She tried to hit him again, but he yanked the rock from her grasp. Before he could grab her wrists, she flung her roped hands around his neck and yanked him under. He immediately grabbed her waist, pulling her down with him.

Her lungs screamed for breath. She swung and punched him, desperately trying to swim up for air, but the man wasn't letting go. He was going to drown them both.

She tore at the arm around her. She was vaguely aware of the falls pounding above them. When she couldn't hold her breath any longer, she opened her mouth and sucked in a gulp of water.

AIDAN DOVE INTO THE WATER. Two guys jumped on his back to try to stop him, but he kicked them away. The assholes were trying to slow him down so Elijah could drown Cass.

No fucking way.

He plunged beneath the surface and swam. His team would take care of the others. They'd already shot a few people swimming toward Elijah and Cassie. Several of Elijah's guards had pulled their guns, but his team took care of them too.

His eyes were open as he propelled himself forward. When he finally spotted Cassie and Elijah, his stomach clenched.

Her eyes were closed—and she was drifting to the bottom of the pool.

Elijah released Cassie and pushed away from her, but his movements were slow, sluggish.

He hadn't breached the surface by the time Aidan reached them.

Aidan didn't give a damn. He ignored the other man and grabbed Cassie's arm. The second they surfaced, he swam for the nearest bank and laid Cassie on the cold ground.

Bile rose in his throat at the sight of her, so still and pale, lips blue. He shoved the hair from his face, held her nose and leaned down. Then he breathed into her mouth two times.

Come on, Cassie. Come back to me.

When the breaths didn't work, he began compressions against her chest.

"Come on, Cass! Breathe! I need you to breathe for me! I can't lose you. I *won't* lose you!"

He stopped compressions and breathed into her mouth again,

just as Tyler appeared beside him. Aidan lifted his head and pressed once more on her chest—and her back arched as she coughed violently, water spewing from her mouth.

His heart damn near stopped. He quickly rolled her to her side. He pressed one hand to her back and used the other to hold her forehead. The blood in his veins stopped racing, and finally he could breathe, because *she* breathed.

"You're okay! You're alive," he whispered. He wasn't sure if the words were meant to comfort her or him. Maybe both.

Finally, the coughs stopped racking her chest, and air wheezed in and out of her. She looked at him, her eyes watering. "Aidan!"

She reached for him, and he tugged her against him. He held her tighter than he'd ever held her before, pressing his face into her hair, breathing her in.

"You're alive," he repeated. He couldn't stop saying the words.

She dug her head into his chest. "I'm alive."

CHAPTER 30

Cassie threw back her head and laughed at Willow's story. She was recounting her morning and how her daughter had tricked her dad into eating a teaspoon of salt.

They stood around a tall table at Tucker's Bar. All the women were here—Grace, Courtney, Willow and Carina, while all eight men sat at a long table near the back. She'd looked their way countless times. Had she not known them, they'd be an intimidating sight. All big and muscled and… Had she said big?

Every time Cassie looked over, Aidan's eyes were on her. It left her feeling hot and tingly. She almost wanted to squirm.

This was her first night out since the kidnapping a week ago. It felt amazing. She thought she'd be nervous. Maybe end up looking over her shoulder the entire evening. She wasn't. It was impossible not to feel safe with all the guys watching over them.

Grace nudged her shoulder. "You doing okay?"

She turned to the woman and smiled. "I'm doing so good. Aidan's been…" She smiled. "I can't even explain. Incredible."

"He hasn't been treating you like you're fragile?" Courtney asked, leaning across the table, cocktail in hand.

Cassie laughed. "Oh, he's definitely been doing that. But I kind of love it." Actually, there was no "kind of" about it. "After years of taking care of myself while trying to shut down a crazy cult, it feels good to have someone looking after me for a change."

Not someone. Aidan. The man she loved. The man she'd always loved.

"How are you feeling about Mia?" Willow asked quietly.

There was a little pang to her heart at the mention of her sister. "I'm glad she got a job and an apartment. And she's only a couple of towns away, so still within driving distance."

Mia was working in a coffee shop. It was a start. There was still a lot of friction between them, and she didn't know when or *if* things would get better. For Cassie, it would take a while for trust to build.

Grace touched her hand. "It sounds hard."

She traced her finger along the rim of her glass of OJ. "We're both trying to find our way back to each other. She blames herself for everything that happened to me, and, while I don't blame her for anything Elijah did, there's still a lot of hurt that she couldn't trust me."

"Family can be complicated," Carina said gently.

Cassie gave her a small smile. She wasn't wrong. But that didn't make any of it easier to accept. She didn't know if the hurt and betrayal she felt for Mia choosing Elijah would ever fully disappear. But...Mia was her sister. The only blood relation she had left. So she was choosing to work on her feelings.

"I'm just glad Elijah's gone and everyone who played a part is in jail."

By the time Elijah had been pulled from the water, it was too late. The knife wound and blood loss had made him weak. He was unable to reach the surface on his own. He drowned in the very waters he'd attempted to use for Cassie's death.

Everyone at the waterfall who wasn't dead had been arrested, and those who hadn't been there were shocked to learn what had transpired. They had no desire to go back to that life. The cult was officially dead.

"You'll always have us," Grace said.

"And the guys," Courtney added. "Aidan may be your guy, but every one of them would stand in front of a bullet for you. They're basically the big protective brothers you never asked for."

Her heart warmed. For so long, she'd lived in a community with people she felt no connection to. She'd lived with a husband she loved as a friend but nothing more. For years, she'd felt alone, but she hadn't dared admit that to herself because it would have made everything ten times harder.

Now, she had it all. Love. Beautiful women she got to call friends. People looking out for her.

Carina smiled at her. "I heard a rumor that you might be taking over the reception at Blue Halo."

Cassie chuckled. "That rumor is correct. I was an executive assistant before I went back to Paragons of Hope, and, although working admin and front desk at a security company won't be quite the same, it will be a good entry back into the workforce. Aidan's excited because he thinks he's going to get to boss me around all day."

The women all laughed.

"Bet you told him what you thought of that." Carina chuckled.

"Don't worry, I told him exactly who's in charge, his business or not."

Willow took a sip of wine. "Thank the Lord. I've been on the boys' backs for a while to hire someone for that job. Whenever Blake has admin duties, he's in a bad mood for a week."

"You should see Logan." Grace shook her head. "It's like he's been asked to work night shift in a morgue."

"Yeah, the boys are definitely built for action, not desk jobs," Carina agreed.

"Lucky for them, I love admin," Cassie added.

Willow's voice softened. "How's Damien doing?"

Her heart lifted. "Amazing. We signed the marital separation agreement and because the divorce is uncontested, it should be quick and easy. We're just waiting for the judge to sign off on it. Oh, and he moved in with Dean."

Seeing those two together... God, it was everything. She'd been Skype calling them at least once a day. Damien smiled more during those Skype calls than he had in the last thirty years of his life. He could finally be himself.

When Aidan rose from the table, her heart sped up. He wore a tight white T-shirt that pulled across his chest and thick biceps. And when he walked, his blue jeans hugged his powerful thighs. Women around the room stared as he passed, but he only had eyes for her.

"YOU CAN'T TAKE your damn eyes off her."

Aidan couldn't even argue with Liam. "Nope. I came too close to losing her again. I won't be taking my eyes off her for a long time."

Fuck. He hated even thinking about it. Those two minutes she'd been unconscious had been the worst of his life.

"How's she doing?" Blake asked.

Aidan lifted a shoulder. "Highs and lows. Things with Mia are complicated. But she's relieved the cult's dead and Damien's healthy and happy. The divorce is going to be finalized soon."

Cassie's gaze met his for a second, and her eyes heated.

God, he loved her. It was a can't-get-her-out-of-his-head-or-breathe-without-her kind of love. It was annihilating, but also exhilarating.

"Looks like we're the last three standing," Callum said, looking across to Tyler and Liam.

Liam scoffed. "I haven't come close yet. Can't see it happening anytime soon."

Tyler barely seemed to be listening. Instead, he was looking toward the bar. Again.

Aidan followed his gaze to take in the woman sitting there. She looked to be mid-to-late thirties. She wore tight jeans with rips in the knees, paired with high heels. Her snug black top had long sleeves, and the glints of red in her brown hair shone in the lights behind the bar.

Aidan looked back to his friend and raised a brow. "Someone caught your eye?"

Tyler looked back at him. "No."

Liar. He'd had been looking at her all night.

Aidan pushed to his feet. "All right, I'm going to see my woman."

"Whipped," Liam coughed under his breath.

Aidan thumped him on the shoulder and moved across the room. When he reached Cassie, he slid his arms around her waist and tugged her against him. "You shouldn't be on your feet for too long."

She turned in his arms and wrapped her hands around his neck. "I'm okay, but if you want to hold me up for a while, I wouldn't complain."

He kissed her, then whispered into her ear. "I'll hold you for a lifetime, Cass."

She sucked in a shuddering breath.

"Dance with me," he whispered.

"Always."

Her one word hit him right in the chest. He tugged her away from the women, but he didn't go to the dance floor. Instead, he led her outside to the empty deck and pulled her into his arms. They could still hear the music through the door, but they also had privacy.

"I want you alone for a couple of minutes," he whispered at

her raised brows. "But if you get too cold, let me know and we'll go back inside."

"Mm. Being cold is a small price to pay for alone time with you." Her arms wrapped around his waist, and she lay her head on his chest, right over his heart.

"Are you feeling okay?"

She hummed. "Amazing. I haven't felt this happy since before."

Before. As in, before he was taken. Before they were torn apart, and they'd had to fight to get back to each other.

He pressed his mouth to her hair. "Me too, honey."

For a couple of minutes, Aidan just held her as they swayed to the music. This was his peace. His sanctuary. When he held her, everything in the world felt right.

"When I lost you, a lot of the world stopped making sense," he said quietly. Her head rose, and she looked at him. "Nowhere felt like home anymore. Nowhere felt happy and familiar and comfortable."

"Aidan..." She pressed a hand to his chest.

"I lived for the memories of us. The moments in my head. But there were so many things I regretted. I regretted not telling you I loved you every day. I regretted taking our time together for granted because I thought I'd always have you."

She shook her head. "You told me you loved me all the time."

"Not enough." But then, no amount would ever be enough. "And something I *really* regretted was not asking you a question."

Her voice quieted. "What question?"

"I know your divorce isn't finalized, but I can't wait any longer." He'd already waited long enough.

He took a small step back and slipped a hand into his pocket before pulling out a velvet box. She gasped softly and he heard her heart speed up. He knelt in front of her, and her breath caught.

"Cassie. You're my entire world, and you have all of me. My heart. My soul. The little fragments that only pull together when you're close by. I love you. And I want you to marry me." He opened the box to reveal a diamond ring. It was one he'd had his eyes on for a while. One that made him think of her every time he saw it.

Tears welled in her eyes, and for a moment there was silence. Then the words he'd waited three long years to hear came out.

"Yes. Yes, Aidan Pratt. I'll marry you!"

He took her hand and slid the diamond onto her finger. Then he rose and pulled her off her feet and into his arms and kissed her.

His. The woman was *his*. Forever.

"One more thing," he said when they finally parted.

"What on earth *else* could there be?" she asked with a watery laugh.

He lowered her and slid a hand into his other pocket...

And tugged out her necklace. The one he'd given her years ago.

She gasped. "How did you..."

"A few of the guys and I walked the road Elijah took." He slid it around her neck and fastened the clasp before lifting her hair over the delicate chain. "It wasn't too hard, since you told me the approximate area where it was taken from you."

She held his face in her hands. "You are my everything, Aidan. I love you so much."

He kissed her again. "You have no idea how deep my love for you goes."

He'd just tugged the woman into his arms again when he heard the quiet murmur of familiar voices. He looked to the side to see all of their friends a few feet away, standing in the open door, watching. There were tears in the women's eyes, and the guys wore knowing smiles.

He grinned and motioned his head toward Cassie. "Okay, come on."

The women ran forward, tugging Cassie from his arms into theirs. The guys did the same to him.

Yep. Everything was as good as it could get.

CHAPTER 31

"What a night," Logan said quietly, leaning back in his seat, his arm around Grace.

Tyler smiled, lifting his beer to his mouth. The entire team, men and women, were sitting around the table now. The danger surrounding Cassie was gone. Aidan had proposed to the woman. Life was good.

His beer had just hit the table when he felt it. The woman's gaze on him. *Again.* Not just him, though. The other men at the table as well. She'd been looking over at them the entire evening.

He turned toward her. Immediately, her eyes widened and she looked down. Unlike her, Tyler didn't look away.

Beautiful. The woman was *beautiful.* The black top, although showing little skin, pulled tightly across an ample chest. The red highlights in her hair were bright under the dim lighting of the bar, and the thick waves fell over her shoulders and down her back.

But what *really* had him captivated was the light amber of her eyes. When their gazes clashed, those eyes hit him right in his chest, almost stealing his breath.

Fucking radiant.

"So, when's the wedding?" Blake asked, his voice booming over the table.

Tyler dragged his attention back to his team.

Cassie laughed. "Give us a month or two to be engaged."

Aidan pressed a kiss to her head. "I'd marry you tomorrow."

Courtney shook her head. "No. Nope. No. You need time to be engaged. To choose the venue. The food and wine. The *dress*. And we need time to plan the bachelorette party."

The women started talking excitedly about the party while the men chuckled and rolled their eyes.

From his peripheral vision, Tyler noticed a younger guy sidle up to the woman at the bar. His muscles tensed, though he had no idea why, and he looked directly at them. He watched her closely as she gave the guy a polite smile. Definitely no affection there.

When the guy leaned closer, her smile dropped. Tyler was a second away from crossing the room when the woman pressed a hand to the man's chest and pushed.

A smile played at his lips at the way the guy blew out a breath and walked away.

Good. The only thing he hated more than an asshole, was an asshole who harassed women and couldn't understand the word no.

Her gaze skittered over to him from beneath her lashes. One side of his mouth lifted. She bit her bottom lip and looked back to the bar.

Yeah, honey, I see you looking. He just wanted to know why.

An arm swung around his shoulders. Liam grinned at him. "She's pretty."

He glanced at his friend. "She is. Not why I'm looking at her, though." Well, not the entire reason. "Just wondering why she keeps looking over here."

Liam lifted his brows. "Maybe someone caught her eye."

It was more than that. Her glances were too frequent, and

each time they locked eyes, she looked away too quickly. "It's something else. And it's not just me she's looking at—it's all of us."

Callum lifted his shoulders from the other side of the table. "Everyone in the country knows our faces after we were in the media."

Liam nudged his shoulder. "Yeah, maybe she just wants an autograph."

Tyler shook his head.

"You should go talk to her," Carina said from beside him.

He was considering it. She looked maybe a couple of years older than him. At twenty-six, he was the youngest on the team, but age differences never bothered him.

He was just pushing his chair back to head toward the bar when she lifted a phone to her ear. Right away, he knew something was wrong. A frustrated, almost angry look came over her face. Her knuckles went white as she clenched her phone. She covered her other ear with her free hand, stood, and started moving through the crowd toward the exit. Even her movements were beautiful. Could movement be beautiful? Graceful, maybe. Yes. She was graceful. And the sway of her hips... *Damn*, that was sexy.

Tyler would have left it at that—but he wasn't the only person watching her leave. A man began walking through the crowd, eyes focused on the woman. The guy who'd approached her at the bar.

His gut clenched. What the hell was he doing? She'd already told him she wasn't interested.

When the man stepped outside after her, Tyler rose from his seat. His friends threw questioning glances his way, but he ignored them. He moved out of the bar and spotted her immediately. She stood a little way down the sidewalk, in the shadows, and the guy was approaching behind her.

When he slid an arm around her waist, she spun around, startled, and shoved his chest. Only this time, he didn't move.

Tyler saw red. He was behind the asshole in a second, shoving him away.

The guy spun around, planting a belligerent, drunken glare on him. "Hey!"

"Her shove wasn't clear enough?" Tyler growled.

The guy frowned. "Mind your own fucking business."

Tyler stepped closer, and his voice lowered. "When I see drunk assholes harassing women, I *make* it my business. Leave."

"Or what?"

Was this guy always an idiot or did the alcohol do that for him? "You really want to know the answer to that?"

There was a moment of silence. Then the guy's jaw clicked. "Whatever."

He'd just brushed past him when Tyler grabbed his arm, his words so low, he knew only the guy would hear. "Come near her again, and I'll hit you so fucking hard you won't talk for a week. Got it?"

The guy's eyes widened a fraction, fear transforming his expression. It wasn't until he nodded that Tyler finally released him.

He turned to look at the woman. She didn't seem scared. More shocked, really.

He stepped closer. "You okay?"

"Yeah. Um, thank you."

Her voice was soft. It strummed through his veins, heating his blood.

"Miss Charles?"

At the murmur of another voice, he frowned, gaze shooting down to the phone in her hand. "Someone's still on the phone."

For a moment, she didn't drag her eyes away from him. A full beat passed before she seemed to hear what he'd said, then she jolted and lifted the phone back to her ear. "Sorry, there was… Sorry."

"The situation hasn't changed, Miss Charles," the guy on the line said. "You're still going to have to pay the fee."

Lines of irritation formed beside her eyes. "Fine. Email me the invoice. I have to go."

She hung up and gave him a tight smile. He didn't want a tight smile. He wanted to know what this woman looked like with a full, unhesitant grin stretching her lips. "Everything okay?"

She swallowed. "Yes. Just life."

She wet her lips, and his gaze shot down. Man, they were some lips. Red and plump. What he wouldn't give to be able to—

Shit. What the hell are you doing, Ty? You've just met the woman.

He shoved his hands into his pockets to keep from touching her. "I'm Tyler, by the way."

"Emerson."

Emerson. He liked that name. It suited her. He nodded toward the bar. "I noticed you watching our table."

She looked toward the bar, then back to him. Her mouth opened and closed.

What's going on, amber eyes?

Finally, she said, "Yeah, I, uh…recognized you as the Blue Halo guys."

Why the hell did he feel disappointed at that? Because he wanted her to be looking at him for another reason? For the same reason he was looking at her?

She cleared her throat. "I actually have an appointment there tomorrow morning."

Her words had him pausing. "Everything okay?"

His question seemed to have her looking uncertain. She quickly covered it with another tight smile. "Of course. I'll discuss everything tomorrow." She took a wide step around him. Was she being careful not to touch him? "Thank you again, and I guess I might see you tomorrow."

She disappeared into the parking lot.

Oh, the woman would definitely see him tomorrow. Because he was going to make certain that meeting was with him. Why? He wasn't sure.

It wasn't because her amber eyes had him transfixed, or because he couldn't take his eyes off her hips. And it certainly wasn't because her sweet, melodic voice had him damn well captivated.

Order Tyler Today!

ALSO BY NYSSA KATHRYN

Declan

Cole

JOIN my newsletter and be the first to find out about sales and new releases!

~https://www.nyssakathryn.com/vip-newsletter~

ABOUT THE AUTHOR

Nyssa Kathryn is a romantic suspense author. She lives in South Australia with her daughter and hubby and takes every chance she can to be plotting and writing. Always an avid reader of romance novels, she considers alpha males and happily-ever-afters to be her jam.

Don't forget to follow Nyssa and never miss another release.

Facebook | Instagram | Amazon | Goodreads

Printed in the USA
CPSIA information can be obtained
at www.ICGtesting.com
LVHW042346300923
759799LV00041B/649